PHRYNÉ

ISN'T

FRENCH

EDWARD R HACKEMER

Phryné Isn't French

Edward R Hackemer

Phryné Isn't French

(The Truffaut Novels #1)

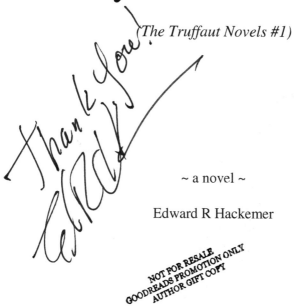

~ a novel ~

Edward R Hackemer

ISBN 13: 978-1975926397

ISBN 10: 1975926390

Other Titles By This Author:

(The Throckmorton Family Novels)

In A Cream Packard
(Book 1)
© 2011, 2013
ISBN-13: 978-1482662801

The Katydid Effect
(Book 2)
© 2013
ISBN-13: 978-1482669831

A Bridge To Cross
(Book 3)
© 2014
ISBN-13: 978-1494972820

Dollar To Doughnut
(Book 4)
© 2014
ISBN-13: 978-1505245110

THE FLYING PHAETON
(Book 5)
© 2015
ISBN-13: 978-1518707858

Sangria Sunsets
(Book 6)
© 2017
ISBN-13: 978-1542615945

Plus:

Fables Foibles & Follies
© 2019
ISBN 13: 978-1790613717

Phryne Crossing
(The Truffaut Novels #2)

© 2020

All titles are available in print and/or electronic format at online booksellers.

Visit the author's web page:
www.edhackemer.info
"They come and they go."

Acknowledgements Are Due

My beta reader & proofer − Edny,
my editor − Letitia,
my advocate & reader − you,
and the songwriters, musicians, vocalists, actors,
actresses, writers, directors, producers and crew.

And for the unwavering support of:
The Flying Porcine Air Defense League
and
The Pirkle Woods Packard Parkers.

The Story Is Dedicated To

the thespian and her understudy ... because they know drama.

Photo Coordinates:
Latitude: 48; 51; 27.05
Longitude: 2; 17; 36.15
Altitude: 132.57
Location: Paris, France

The Fine Print

It's to be expected that winters are colder than summers, but it came as an anomaly that this author's entries into THE FINE PRINT now require more than one page. It is therefore likely that our self-published wordsmith deems that what he has to say in the following seven paragraphs could be interesting to the reader. Bearing that in mind, and while understanding his propensity for claptrap, it is advised that you proceed with due caution.

Sincere effort has been taken to ensure that *Phryné Isn't French* contains the straight stuff for 1935 through 1945. Please realize that much of this novel is fiction except the scattered special little parts that are not. The needle and names were changed to protect the record and only the record, because the extended-life lithium batteries in the MP3 player are dead and the charger is lost.

This novel is a work of fiction and the reader may safely assume that some of the featured characters in this book are the author's imaginary friends. Privately collected DNA samples can reveal unique genetic markings and personality traits that are exclusively dependent upon family lineage. Therefore, any resemblance in the description or name of any real person, living or dead is merely coincidental. No endorsement is given or implied for the surreptitious activity of any character, organization or institution described in this novel. All opinions, conversations, actions or interplay carried out or expressed by any named character acting individually or on behalf of an organization either actual or fictional, are used solely for descriptive and entertainment purposes. Please note that teleprompters, margin notations or cue cards were not used for the final transcription edits of dialogue.

Any lyrics, songs or music annotated in this book are the intellectual property of individual copyright holders and are referenced only for descriptive purposes. The reader is encouraged to purchase the music, listen and sing along, hum, snap fingers or tap feet. Except for the most experienced users, finger snapping while texting is strongly discouraged. Do not read distracted, test and drive or drive while test texting. Practice safety first.

Cinematic compositions, including all titles, dialogue and associated soundtracks described in this novel are the exclusive intellectual property of their respective copyright owners, excepting those which may have fallen into public domain. It is suggested that the reader purchase, rent or download any readily available lawful content to further enrich the total entertainment experience. Please note that 3D glasses are not required. Popcorn and candy are available in most motion picture lobbies throughout the country. Plastic is nice, but cash transactions are preferred.

Governmental, military, political or ecclesiastical institutions mentioned in this book, actual or fictitious, are included neither as an endorsement nor as an editorial rejection of their function or doctrine. The descriptions of public entities, private enterprises or government agencies within these pages, whether they are actual or apocryphal, are included with literary license and no negative inference or implication to any past or present entity is intended. Civil, military or personal violence is recounted solely for editorial reality. No animals were harmed during the creation of this novel.

Snowflakes are encouraged to research the history. The reader should understand that early twentieth century French prisons were not resorts. History can be multi-faceted and difficult to accept because it's true: bad guys exist and jails are not five-star hotels.

☞   Verbiage used in this novel is contemporary with the story except what ain't. Mid-twentieth century terminology, slang and colloquialisms are indicated with a *Single* * *superscript asterisk* and can be found in *THE WORDS* at the back of the book. British English can be smashing! And let the truth be told: for some readers, French, Spanish and German may as well be Greek.   ☛

☞   Points of Interest, Curiosities and General Footnotes are pinpointed with *Double** superscript asterisks* and transcribed as handnotes in a section titled *THE END NOTES.*   ☛

☞   Weird Things & Oddities are indicated by *Triple*** superscript asterisks* and listed in *THE ODD STUFF.*   ☛

THE JAZZ

THE QUIRKY PRONUNCIATIONS:
Phryné – (Free-NAY) {French}
Phryne – (FRI-nee) {English}

THE STAGE:
Margate, Kent, United Kingdom
Hollywood, California
Pre-war Paris and German-occupied France

THE CHARACTERS:
Phryné Althea Truffaut, Desmund Cuttleford,
Hugo-Henri Grétillat, Guilermo Gaeta, Dieter Dientz,
Renée-Ffion Delacroix, Morris Sutcliffe

THE PLOT:
A young woman in pursuit of happiness.

THE THEME:
Interpersonal and geo-political conflict.

SELECTED SCRIPT:
*"An American who knows tango is as rare as snow on the streets
of Barcelona! An American who can dance the tango is a gift from
the Saints themselves."*
~ Guilermo Gaeta, October 1935, Aboard the SS Normandie ~

*"France has fallen. Paris has fallen. Pathé has fallen. The Reich
is a thousand years."*
~ Hugo Grétillat, July 1940, Poissy, Île-de-France ~

*"It seems that I have been forever blowing bubbles; bubbles that
just float away, pop and disappear into thin air."*
~ Phryné Truffaut, August 1945, Margate, Kent, UK ~

Map Of The European Stage

Scotland

Ireland

England

London★

☆ Margate

Southampton↑

⚑ Le Havre

Rouen ☆

★Paris

France

Portugal

Spain

(Alella)
Barcelona ⚑

What's Inside

1. MARGATE, KENT
~ 1945 ~

The White Cliffs of Dover

3:00 PM, Friday, August 31:
Inn at The Flying Pig, at the corner of Market Street &
Newby's Alley, Olde Towne

Desmund Cuttleford closed the heavy oak door behind him, walked through the narrow vestibule into the pub, propped his cane on the coat rack and took his usual seat at the bar. He never found it occupied. It was his alone: a seat of honor reserved for only him.

He'd lived through Zeppelin[**] bombing raids, periods of dire economic strife, coal shortages, buzz bombs and the reigns of three kings since his birth in 1874. Not once during his seventy-one years, however, did he venture more than fifty miles from Margate, and he held steady employment for forty-two years as a millwright in the maintenance shop at Willis Ferry Works in Ramsgate; a fifteen minute, five mile commute on his Ariel motorized bicycle. During times of harsh weather, he would ride Coastal Coach Lines for a shilling[*].

Although he'd weathered two world wars; each time his age shielded him from military conscription. Still, Desmund had managed to serve his country honorably. He spent nearly four years during England's most recent war with Germany patrolling the eastern shores of Kent from Herne Bay to Dover, keeping watch over the English Channel coastline as a Sergeant with His Majesty's Home Guard[**].

Thin and wiry, he stood five-feet-four and the easiest thing he could do was smile. His hat couldn't cover all of his thinning hair and allowed snow-white tufts to drift around his ears and onto his collar. He hadn't drawn a razor across his face that morning and a one-day stubble of whitish whiskers covered his cheeks. His bushy eyebrows could pass as little white mice trying to hide under the small brim of his linen Welsh flat cap.

Without a word, Roger, the innkeeper, began filling a glass of Allsopp's Export as soon as he noticed that it was Desmund entering the pub. Roger was a tall, sturdy man of six feet, so his head barely cleared the blackened, century-old ceiling timbers over the bar. He had close-cropped, salt-and-pepper hair, and a long face with pronounced cheek and jaw bones that earned him the rude moniker of Horse Face. Some of his closest friends would remark in jest that he was born with a face only a mother could love. Despite his equine features, the innkeeper had a heart of gold that was home to a considerate, outgoing and cheerful personality.

Desmund brought a shilling* and tuppence* from the vest pocket of his brown tweed jacket and methodically, silently set the coins onto the bar. The landlord put the glass of ale down squarely in front of the well-seasoned pensioner with a gentle clunk. A frothy wave of foam silently fell over the rim and onto the time-worn, ash bar. He smiled at his senior customer and greeted him, "There you be, Des. You got the first pull off a fresh keg. I tapped her this morning, just knowing that you'd be in, Mate."

Desmund returned the greeting, "I'll be thanking you muchly, kind sir." His Adam's apple bobbed up and down his lanky throat, fighting with the knot in his dark blue, woolen tie as he spoke. He had a seat at the bar alongside his close friend, postman Dewey Newsome, another life-long resident of Margate and thirty-nine-year veteran of the Royal Mail. He was ten years Desmund's junior, four inches shorter and forty pounds heavier.

Dewey was conscientious about his position in the community and the responsibilities that came with a career appointment to the Royal Mail. He was careful not to degrade the King's Blue with even a single pint**, and would never consume beer while in uniform. His mail frock and cap hung on a wooden peg in the foyer and he sported his standby camel-brown sport jacket and black bowler* in their stead.

Desmund turned on the bar stool, glanced around the pub, nodded, smiled and lifted his glass to his fellow patrons. Low, indiscernibly mumbled greetings bounced back and forth off the timber and plaster walls. It was mid-afternoon and between tea* times, and only a handful of customers sat inside the tavern. Issa, Betty, Clarence and Will were playing a spirited game of whist** at the round table in the far corner. A quiet, disengaged Albert Perkins was sitting on the bench next to the double window, smoking his pipe and reading through a tattered, two-day-old copy of the *Thanet Advertiser and Echo*. The publication was reliably four pages of local gossip, advertisements and, on occasion, included a tea-cup's worth of innocuous Kent County news.

Horribly, two years earlier, on the first of June, 1943 the war came exploding into Margate during one of the air raids that had become commonplace since 1939. A German V-1** rocket-propelled bomb struck the Holy Trinity Church on Trinity Square in the center of town. Sadly, ten civilians, who had sought shelter within the church's stone walls, tragically lost their lives in the blast and ensuing fire. Prudence Cuttleford, Desmund's wife of forty-nine years numbered among the victims.

Prior to the heartbreaking loss of his wife, tragedy had mercilessly crossed Desmund's path on two other occasions. The first piercing anguish resulted from the 1916 death of their son, Harley in the Battle of Somme** in France, during the First World War. Two years later, he and Prudence

3

suffered loss once again with the sudden death of their teenage daughter, Evelyn to the influenza epidemic of 1918[**].

In the two years since the death of his darling wife Prudence, Desmund had managed to muster the courage to carry on, simply putting one foot in front of the other. Six days a week he'd had his pint and afternoon tea of a simple meat pie or sliced meat, cheese and bread at The Flying Pig[***]. On Sunday, he'd usually had tea with his neighbors, Leonard and Hazel Adair in their flat on Cecil Square. Hazel was known throughout the parish for her tasty toad-in-the-hole, shepherds' pie and bangers and mash[**].

Desmund and Dewey were two of more than a dozen, loyal regulars who frequented The Flying Pig and they, like most of their fellow beer connoisseurs, knew everyone in town by name. They considered community awareness to be their civic duty, and on more than one occasion during the past six years their collective knowledge proved to be of inestimable worth to the gossip-mongers at the whist table. And like his postie[*] drinking mate, there wasn't much that Desmund didn't know about anyone in the seaside village other than the trippers[*].

World War II had officially ended sixteen weeks earlier, on April 8, with the unconditional surrender of Germany. The post-war enthusiasm had extended the tourist season well into the cooler, somewhat chilly, damper air of August, and had only begun to dwindle down from its bustling peak of June and July. The country was enjoying a long-awaited respite from air-raid sirens and casualty reports. Standing lights-out orders, rationing and the stark reality of war had given way to a long-awaited, yet cautious, euphoria. The troops were trickling back home, the wounds of war beginning to heal and a sense of calm was steadily returning.

From Whitstable to the White Cliffs of Dover[***], the seaside of Kent beckoned vacationers to its shores. It was the onset of another holiday weekend for day-trippers and war-weary Londoners. For them, every weekend was a holiday. Margate's sandy beaches, the picturesque Victorian pier, Dreamland Park and its Scenic Railway drew them like ants to a picnic. Sharing honors with Bristol in South West England, Margate, Kent was synonymous with a weekend seaside holiday.

The pub[*] was part of Margate's Olde Towne, nestled two and a half blocks from the beach and busy King Street. The tavern wasn't the sole force turning the wheels of commerce within the district, but it certainly was one of the main spokes. It was a well-hidden gem that stubbornly strove to keep itself separate from the tacky tourist and souvenir trade, neatly tucked away within a maze of one-way alleys and narrow, ten-foot cobblestone streets. Tudor half-timber-and-stucco homes were nestled neatly among the nineteenth century brick buildings, row-houses and connected mews[*] that stood guard over the neighborhood's sovereignty. Vibrant red geraniums and deep purple petunias crowded wooden flower boxes along Market Street. Since the days of Dickens, the world seemingly stood still inside Olde Towne. Butchers, bakers, tailors, tobacconists, barbers, dress-makers, haberdashers, book sellers, tea rooms and even a blacksmith had storefronts.

The exterior of The Flying Pig was time-worn red brick, almost completely covered with hardy clinging ivy spreading from the stone walls of the basement up to white painted eves and around the windows and shutters. The roof was terra cotta tiles, spotted with green moss and stained black with nearly a century of mildew.

A substantial, four-by-five-foot hand-painted, wooden sign hung from a structural beam jutting out from the northeast corner of the building. It bore the likeness of a smiling, Gloucestershire sow sporting a pair of white-feathered wings;

giving the formidable swine the lift she would need to soar over the sandy beaches, changing tents, funfair and fish-and-chips shops that crowded Margate's white sands, cobbled streets and waterfront boardwalks.

As half-past three approached, Roger tuned the radio behind the bar to frequency 1293, Radio Luxembourg's long-wave radio station broadcasting the British Big Band Hit Parade. Dewey and Desmund watched with detached curiosity as Roger boldly fidgeted with modern technology. Through the static, pops and snaps, he turned the wire-wrapped, circular antenna atop the unit until Vera Lynn could be heard singing *The White Cliffs of Dover*. Her vanilla-smooth voice sweetly resounded from the Pye parlor radio and its extension speaker sitting at the far end of the bar.

Radio Luxembourg and Vera Lynn couldn't hold everyone's attention indefinitely. The sleepy tune's sentimental lyrics became barely audible background noise.

I'm Forever Blowing Bubbles

The sound of the pub door opening and closing was easily ignored by the regular clientele, but the unique tap-tap of a lady's healed shoes stepping through the short hall and into the tavern was something more than a simple audible distraction; it was an unusual happenstance.

Heads turned to see a tall, attractive and shapely woman, possibly in her mid-thirties; a vision about three inches shy of six feet who was wearing black, patent leather two-inch heels. Whether they were casual customers or loyal punters[*] like the table of whist players, everyone in the tavern immediately realized that the woman walking into the public house was certainly not of Margate or any of the surrounding the seaside communities. In fact, it was highly likely that she wasn't British at all.

Her clothes were continental and she appeared to be dressed for a proper meeting, such as an elevenses[*] with a business associate, a reunion with a former acquaintance or an informal appointment with a local solicitor[*]. As she entered the drinkery, she removed a floppy, wide-brimmed, dark grey hat with a bright red band that she had been wearing cocked fashionably to the left. A short, black lace veil had partially obscured that side of her face. She then placed the hat in her right hand, where she was holding not a handbag, but a black calfskin clutch. The woman was sharply dressed in smoky silk stockings and a light grey, knee-length, half-sleeved linen dress with a vertical pattern of large, soft-pink roses down one side of the bodice with a deeply pleated skirt and a matching cropped jacket. She wore one-inch, red button earrings and an ornate, round bejeweled broach that matched her crimson lips and lacquered nails. Her cosmetics were perfect and her wardrobe was certainly neither wartime nor rationed.

All eyes were upon her, wondering who she was and what her matter-of-course, yet assertive entrance could portend. The woman walked straight to the bar and stood front and center at the row of draft beer taps.

A tempting slice of real-life mystery was developing in front of a handful of patrons inside the pub. A curious excitement fell upon the captive audience.

The lady smiled at the barman, "A glass of your sweet sherry[*], please, Roger. Like the one I enjoyed this morning after my coffee, toast and those lively, gingered rhubarb preserves." Her voice cracked ever so slightly as she spoke.

In stark contrast to her entrance, her tone was demure; almost cautious. First impressions and suppositions were drifting through the pub like the first snowflakes of winter.

Curiously, the customers noticed that she had called their neighborhood innkeeper by name and freely mentioned that she'd had breakfast at the pub. It was immediately obvious that she was an overnight guest at the least, and had certainly rented one of the three rooms that the humble public house had to offer.

The woman's accent was foreign, but of uncertain origin. Everyone was attentive, fascinated and guessing. She didn't seem grandiose, but had an air of self-achieved refinement without the pomposity. She walked with poise and purpose, and while her words were refined, it seemed that she was a bit on edge; perhaps stressed, or simply tired from travel.

Desmund and Dewey exchanged glances, and looked to Roger first; then the woman and back again to Roger, all the while hoping for some clue or sign of who she was and what could have drawn her to Margate, and of all places, The Flying Pig.

Roger spoke, "Certainly, Miss Phryné." He was wearing a mischievous smile.

Her name certainly sounded foreign. Someone at the whist table whispered *"French"* and another proclaimed *"no, it's Flemish"*.

Issa Dunn suggested, "She may be Italian."

"I call bollocks* on Flemish." said Will. "I'll wager she's a Belgian."

Clarence muttered, "Flemish *is* Belgian, you twit."

Betty put a tobacco-stained finger to her lips and, "Shhhh!!!"

The bartender turned, filled a small, long-stemmed glass with the amber elixir and set it on the bar. Desmund, Dewey and the others were beyond curious as to why Roger and the woman were already addressing one another on a first-name basis.

"Please, how much do I owe you for the drink, Roger?"

"Two and six, but no need for the silver. I will simply charge it to your account, Miss Phryné."

"Thank you, Roger. You've been so kind to me. It's comforting to know that there are still caring people in this world. It means a lot in times like these. And it certainly means a lot to me, while considering the day that I'm having."

After that exchange, every member of the captive audience released a barely audible gasp. Everyone knew that Roger's wife Georgina was away and spending a fortnight[*] visiting her sister Gwen in Suffolk, East Anglia.

The woman whom Roger had called Phryné, acknowledged her nearest neighbors, Desmund and Dewey with gentle nods. She smiled briefly at them as she picked up her little glass, then turned and walked to the small table adjacent to the foyer wall and dart boards. Desmund watched her glide away from the bar and noticed that the seams down the back of her hose were straight and true. For him, such attention to detail was a sign of self-esteem.

He and everyone else in the barroom now felt certain that Roger knew this woman far better than they did. Desmund, especially, was quite perplexed and peeved as to why his favorite landlord didn't mention this mysterious visitor early on. He wondered how Roger was able to muster the nerve to keep this exotic visitor a secret. Desmund was anxiously anticipating Roger's explanation, and wondered exactly how intriguing, detailed or adventurous it could be.

Desmund focused on Roger, waiting, hoping for even the tiniest bit of information. He felt that the innkeeper needed to fully explain why he had been keeping the news of this glamorous traveler to himself and what could have prompted him to hide this new, tantalizing and potentially scandalous information from his loyal customers.

Roger ignored Desmund's steely gaze and deftly began wiping glassware as a matter of blind habit. The barman's silence was certainly out of character. Roger was never known to keep secrets, and never backed away from boasting about his romantic expertise and affinity toward women.

Desmund's curiosity became more than he could bear and he decided that he could no longer wait for Roger's explanation. Desmund knew all too well that the innkeeper enjoyed telling dramatic stories and when the time came, he would draw them out much longer than necessary, simply to add to the suspense. Desmund believed that it was an unscrupulous sales tactic that Roger used to sell more beer.

After quick consideration of all the options available to him, Desmund resolved that his only recourse was to take control of the situation. Without a word or warning, he decided to tempt fate. He slid sideways off the barstool and boldly approached the beautiful, tempting and mysterious invader of The Flying Pig.

Left behind at the bar, stranded, surprised and shocked nearly beyond belief, Dewey and Roger could only watch. Desmund had acted inexplicably bold and dangerously out of character. The others sat amused with mouths slightly agape and watched as the usually reserved old man approached the exotically entrancing stranger.

Desmund stood at the woman's table, smiling timidly and holding his half-empty, pint beaker of Allsopps, ready to apologize and fully expecting to ask for her forgiveness. He worried that his presence was on shaky ground at best, and that his foolhardy experiment in fortitude would certainly be short-lived and could easily result in crushing embarrassment.

The possibilities for personal humiliation were endless. Nervous thoughts bounced around his brain like corks on a storm-driven sea. He reached inside and found the words,

"Desmund Cuttleford here, Miss. May I be so bold as to ask for a seat at your table?"

The lady visitor heard a gentle, kindly voice forming the words with the nervous precision of a sixth-grader reciting memorized verse in front of classmates. She heard a curious, compassionate soul, an elderly gentleman offering open, friendly companionship.

Desmund felt a flush come to his cheeks and his heart jumped. He hadn't felt so giddy in decades. Furthermore, he couldn't remember the last time he could withstand the punishing pain in his calcified* knees and stand without his walking stick, unsupported and not wobbling. He temporarily scolded his impetuously poor sense of judgment and considered apologizing to the hazel-eyed beauty, walking back to his barstool and retaking his rightful seat next to his closest mate, Dewey.

Time stopped and he bravely stood his ground at tableside. He was prepared to face the music and accept his impending humiliation. From such a beautiful woman, rejection could be forever worn as a badge of honor. Desmund refused to turn away and start back toward the bar. He was beyond the point of no return.

The lady traveler looked into his eyes for a second, admiring the aged fellow's boldness yet apparently questioning his motive and searching for a reason why this man was standing at her table. She evidently found enough solace in the man's calming presence and the serenity in his voice to reassure her.

Desmund could feel her inquiring gaze. He boldly mirrored her stare, and bounced off hers. They shared smiles that instantly, inexplicably bridged the difference in their years.

He had experienced a fleeting moment of uncommon emotional bravery, but still felt strangely uncomfortable, like an elementary pupil in the headmaster's office. Standing in front of her, he felt the goosebumps at the nape of his neck and swarms of mayflies in his belly, but he managed to frighten them away like fairies into the wood. He paid no attention to the audience behind him at the bar and the eyes that were watching from the card table and window seat.

Desmund nervously awaited the woman's reply and noticed that the color of her eyes was exactly that of his dear, departed wife, Prudence. He felt relief as the woman smiled up at him and her lips breathed a melodious answer that was heard by his ears alone, "I am Phryné Truffaut. And yes, you may share my table, Desmund."

It was an intimate invitation exclusively for him. For Desmund's ears, her voice tasted like sweetened cream on Christmas pudding. Her gaze warmed his heart. His derring-do was vindicated. Selfishly, privately Desmund drifted away into cherished memories of his Prudence in times and places gone by.

The visitor spoke without forethought, and, like her unsuspecting, seasoned guest, she couldn't find a precise reason for the words she had uttered, other than the gentleman seemed kindly and quite harmless. Common sense floated away at the mercy of the evening tide like an unmoored skiff. Practical, cautious thinking was set adrift on a sea of happenstance.

Desmund pulled the wooden chair back from the little table, causing the legs to squeak in protest across the century-old fieldstone floor. He found himself sitting directly opposite a beautiful, mystical traveler at an impromptu rendezvous for reasons unexplained. Two unsuspecting strangers had defied destiny for one uncharted reason or another, driven by forces undefined. For Phryné it was comforting. For Desmund, it was magical. It was then that he noticed the one-inch scar over her left eye and assumed that it was the reason for the camouflage provided by the lace mask of her short-brimmed cloche hat.

Phryné sipped at the fortified Spanish wine, looked over her glass at Desmund and momentarily became lost in a daydream of her own. His mannerisms made such an impression on her that she thought: *If he hadn't jumped into that icy river sixteen years ago and killed himself, this Englishman could be my father.*

The mystery woman abruptly dismissed her fantasy and questioned her train of thought. She returned to the *here and now*, finished her sherry and motioned to Roger for a refill.

Desmund jumped at the opportunity to ask an innocuous yet pointed, question, "Tell me; what brings you to Margate, Phryné?"

The traveler felt that whatever the reason, she owed this man an answer and it needed to seem genuine, however brief she wanted it to be. She began to consider all of her options and decided that the ancient proverb was correct: *Honesty is the best policy.*

She found herself unusually at ease in this man's presence. Once again, she looked deeply into Desmund's pale blue eyes and believed that she had discovered a long-lost friend: someone she knew in another life at another time, or perhaps in childhood, her youth or somewhere hidden far within her deepest sleep and her most intimate dreams.

Her progression of thoughts was rudely interrupted yet again when Roger appeared from nowhere with another sherry and a fresh pint for Desmund. She and Desmund felt annoyed yet unified by the inconvenient, innocent, but well-intentioned, unavoidable tableside disruption. There was an awkward silence. Not a word was spoken between the landlord and his customers. Roger left sullenly after he had set the drinks on the small table.

Phryné sipped at her sherry like a duchess at high tea as she considered her answer to Desmund's elementary question.

She began, "What brought me to Margate is quite simple ... and yet very complicated without a proper explanation.

"What drove me to this corner of the world was a poem ... a private, personal message I received from a citizen of your country who was very dear to me ... and it was written almost like a coded message. His words were a riddle, but his note wasn't unusual or surprising; it was his way. He talked to me between the lines of his poetic musings and could say things that touched my heart like no man had done before.

"He often found it difficult to express how he felt and to say the right words, so he would write little poems or a few small, romantic sentences for me, and he tried instead to explain his thoughts and feelings with a few tender words written in pencil on little bits of paper.

"We met two years ago, in France, a year before D-Day, under strenuous circumstances that limited the time we could spend together. And because of the war and our combined personal histories, our future together was highly doubtful in a perfect world and very much impossible in the real one.

"His last little message was the hardest one for me to understand. I tried to put him and his words out of my mind and I tucked his silly little poem inside my jewel box for a time. But I couldn't forget it. I wouldn't accept his absence. His memory couldn't be locked away. Through no fault of his own, he left me behind. He took with him the key to my heart.

"It wasn't easy, but I finally figured out what his last little rhyme meant and it led me here ... to Margate, Kent. I was so excited when I arrived on the train from London this morning; I thought I was walking on the moon. I thought I was on my way to the stars, on track to my future ... and following my dreams all the way to the end of my own private rainbow in my own personal paradise. For a while, I thought my search for lasting love and happiness was about to come to a perfect end. I believed that my fortunes had changed, and finally it was my turn to grab the golden ring off the twirling merry-go-round that has been my life so far.

"But now ... all that's in serious doubt and it looks like I may need to start my life all over again ... again. I've done it so many times in the past. But now I don't know where to begin ... if life could only be a board game ... it would be more predictable if I could simply throw a pair of dice."

Her voice trailed off with her last words. She sipped at her sherry, took a breath and worked to regain her composure. Desmund could only watch sympathetically as she took a lace-bordered handkerchief from her clutch and wiped a tear. He noticed that it was neatly embroidered with the initials *"PT"*.

She continued, "For years I have searched for answers ... just like that song that's playing on the radio right now. It seems that I have been forever blowing bubbles; bubbles that just float away, pop and disappear into thin air. It's like they're playing that song just for me.

"I'm forever blowing bubbles ...

"Just listen to those words ...

"I'm forever blowing bubbles ...

"Pretty bubbles in the air.

"They go up in the air and burst and then they're gone. They disappear never to be seen again. Gone forever."

She tasted her sherry and closed her eyes for a moment, drifting into her dreams. Slowly, pensively, she reopened her clutch, replaced her hankie and brought out her Rothman's filter tips. She pulled one from the pack, held it between her fingers and allowed her daydreams to take her away once again.

It was a few seconds before clarity returned and she could look Desmund in the eyes and continue, "That's my story, kind sir. That's how I ended up in Margate. My life is like a song on Radio Luxembourg. I'm here in Kent, a guest at a local bar on a dead-end railway line that stops at the cold, blue sea. My fate has been reduced to a rhyming riddle that has sent me off course and into stormy waters."

Desmund brought his half-penny box of matches out of his coat pocket and lit her cigarette. He couldn't explain his empathy for this woman.

She inhaled, smiled at him and slowly expelled the smoke from the corner of her mouth.

Desmund was caught in the web that Phryné had woven. He wanted to help, had plenty of time and was willing to give some of it away to rescue this wonderfully attractive tripper and try to resurrect her dream. He picked up his pint of Allsopps lager, took a draw and looked her in the eye.

"I dare say that you have landed at the right place at the right time, Miss Phryné. Here at The Flying Pig we pay homage to the airborne porcine and all the improbabilities that give lift to her wings and credence to the stories we hear.

"I enjoy wetting my whistle during a chat and nibble. And I'm fair enough at working out puzzles and riddles, so please, tell me more."

Her captivating smile signaled that she had accepted his invitation and was about to begin an adventurous narrative that would hold Desmond's attention for hours.

It was truly a story that was meant to be told.

2. Hollywood, California
(Ten Years Earlier)
~ 1935 ~

Let's Misbehave

7:00 PM, Saturday, September 7:
Studio 4, Lot 2, Balaban Way, Paramount Pictures

Phryne and her guest had just dropped in and claimed a spot on the right side of the studio, away from the action and about fifteen feet behind the director, sound, and camera crews. They sat in folding wood and canvas chairs not for comfort but because the seats were lightweight, portable and the only option on a Paramount set. Whenever she anticipated a lengthy shoot, Phryne would bring along her own seat cushion, but didn't believe she would need one on this visit. It was the eve of a party and she certainly wouldn't be lingering on the set. She was acting as an ambassador of Paramount studios and was there for one reason only: spread goodwill and grease the gears. Congratulating the director for a successful shoot was merely studio feel-good fluff.

Seated close and immediately on Phryne's left, was her companion, Hugo-Henri Grétillat, a promising young French director. He'd arrived in New York from Le Havre, France six months earlier, on March 6 aboard one of French Line's[**] premier steamers, *Île de France*. Four and a half days later, thanks to the New York Central and Union Pacific Railroads, he reached his destination on the Paramount lot. His journey from Paris to Hollywood had consumed a total of eleven days.

Hugo's American experience had begun as soon as he arrived at Paramount. He'd begun working with director Lewis Milestone on the Balaban and Glazer production of *Paris in Spring*, a musical comedy about a heart-broken man and woman, both disappointed in love, who climb the Eifel Tower and contemplate suicide. They plot a fake love affair to make their original partners jealous and instead fall in love with one another.

Because the film was set in Paris, it was an exciting first motion-picture project for the promising young French director. The illusion of the Eifel Tower on a Hollywood lot was especially surreal to him.

Four months later, in late August, Phryne couldn't help but notice the dashing Frenchman on the set of Gloria Shine's newest film. Hugo was in his mid-thirties, six-foot-four, wearing a black silk shirt, an ivory, silk ascot and dark grey, wide-leg pleated trousers and two-tone, white-over-black wingtips. He had a swarthy, Mediterranean complexion and thick, black, wavy hair.

Assistant Director Mort Silver's introduction was all that Phryne needed to be smitten. Hugo's sky-blue eyes and the deep, soulful timbre of his voice sealed the deal. On the evening they met, they dined, drank, danced and gambled until daybreak at the Clover Club on Sunset Boulevard. Hugo-Henri was receptive and Phryne's charms worked. They became inseparable almost instantly.

When Hugo arrived in Los Angeles, he became the first French film director to participate in a new cultural, technical and professional exchange program between Paramount Pictures and Pathé Frères Productions** of Paris. The cinema giants believed that Pan-Atlantic cooperation could be beneficial to the art, entertaining for the public and an enhancement to both studios' bottom line. Phryne hoped that Hugo would indeed prove to be all three for her; enhancing, entertaining and beneficial.

Outside, twilight was blanketing the lot. And like the movie, daylight was ready and waiting to be put to bed. By industry standards, the production was a success. The film finished comfortably under its $400,000 budget and wrapped three days ahead of its projected thirty-day schedule.

The final day's shooting, however, could be written off as nothing more than an exercise in futility and exasperation, and no one was happier than the film's director, Hal Tuttle, that the project was finished. From the first read-through, one actress, Gloria Shine, was the fly in the ointment. At half past six, when the director announced "that's a wrap" and thereby declared that filming was over, the film's leading lady was still recovering from her brunch of gin and milk. She had spent the afternoon in her trailer guzzling Bromo^{**} seltzer, moaning, munching on saltine crackers and throwing up.

Fortunately, despite the antics and headaches of headliner Gloria, the production crew promised the film's producers Balaban and Mandelbaum, and director Tuttle that they would be able to piece together enough shoots with stand-ins and doubles to stick the film in the can[*] by the next evening.

The final obstacle before ultimate release to theaters was The Hays Code^{**}, but the legal department assured the producers that with a few minor cuts, it should pass muster with flying colors. And lately, perhaps because the restrictions were so new, the censor board hadn't been looking that close. They really had no idea how much skin was too much and what dialogue went too far.

All the Queens Men was a loosely scripted, innuendo-laden, campy comedy about two men from the borough of Queens who were trying to break into the world of fashion in New York's Manhattan Garment District. Ari Robertson played an extremely talented twenty-year-old amateur artist with only an eighth-grade education and a proclivity for ladies' undergarments. Milton Laird, an aspiring dancer and recent dropout of the New York School of Fine and Applied Arts, was cast in the role of Ari's roommate. Gloria Shine topped the marquee as the tyrannical fashion mogul Wanda Moore, a former model with a penchant for money, men and more men. *All the Queens Men* wasn't expected to garner critical acclaim or gather awards, but rather, give the public what it wanted: an opportunity to forget about the ongoing Depression with an hour and ten minutes of black-and-white vaudeville humor, suggestive sex, playful depravity and mildly scandalous behavior. First and foremost, however, the goal was to make money and help keep Paramount in the film business at the cost of a movie ticket, one dime at a time. Times were tough and Paramount Pictures was facing steely competition from Meyer Films and their burgeoning stable of sparkling, steamy starlets. Risqué subject matter, evocative dialogue, skimpy costumes and subdued lighting were the new production techniques in the toolbox. Torch singers and thinly veiled, lurid lyrics also helped the box office. Hollywood learned early on that sex sells and Paramount looked for some professional assistance from their very continental and cultured French counterpart.

When the second cameraman snapped the last clapper board[**], it signaled that party time was imminent. The usually whisper-quiet set came to life with a steady hum. It was as if the crew breathed a sigh of relief in unison. Conversations started and the click of cigarette lighters and small talk bounced through the huge, echoing studio. The extras mulled around like lost puppies and the stand-ins scurried to see what titles were filming where the following day. Reels of cellulose safety film were stripped off the cameras, stowed in cases and either tied or strapped shut. Lights went out one by one, cluster by cluster, click after click and turned the yellowish, artificial, incandescent daylight into shadowy dusk.

The air was mired in relief and thick with anticipation. The good times and high jinx were only a few hours away. The post-production bash was to be held in the private rear banquet room of the Café Trocadero[**] on Sunset Boulevard.

Phryne had attended nearly every cast and crew party that was thrown for an Abner Mandelbaum film since the winter of 1930. As the wife of one of Paramount Pictures' premier producers, she always had a seat at a head table. By the time of this party, however, Phryne no longer hung on the arm of roaming husband, Abner. In fact, she had been stepping out for years. For most of the previous twelve months, she and her husband had been in an 'open marriage', which in Hollywood meant *whoever, whenever and wherever,* publicly. A week ago, Hugo may have begun his platonic relationship with Phryne as a *whoever,* but he had been a regular fixture every day since. Phryne had cut her husband out of the script and wrote her Frenchman into the role of leading man. For the first time in years, she had a man on her arm who wasn't just a flash in the pan. Hugo wasn't yet a steady flame, but one that had possibilities to grow warmer and stronger with time. Phryne was softly fanning the flames and hoping that the heat would build. Now that Abner had all but left the paddock, she needed to hook her wagon to a new steed and set out for greener pastures.

After the limp handshakes, token back-pats, cursory kisses and tepid smiles, the serious post-production congratulations and invitations were passed around. Phryne introduced Hugo-Henri, who then congratulated director Hal Tuttle with the usual French *faire la bise*[*] on both cheeks, and passed him a bottle of Moët & Chandan champagne.

The haughty, snobbish Tuttle accepted the gift, looked to Phryne, thanked the Frenchman, and said, "I will anxiously await working with you and Phryne on your next film here in Hollywood. Not Europe. There's too many of them damn Nazis over there."

Hal Tuttle gave what had become expected of him: the truth, crude and rude. He was too self-absorbed to indulge in fluff.

The champagne transfer freed up Hugo's right hand, and Phryne immediately took it.

She gently pulled him to her side and breathed, "Forget him, Hugo. I want one, my darling."

Hugo was a bit perplexed by her request. "Why, of course you may have one. I'll give you a bottle when we return to the Garden, ma chérie."

She cuddled closer and whispered in his ear, "When we get back to your suite, my darling, you'll give me more than a bottle of Moët. Besides, it's not the bubbly I want now, you silly ... I want a kiss. Not on the cheek ... on the lips. I want a proper kiss. Show everyone here how it's done in France."

Hugo scolded his naïveté. Although it was still early in their relationship, he knew fully well that Phryne was all about the glitz, glamour and presentation. Only a few hours after they met, he recognized that Phryne was all Hollywood. During their first night together at the Clover Club, she lived it. Hugo believed that he had already experienced every taste and breath of life Hollywood could offer, but after that first evening with Phryne, he realized how much he had missed before he met her.

He'd quickly discovered that when he was alone with her, Phryne could flash like the fireworks at a Bastille Day* party. Her personality mirrored the exuberance and excitement of party-goers waving hand-held sparklers along Avenue des Champs-Élysées on New Year's Eve. On the town or at a party, she portrayed a bold and brazen handful. First and foremost, she wrote her own script, a quality that enamored Hugo and endeared him to her scintillating spirit and love of life. She primed his pulse, teased his judgment, challenged his senses and tested his balance. Phryne pranced without bounds.

In return for her vibrant vitality, Hugo gave Phryne what had been lacking in her marriage. Her husband Abner had recently confessed to being in love with a younger woman and demanded that she grant him a divorce. Over the years, Abner had gleaned young starlets from an endless cast of studio hopefuls and harbored one shiksa* after another. Until Phryne met her Frenchman in August, there hadn't been a steady man in her life. The zestful, zingy sex that she once practiced and enjoyed on a regular basis had been a pleasure of the past.

Phryne sidled nearer to Hugo, turned to face him and pushed closer, daring him to make her his alone. He took her in his arms and gave her what she wanted. She returned his kiss, set his soul aglow, sparked the flames and ignited his passion. Her hands on his buttocks pulled him even closer to her own fire.

He whispered into her deep brown curls, "Where is this going, Phryné?"

"To our rooms at the Garden of Allah**, of course ... it's nearing eight o'clock ... but it's time we ready ourselves for the Trocadero, my darling. We have a full plate of parties tonight before we can tangle the sheets."

Hugo was happy to agree, "You are correct, of course, ma chérie. I am especially looking forward to tonight's screening of Leni's film back at the Garden."

She giggled and teased, "Let's get our wiggle* on then!"

Four days earlier, Phryne had left Abner Mandelbaum and moved out of the bungalow that she and her husband had called home since the day they shared wedding their vows. She had telephoned a stage hand and audaciously arranged for the Studio Three property department to move her wardrobe and belongings fifteen miles from 16 Gardner Place in Glendale to Hugo's five-room suite at the Garden of Allah.

During the previous six months, Phryne's lawyer and a bevy of Abner's studio attorneys had smoothed some of the wrinkles and pressed out an agreement that both parties considered to be an amicable dissolution of the nearly eight-year marriage. Disgusted with her husband's verbal abuse, persistent philandering and disinterest in rekindling their romance, she had decided to close her open marriage and move on. There were no children involved and since it was argued that Phryne had brought nothing of tangible value into the marriage, she and her long-time friend and legal advocate Ira Furst, settled on one thousand dollars' worth of five-year-maturation Paramount stock debentures, a cash settlement of two thousand dollars and a stipend of twenty dollars[**] per month for ten years. The divorce had become final on September 1.

Phryne was thirty years young, and acting on a whim. She was moving in with her new leading man and starting over.

Crazy 'Bout My Baby

9:15 PM, Saturday, September 7:
The Café Trocadero, Sunset Boulevard, Hollywood

Everything was a production when Phryne was out and about, whether she was afoot or behind a steering wheel.

The brake pads squealed briefly as she pulled to the curb and set the parking brake. She loved driving the small convertible that she affectionately called *my little windup*. Around town, it was a familiar sight; a flashy woman flaunting a white, fringed silk scarf over a swanky hat. She'd tucked the scarf behind her back and up against the seat in an attempt to hold everything in place.

Phryne's deep burgundy and cream, two-seat roadster wasn't the biggest, jazziest or most expensive car on Sunset Boulevard, but it certainly garnered more than its fair share of double-takes and comments. Five years earlier, it had been a wedding anniversary gift from Abner. The pert, snappy and audacious 1933 American Austin[**] turned more heads than Clark Gable's forest-green Packard Super Eight.

Phryne meticulously unwound her scarf while Hugo walked around the rear of the miniature car and opened her door. As she stepped out of the vehicle, her hemline dashed above the knee, to the lower thigh and just below her stocking tops, giving the valet an intended, visual tease. Phryne always dressed for the maximum optics. She briefly feigned embarrassment, handed her key to the attendant, gave Hugo her hand, and started up the sidewalk to the portico.

The gold-colored threads woven throughout her soft yellow, lamé dress shimmered with every step she took. It clung to her hips like a second skin and ended just below the knee in a ruffled hemline. She had fashionably donned an oversized, moss-green beret, matching T-strap heels and a small, white ermine tippet around her neck that camouflaged her single strand of natural pearls. Abner may have been inattentive and unfaithful, but when it came to her material wants, he never skimped with Phryne.

Hugo's fitted three-piece suit was golden brown, with a double-breasted jacket, full shoulders and a six-button vest that presented a broad, masculine look. The pants fit high on the waist, bulging at the thigh and knee, and tapering to the ankle. Atop his black curls was a soft, coffee-brown fedora with a wide, cream-colored, silk band.

Flash bulbs popped as the pair approached the heavy oak and brass doors of the night club. While Phryne played to the cameras, Hugo turned a cheek and shied away from the photographers. White-gloved doormen in crimson jackets and black slacks stood stoically on either side of the entrance.

The entertainment reporters and photographers lurked outside the Trocadero on Saturday nights, especially when there were post-production parties like the one Phryne and Hugo were attending. The Monday edition of the *Hollywood Reporter*^{**} invariably printed photographs of the glitziest entrances, while the *Los Angeles Times* generally gave their coverage only to the leading ladies and headliners. While Phryne was certainly theatrical, her printability status with the Reporter and the Times was currently in question. Her divorce instantly lowered her standing from an influential producer's wife down to a front-line dancer, cast stand-in, body double and studio chorus girl who happened to be clinging onto the arm of a young, unknown French director. She knew all those things going into her situation, and they were of no consequence. Phryne was focused on her own happiness, and she believed that she had everything she needed to be and remain happy. She still had plenty of close friends in and out of Paramount Studios who had plenty of professional clout and social pull.

Having attended these post-production affairs more than once or twice, Phryne cleverly timed her and Hugo's arrival to be after the first wave of guests and before the club would begin open seating at the secondary reserved tables. She and Hugo were met in the main foyer by the maître-d and a bevy of hostesses decked out in cropped tuxedo jackets, short, black taffeta skirts and fishnet^{***} hose.

Their hostess seated them one row of tables back from the stage and small dance floor. Phryne and her French director Hugo-Henri would share a table with German director Arthur Robison, Austrian actress Hansi Knoteck, German actress Brigitte Helm, Russian director Rouben Mamoulian and German director Josef von Sternberg.

In the tenth seat at the round table, next to von Sternberg, sat the exotic and glamorous Marlene Dietrich, wearing a semi-sheer, ruffled white silk blouse, black blazer, slacks and white-over-black loafers. Since Marlene Dietrich first arrived in Hollywood from France and signed her contract with

Paramount in 1929, she and director von Sternberg had been inseparable, either on the set or while attending studio social gatherings. Marlene successfully traded on her glamorous persona and 'exotic' looks, and immediately became one of the most highly paid actresses in Hollywood. She and her producer had cemented a strong, dependant relationship since they finished their first Hollywood collaboration, *Morocco* in 1930. Their current box-office draw and most recent film together, *The Devil Is a Woman* had wrapped in March. But unlike Phryne and Hugo, von Sternberg and Marlene's relationship was strictly professional. It was common knowledge in Hollywood social circles that Dietrich led an active, varied and commitment-free private life.

Although pioneering director Mamoulian had just completed *Becky Sharp;* the first three-strip Technicolor film[**] for Paramount, it was German director Robison who was in possession of the highly anticipated late-night entertainment. The pièce de résistance[*] was two reels of Leni Riefenstahl's widely acclaimed, Nazi-financed *Triumph of the Will*[**]. Hugo was aware that Robison had a smuggled copy of the film, and had mentioned it to Phryne weeks earlier.

Phryne had quietly finagled the Trocadero seating arrangement both as a surprise for Hugo and as a curiosity-driven personal test of what clout the name *Phryne Truffaut* still carried around Paramount Studios. Her plan came together well. The directors were the first to accept Phryne's invitation, and when she discovered that two beautiful, young, blue-eyed, blonde actresses would be in attendance, getting von Sternberg and Marlene to attend was as easy as drawing ants to Sunday picnic. Phryne's table and about a half dozen other directors and their guests had been invited to a private midnight screening of the German film at Clark Gable's villa at the Garden of Allah.

Surrounded by actors from nations around the world, film directors and producers from all over Europe, Hugo-Henri Grétillat now believed that this American fireball who he called Phryné could hang the moon.

Phryne believed that she and Hugo were about to walk on it. At the least, they were walking on air.

After dinner, they danced until half past eleven to the Harlem stride*** piano of Fats Waller, his Rhythm and the vocal talents of Elizabeth Handy teamed with Fats' scat*.

You Oughta Be in Pictures

The private, two-hour screening of *Triumph of the Will* began just past midnight under the stars in the central atrium of the glass-domed patio lounge. Of the thirty or so people in attendance, less than half were viewing the film. The truly engaged members were perhaps a baker's dozen of directors who had gathered around the Kodascope K-52 projector. Black and white images were being cast through clouds of cigarette smoke, across the flagstone floor and onto a portable roll-up screen as flickering bits and pieces of flashing light. The electric hum of a motor and the rhythmic click-click of celluloid film passing through the projector were mood music for the cinematic enthusiasts. They were mesmerized and lulled into a transcendental trance by Leni Riefenstahl's production, mastery of the camera and editing. The powerful imagery and the hypnotic vision of the subject matter that she captured were tertiary by-products of her cinematic genius.

The remaining guests were scattered throughout the courtyard and adjoining lounge in various stages of sobriety and undress. Bodies were strewn across chaise lounges, white wicker sofas, dual loveseats and simple patio cushions. Amorous guests were either giving attention to, or receiving attention from whomever else was in a receiving or giving mood. Some couples or groups of three or more escaped and made their way indoors to dimly lit, secluded enclaves or the bedrooms.

Hugo was one of the dedicated dozen who were fully immersed in the film. He was intense; his eyes glued to the screen. Except for a half-hour interlude with Paramount actress Carole Lombard and her beau Clark Gable, Phryne roamed no further than arm's length from Hugo, but continued to observe the ballet of bodies around her. Secretly, she would have preferred mingling with the sensually active guests rather than the technically involved. The screening wasn't her cup of tea, but she considered it a necessary inconvenience for growing a comfortable relationship with her director. She realized that she could give Hugo a personal and especially intimate screening back at their rooms. Now that she had left Abner and moved into the Garden of Allah with her Frenchman Hugo, there were things that they needed to discuss.

Phryne however, wasn't the only one who recognized that Hugo had promising talent. Austrian-American director Volker Ufaltz had Hugo's ear much of the evening.

The screening of *Triumph* ended about two o'clock, initiating spirited editorial discussions among producers and directors. There was no shortage of critical opinion; however, the majority of assessments were positive. It wasn't until an hour later that Phryne was able to pry Hugo away from Rouben, Arthur, Josef, Hal, Volker and the rest. At long last, they left Gable's opulent villa, walked across the Garden of Allah courtyard back to Hugo's modest, five-room suite.

Masculine Women, Feminine Men

It was too early to settle in for the night. Phryne's thoughts and senses were still too much aflame to snuff out. She kicked off her heels and walked in stocking feet through the hallway and into the carpeted lounge. She was hanging onto Hugo, and pulling him along hand-in hand.

Once inside the living room, she released her grip on him, tossed her pocketbook onto a plush, cream-colored chair and coyly said, "I think I'll go into character as Mary Magiz and make up a couple of champagne cocktails*** for us just like Carole Lombard did last year with that screwball Zasu Pitts in Goldwyn-Mayer's gangster, comedy train wreck that they called *The Gay Bride*. It was their biggest disaster of the year, but the drinks were good!"

Phryne wasn't about to wait for an answer, and already had started toward the bar. Glasses, bottles and ice cubes tinkled cheerfully as she began working on their drinks.

Hugo watched her from across the room as he removed his suit jacket and vest, loosened his tie, and settled into the sofa. He spoke frankly, "I don't think I've seen that film. But I have seen Carole Lombard. It would be difficult not to." His tone was deadpan.

Liquid libation was already pouring and crystal champagne flutes were being filled. Phryne was exuberant and giggled, "The movie was nothing special, but I think that you'll agree that these drinks are!" Her mood was upbeat.

She smiled and corked the champagne with a gentle thump from her open fist. Wisps of dark brown hair fell from her gently curled tresses down across her temples and cheeks. She carried the drinks from the bar, one in each hand and cupped in her open palms, offering one to her director as she carefully maneuvered her form around the cocktail table and took a seat next to him. She offered a toast, "Cheers!"

Hugo leaned in, kissed her on the lips, and returned the sentiment, "À la votre*, ma chérie." He tasted the drink, feigned surprise, smiled and said, "I would never think anyone could use French champagne in a cocktail and not ruin it, but Phryné, my dear, you have succeeded. What did you mix in here?"

"I'm glad you like it ... there's champagne of course, a slosh of brandy, and some orange juice from breakfast."

She snuggled closer and asked, "What did you think about the film? You seemed all taken up with it. I myself thought it was too dark ... too serious ... and very close to intimidating. It was far too serious."

Hugo paused in thought, took a drink and set his glass on the table before he answered, "I don't agree, but I believe I can honestly speak for the others; in that we all would critique the film as a cinematic masterpiece. Leni Riefenstahl created a work that will become the standard for all film, from documentary to musical farce. Her camera direction and post-production editing were superb."

He took an Old Gold from his cigarette case. Phryne picked up the Ronson lighter off the coffee table and lit it for him. She offered her opinion, "I still think it was too dark. I don't like dark movies. Everything about that movie was dark."

"The whole point of the film wasn't about the Nazis or their politics, Phryné. It was about people believing in something.

"It showed that the true art in cinema is how you edit the film. The images are already easy to comprehend; black and white, clear and simple. The cinema spoon-feeds the public like little babies and gives them moving images and lets them see what we want them to see. How we edit those images can influence history! Don't you see! Volker and Rouben and I talked about this and everyone else agreed. It is so encouraging that some people understand the power of the camera, know how to use it and possess the courage to do it.

"We can change the world when we permit the audience to see things the way they should be seen! That's the beauty of this film. You don't believe anything until you see it right in front of you with your own eyes. Without dialogue, without a single word, the film allows the audience's eyes to tell their warm, mushy, porridge brains what the truth is.

"There's unlimited potential here. With editing like we saw tonight, I mean. It is possible to shape the way people think.

"Don't you see it? The German Chamber of Film** and The Fuehrer himself recognize the power of the cinema.

"It's exactly like your Paramount film that Hal just wrapped, *All the Queens Men*. It's exactly the same, except one has Nazis and the other has queers. In your Paramount movie, the boys are trying to be girls and the girls are trying to be boys. And in Leni's film, the German men and women want to be supermen and amazons and they believe that the Nazis can help them be what they want to be.

"*All the Queens Men* ... think about it ... even the title has a double meaning ... a triple meaning ... and that's what the studio intended. They want everybody to see that movie ... they want the queens, queers, paupers and pampered to come in, pay money and watch that trash.

"It's films like *All the Queens Men* and this Nazi *Triumph* propaganda that fuel our paychecks now and will continue to do so in the coming years, Phryné. And these films give the producers what they want. They can change public opinion to whatever they wish. It's harmless, really.

"We all know it ... some of us do it ... everybody dabbles but not everybody diddles. You know what I mean.

"You allow one part of the audience to believe that it's normal to be queer and another part will see it as decadent, sinful behavior and still another part will see it as comedic nonsense and go home laughing their pants off.

"When people have things presented to them in pictures, they believe that they're seeing things the right way. They want to believe that they, themselves can determine the way things should be.

"When the film shows the audience what it wants to believe, they perceive the images to be the absolute truth. People want other people to agree with them. The producers have them in the palm of their hand and the viewing public will believe whatever they want them to. The power is there for the taking.

"This kind of film production is the future. We have the power! As artists and as technicians, we can be the force of permanent change."

Phryne took a deep breath, finished her drink and lit one of Hugo's cigarettes.

There were a few seconds of silence before she said, "Maybe I'm reading too much into this German movie. It's just that seeing all those thousands of people cheering for something that they don't understand and what nobody has ever seen before is daunting. You must admit that much."

"It's harmless film, Phryné. It gives people something to cheer about and gives them hope for the future. It's all good. You'll see."

"No, it's not good, Hugo. Not really. It's not good. I think the world would be a better place if kings and kaisers didn't trick people into believing that the grass is greener on the other side of the fence. The grass is greener on the other side of the fence because that's where the horses poop. All of humanity would be safer if people simply knew the truth."

Phryne was tired of direction tips and production pointers. Her discussion with Hugo left her frustrated. She swallowed two aspirin tablets and fell asleep wondering who was sharing Marlene's pillow that night.

Let's Do It

Hugo and Phryne had just finished brunch and were relaxing, sitting in the living area, enjoying coffee and listening to *The A&P Gypsies* on radio 930, KHJ. The volume was turned low on the Crosley parlor radio, allowing the bass tones of Harry Horlick's big band to softly resonate from the ten-inch speaker. Hugo was paging through the morning's *Hollywood Reporter* and Phryne was reading the gossip pages in the August issue of *Movie Mirror* with Myrna Loy pictured on the cover.

Hugo wore a grey, brushed silk smoking jacket tied at the waist with a red sash over his black satin pajamas. His bare feet were inside black lambskin loafers.

He was between pictures at the studio and eagerly awaiting his next project, a drama titled *Peter Ibbetson****. The final dialogue edits and stage directions were expected at anytime, which would enable him and director Henry Hathaway to begin work on the technicals, cutaways and final read-through. Shooting was tentatively scheduled to begin the coming Saturday, September 14th under the innovative cinematic direction of Charles Lang.

The project had Hugo especially excited because the lead character spent his childhood in France, and fellow Frenchman George du Maurier's novel of the same title had inspired a successful production on Broadway. Lang and Hathaway also hoped to experiment with new filming techniques to help create a transcendental experience that would take the audience into the world of dreams.

At exactly quarter past noon, Hugo and Phryne's quiet interlude was interrupted by the rap-rap-rap of knuckles on the oak, round-top entry door.

It echoed through the tiled foyer, down the hall and into the living room. Snooker, Phryne's blonde cocker spaniel, was curled up in her favorite chair. The dog sat up and barely woofed at the interruption. True to form, she remained in her chair, laid back down and simply observed.

Phryne stood, gathered her plush, soft pink house coat closer together at the top and pushed a few wayward locks of curls off her face. She walked down the hallway with her slippers swishing across the tiles like a jazz brush on a snare drum. She stopped for a split second at the hall mirror to check her lipstick. She had a tube of Max Factor *Really Red* in her deep pocket, but didn't need it.

At her destination, Phryne pushed the down the black iron latch, opened the door and recognized the fellow on the stoop for who he was: a Paramount studio messenger wearing a navy blue newsboy cap, white shirt, mustard yellow twill pants and a cropped red blazer with the gold company insignia emblazoned on the breast pocket.

The messenger stood straight and tall at the door, "I have a Cablegram from Paris, France for Mister Hugo-Henri Grétillat." The young fellow had trouble with Hugo's surname and stammered trying to wrap his tongue around it. It came out sounding like *great-a-lot*, which was not that far off. He stood holding a delivery log and pencil and added, "You can please sign there at the bottom, Miss."

Phryne signed the book, stepped sideways to the entryway credenza for her clutch and pulled out a dollar bill. She smiled, handed it to the courier, accepted the 5x7 inch envelope and thanked him.

Back on the sofa, Hugo wasn't the least bit curious, and kept his nose in the newspaper and his eyes on the print until Phryne announced, "A messenger just brought another cable from Paris, my darling."

The event was nothing out of the ordinary. Hugo's employer, Pathé Frères had sent him cables of no real consequence a few times in the past. Phryne often signed for them and dutifully delivered them to Hugo, only to have the correspondence read, torn up and unceremoniously discarded. He paid much more attention to the occasional letters that his family sent with bits of news from home.

Phryne watched as he tapped the envelope on its edge onto the cocktail table, tore open the flap and destroyed the envelope pulling out the contents. On different occasions over the last months, Hugo grew impatient with and mildly irritated by Pathé's trivial correspondence. This time it was different. He was acting out of character.

After his is eyes ran across the three-line message, he tossed it onto the table in apparent disgust. Hugo was unusually animated.

"Damn them all! They're calling me back to Paris! *C'est la fin des haricots**! They will not allow me to have a hand in *Peter Ibbetson*! Damn them, damn them all straight to Hell! Damn that dog Lenard to the Devil's bottom level! And all the rest of the bourgeois* bastards at Pathé!"

Snooker briefly raised her head, but quickly decided that there was nothing really to get upset about and settled back down.

Phryne sensed a chasm opening in her chest. She knew going into the relationship with her French director that it could be forced into an untimely end, but she would be the first to admit that she had been running her race around the Paramount track like a filly wearing blinders.

Suddenly the Finish Line came into view and she was falling behind. Her dream was crushed. Unexpectedly faced with an emotional disaster, she immediately began assessing the probable outcomes and probing her brain for possible solutions.

Her thoughts still swirling, she asked him, "When? How soon do they expect you to leave? How much time do we have?"

Hugo didn't offer an immediate answer. He was on his feet and walking toward the set of crystal liquor decanters and glasses atop the sideboard. The heat had been turned up and he seemed to be on a slow boil. He poured unmeasured volumes of DOM Bénédictine liqueur and brandy into two glasses and brought them back to the sofa where Phryne was seated.

He turned to her, became animated once again and spoke with forced emotion, "The Head of Production, Lenard, said in the telegram that the Production Board has decided to end the exchange program. And they have purchased passage for me from New York to Le Havre for 13 October on the *SS Normandie*. The ticket is forthcoming, as are additional funds for my rail travel from Los Angeles to New York. My boss at Pathé has given me the *coup de gras*[*], ma chérie."

Phryne imagined the worst, and saw her hopes and dreams sailing away and disappearing beyond the horizon. Her director was about to leave her stranded on the shores of a deserted island. She scooted across the divan cushion, moved closer to him and frantically searched for the right words.

"I am so sorry. It's not right. It's not fair. They want you to leave much too soon ... much too soon. There must be something we can do. Perhaps you should protest and question their reasoning as well as their untimely, flawed decision ... without allowing you to develop your work."

He swallowed half his drink and lit a cigarette. He looked into his lover's hazel eyes and said, "I cannot imagine what you or I could do to change this. I work for the Gods at Pathé Frères. They and they alone decide what I do. Like the Ten Commandments, when they dictate something, it is written in stone. I must smile and obey or Lenard will stake me upon a pole of tinder and ignite me like The Maid of Orléans[*], or send me straight to the guillotine at Place de la Révolution[**]."

He drew on the Old Gold, exhaled and stared at the cigarette between his fingers. He became philosophically sentimental, "But to be honest, it will be a treat to hold and smoke a Gaulois Bleu[**] again. And eat a cheese other than your innocuous American cheddar."

His inane comment only irritated Phryne's sense of urgency. "That's too bad about your cigarettes and cheese. But what do we do about the real problem? Where does this leave us ... you and me? Where are we now? What am I supposed to do? I was beginning to hold you so dear to my heart, my darling."

Unwittingly, Phryne had presented her question to Hugo as a test for his feelings toward her. She secretly had all her hopes and desires stowed away below decks, but like the Titanic, her ship of dreams had hit an iceberg and was rapidly taking on water and starting to list heavily to stern.

She and Hugo had never spoken about their future together. Now it was forced upon them. Now it was either head for the lifeboats, hope for the best, jump over the rail and start swimming or go down with the ship.

He turned on the small sofa, lovingly took her hands in his and didn't hesitate a second before he answered, "You will travel with me. We will live and love in France. There is nothing to hold you here, my dear Phryné ... nothing at all."

He leaned to her and kissed her lips.

He continued, "Like caged doves, we have been set free. You will come with me to Paris. You may work with me on my films, and dance so well like you do, and you may be the stand-in and the walk-on, and certainly you may have some lines ... perhaps in French or perhaps in your English. You can have anything you want. Why not? You are still very young and beautiful. Your body is magnifique* and you have the best legs. Dietrich has nothing compared to you. You and I will flourish and our love can only grow stronger. You have never loved until you love in Paris, ma chérie. We will love together in Paris."

Phryne's thoughts were treading water in a tidal wave of dreams. She asked, "Where will we live?"

"We will live in Paris, of course ... I have a flat ... not in the city proper, but in the Marmottan District. It is different from Hollywood. It is most charming and I know you will love it."

She was overwhelmed and momentarily unable to speak. A single, tender teardrop tried to run away down her cheek but he kissed it away.

She kissed him back like the world was coming to an end.

"I will go with you. Let's do it, Hugo. Let's go to Paris."

Phryne tugged gently at the red satin sash of Hugo's jacket. He stood, and allowed the silky cummerbund to fall to the floor. Hugo removed his jacket, kicked off his shoes and pulled his pajama shirt over his head. Phryne patiently waited as he disrobed, then stood to face him as bared his top half. Her eyes were glued to his.

Snooker stayed in her chair, watching with her head resting on folded front paws.

Phryne untied her robe, gently pulled it open, and pushed it smoothly off her shoulders. It fell to the floor with a soft, nearly silent swoosh. She reached for her drink, took a swallow, went down on one knee next to the sofa and set her glass back onto the table. She clumsily tugged on his pajama bottoms until they slid off. Hugo slowly sat down on the sofa, his eyes locked on hers.

Her fingers moved up his legs, over his thighs, across his abdomen, up to his chest and through sparse, soft tufts of black hair; pressing, kneading his flesh with her touch and devouring him with her kisses.

"You're a man-eater, ma chérie."

"I love my French delicacies, my darling."

The consummation was ardent, passionate and complete. After their emotions settled, they fell asleep in one another's arms and napped.

A String of Pearls

8 PM, Wednesday, September 11:
Bar & Café, Chateau Marmont, Sunset Boulevard, Hollywood

They awoke about two o'clock refreshed and feeling renewed and spent much of the afternoon talking about the trip ahead, what they needed to accomplish and what Phryne could bring along. Realistically, Hugo only needed to pack for a return trip home. On the other hand, Phryne needed to prepare for a complete relocation half-way around the world. She had about three weeks to put her ducks in a row and get ready for the trip.

Phryne contacted Starr Travel on Hollywood Boulevard, an agency that was well connected with all the major studios. After a lengthy, helpful telephone conversation with agent Agnes Meade, Phryne finalized her plans and completed a ticket portfolio that included cross-continent and trans-oceanic travel. It was decided that she would sell her American Austin and use the money to help pay for her ninety-dollar passage on the Union Pacific and Pennsylvania Railroads, and the three-hundred-thirty-five-dollar fare for the French ocean liner. Although a passport was not a requirement for travel to France, Agnes strongly suggested that Phryne apply for one at the Department of State annex on Fifth Street in East Los Angeles.

Not only a knowledgeable agent, Agnes was a skilled saleswoman and she easily convinced Phryne that they should spend at least one night in New York and enjoy a Broadway show before they were to set sail on Sunday, the 13th of October. The agent said it would be a once-in-a-lifetime experience for them, and an opportunity much too precious to ignore. Agnes confirmed a reservation at the Belvedere Hotel and reserved seat for the new Cole Porter musical, *Jubilee*[**] that will have opened at the Imperial Theater on 45th Street. The hotel and theater were within a five block radius of the ocean liner SS Normandie moored at Pier 88.

Immediately after he learned that Phryne was leaving Hollywood, Dana Mulbauer, a cosmologist at Paramount's Studio G, telephoned and eagerly offered to adopt Snooker, the spaniel.

Phryne and Hugo's journey would begin on Tuesday, October 8 with First Class Pullman sleeper service aboard the Union Pacific's *Los Angeles Limited* to Chicago, where they would connect with the Pennsylvania Railroad's *Broadway Limited* on Friday and arrive in New York City on Saturday morning, October 12.

Agnes proved that she was an agent with ample experience in overseas travel. She suggested that Phryne pack her clothing and personal effects in one or two roomy steamer trunks and ship them via a Teamster Union freight company directly to the French Line's ocean liner Normandie at the Port of New York. She explained that the bulk of Phryne's belongings would travel with her to France untouched and without the worry and hassle of railroad baggage service or any of the roadblocks that the International Longshoremen's Association could create at the pier in New York.

After the travel agency, Phryne telephoned her attorney, Ira Furst. The lawyer advised her to put her cash assets into a Swiss bank as soon as possible after her arrival in Europe, citing political unrest and the growing tensions in Czechoslovakia and Spain as the justification for his suggestion.

Following the initial surprise of his recall to France, and after Phryne had firmed up their travel arrangements, Hugo's anger at his unexpected transfer was replaced by cautious expectation. The thought of returning to Paris with his Phryné by his side appeared to refresh his outlook on life. Phryne was giddy with joy.

They decided to celebrate their adventurous move and dressed for dinner at the posh and polished Chateau Marmont[**]. Hugo wore a medium blue, large plaid-patterned, double-breasted suit with a deep, wide collar, baggy slacks tapered to the ankle, a black felt fedora and white-over-black wingtips. In lieu of a tie, a white silk ascot was tucked into his shirt collar.

Phryne donned a silver-embroidered lace evening wrap over a clingy, soft yellow, open-back satin gown with wide, cross-over bodice shoulder straps that revealed a deep V-neckline. Her gown's hemline danced from mid-calf in front to the tops of her turquoise, ankle-high Louis XV heels in back.

They walked hand-in-hand through the bougainvillea-lined walkways of the Garden of Allah to the sidewalks of Sunset Boulevard. The restaurant was barely a few hundred feet down the block with flickering gas lights glowing along the way. They met Grant and Crawford walking in the opposite direction, but shared minimal pleasantries. Phryne felt miffed at first, but she reasoned that Cary and Joan must have had a pressing engagement, which by itself, would not be out of the ordinary for either the actor or red-haired bombshell. Moreover, Hugo and Phryne had a lot more on their evening dinner plate than idle chit-chat with passersby.

The Café at Chateau Marmont was always bursting at its doors. Hugo requested a dining table away from the ballroom and its activity, and gladly accepted a secluded booth in the lounge, near the bar and tucked into a quiet corner alongside the coat-check, restrooms and valet stand.

A spry, young hostess in a black rayon skirt and white bib apron promptly led them to a table covered in immaculate linen, accented with a small vase of mixed freesias and two candles flickering inside red votives. Gold, satin pillowcase backs adorned the chairs. Notwithstanding the foot traffic and chatter, it was the perfect setting. Regardless, they were in a world of their own.

Hugo ordered two Tanqueray gimlets^{***} as apéritifs.

"You look wonderful tonight, my dear Phryné. You are simply radiant. You are my private bijou[*]."

"Thank you, I love to dress for you ... and it makes me feel good and lifts my spirits. Ever since I was a little girl, dressing up made me feel special. Lord knows how much I love feeling this way."

"You dress wonderfully, Phryné. You are always beautiful, but tonight there is something special. You are radiant. You are glowing."

She smiled, reached across the small table and took his hand. She waited a moment, and said, "Thank you, darling ... but listen ... I don't want to sound silly. I'm serious. I'm happy, extremely happy. It seems everything in my world is sparkling and glistening. I am so excited about moving to Paris with you that I've got the tickles all up and down and inside me. It almost feels like I'm about to peak. No, not really, but almost. I love it."

"Wonderful. That's what I say: wonderful. I am so happy to begin a new life with you."

She spoke sensually, nearly whispering, "Hugo, my darling, I want to change my name."

She unwittingly created a shockwave.

Her out-of-the-blue statement gave him nervous pause and instant worry that she may have misunderstood his words and was racing full-bore down a different road. Phryne had indeed ignited a flame within him that burned as the deepest, hottest blue, and he held strong feelings for her, but this was something he didn't anticipate. His nerves tightened and his heartbeats quickened. He felt his intestines twist.

Temporary relief came when their waitress delivered a welcome silence and arrived with their drinks. After Hugo slid two one-dollar bills across the table and thanked her, she turned on her heels and disappeared.

Hugo's head began to spin. Phryne had thrown what could be the knockout punch. Suddenly, he found himself worrying about his future and searching for a reply to his lover's off-the-cuff proclamation. She was a delicious, sparkling, well-packaged handful, but a firm commitment wasn't the type of Hollywood souvenir he wanted to bring back to Paris. His independence and pride were in jeopardy.

Bit by bit, he allowed Phryne's next words to soothe his nerves.

"I want my name to be more French. I love the way you pronounce my name. I want my name to be French. I want it to sound French. Do you know what I'm trying to say? If I am going to live in France, I want my name to sound French. I want people to say my name in French ... like you do."

"Your family name *Truffaut* is a very French name, ma chérie."

"No, no, no, Hugo. I mean my given name, my first name, *Phryne*. It is actually a Greek name, but you make it sound so French. You say it differently than most people. You accentuate the last part when you say it, right at the end with the accent on the last little letter *e*."

Her explanation led him to understand and he breathed a silent sigh of relief.

"You can do that very easily. All you need do is add an aigu[*] to the last letter of your name and it will become what you desire: *Phryné*." Like a grade-school teacher, Hugo wrote an accent mark in the air with his index finger, and explained, "You write it just like that: P-H-R-Y-N-É."

Phryne beamed. "That's all? It's so simple!"

She straightened her back, sat up proud and added, "From now on I will be *Phryné Truffaut ... Phryné Althea Truffaut.* When I get my passport next week, that's the way it will be ... that's who I am ... from now on. I'm going to Paris."

Hugo nodded, smiled and finished his gimlet.

He affirmed, "Pathé Frères has rewritten the script. You have a new role, ma chérie."

3. The "Los Angeles Limited" and "Broadway Limited" to New York
~ 1935 ~

Dream a Little Dream of Me

8 PM, Wednesday, October 9.
Evanston, Wyoming

Twenty-six hours after Phryné and Hugo came aboard The Los Angeles Limited[**], they were traveling eastward from Ogden, Utah into southern Wyoming; still about fourteen hundred miles from Chicago. Hand-in-hand, they stepped out of their drawing-room and started down the hall of their Pullman sleeper-car. With six steps down the hall, three past the small lavatory and a final four through the connecting vestibules, they entered the Pullman dining car.

Eleven steps further along a narrow walkway, past the kitchen and into the dining room, a reserved table for two awaited them. The Dining Car was about one-third kitchen and two-thirds dining area. There were six square-top tables with seating for four along the right side of the car and a matching number of smaller tables for two on the left side. Each one was dressed with snowy linen and gleaming table settings of pristine white bone china. At first glance, every table seemed occupied. The steward was a tall, young, thin man with a milky complexion and pronounced freckles, dressed in a white dinner jacket and sienna-brown slacks. He carried his left arm outward, bent at the elbow, with a crisp linen towel folded over it. He stood squarely in the aisle as Hugo and Phryné approached. With an air of authority, he slid his right hand inside his jacket, checked his pocket watch, then Hugo's reserved-time seating card. Satisfied that everything was as it should be, he spoke in a voice as sweet as a meadowlark, "Follow me … sir … ma'am."

There were three waiters in the car, all men of color, and like the steward, they were also dressed in white jackets and brown trousers. The steward moved with the grace of a ballet dancer, stepping down the center aisle, moving aside for one waiter, then another.

He stopped at the fifth set of tables and motioned for his guests to be seated. Hugo graciously helped Phryné with her chair before he took his seat, with his back toward the front of the railcar.

Their closest neighbors were sitting inches away at the next table, snuggled close to the bulkhead wall and the vestibule leading into the Lounge Car.

Phryné was almost certain that Hugo also noticed them, but oddly didn't acknowledge so. She began studying the pair, covertly looking over Hugo's shoulders and gathering information without staring. She recognized them. They were, indeed, familiar strangers. Together, they were mesmerizing. He, especially, emitted a strong, pulling magnetism that tested Phryné's better judgment.

The previous day in Los Angeles, Phryné had spotted and pointed out the same well-dressed couple standing on the bustling platform at Central Station among scores of other Chicago-bound passengers. They were about to board the Pullman section and roomette sleeper *Centgarde*, which was coupled two cars further back in the consist[*] than their own accommodations in the *Glen Dee* Pullman bedroom car.

The gentleman and his lady each dressed to the nines; markedly more sophisticated than the majority of their fellow travelers. At the time, Hugo asked Phryné if she recognized the couple, and she replied, "No, but they certainly stand out among the hoi polloi[*], but they're nobody I know ... I've never seen them before and don't believe that they're from Hollywood or part of the Industry."

Hugo added, "They may be well-dressed, Phryné, but they cannot hold a candle to you or me."

The mystery couple was dressed for dinner in the dining car as impeccably as they had been the day before when they boarded the train at Central Station. But it wasn't their appearance or manner of dress that intrigued Phryné; it was the handsome stranger.

Phryné focused her eyes over Hugo's right shoulder and studied the unknown woman. She was sitting straight in her chair with the caution of youthful inexperience, as if she were afraid to set an unfortunate wrinkle onto her soft periwinkle, taffeta dress. She appeared glamorously aloof and could possibly be a rising star, an intimate personal assistant or simply high-end hired companionship. The gentleman was strikingly dapper without the polish of Hollywood, but Phryné couldn't pin a moniker, profession or skill set onto him either. He and his tailored suit did, however, leave a lasting, favorable first impression when Phryné first spotted him on the train platform in Los Angeles. His likeness was burned into her memory.

Phryné was studying him closely and noticed that while he had a full head of black hair much like Hugo's, there were tight curls from the stranger's forehead to the nape of his neck. His dinner companion was a peroxide blonde who could rival Jean Harlow both in looks and figure. Hugo and Phryné's dining-car neighbors at the next table were either ignoring or didn't notice them. Regardless, they were oblivious to Phryné's scrutiny and continued to sip their cocktails and talk low. Phryné strained her ears, but couldn't spoon a single word out of the simmering stew of railroad noise.

She slyly avoided fixing her gaze, and managed to persuade her eyes to roam over the rest of the dining car as well, but her glances always landed on the back of her mystery man's head, neck or shoulders. Phryné kept hoping for a closer look or more importantly, an opportunity to start a back-and-forth. Her unbridled imagination was running freely through a field of fantasy. Phryné tried to picture the gentleman without his jacket, wondering if his shoulders were truly so square and wide.

She guessed that he was about forty, ten years older than she, and discovered that he had the complexion of an outdoorsman, not rugged or worn, but that of a man who wasn't locked up in an accountant's office or a movie studio for twelve hours of the day. She dreamed about running her fingers through the tight little curls of coal-black hair that were dancing atop his shirt collar.

So as not to signal her wandering eye, Phryné smiled across the table at Hugo as an affirmation of her attention to him alone. While she was familiar with the adage 'curiosity killed the cat', she believed that erotic daydreams were harmless fun and merely sensuous catnip. In any case, it appeared that Hugo was too busy studying the entrée menu and full page of à la carte items to notice Phryné's wandering eyes.

Phryné hurriedly, privately plotted her next course of action, hoping to force an introduction. While she considered some opening lines to a conversation, a waiter appeared at tableside with two slips of paper for her and Hugo to tick off their dinner selections. As if their exit had been scripted, the enigmatic couple at the next table wriggled unceremoniously out of their chairs and stood to leave. Phryné's hopes were dashed and her warm, pie-in-the-sky dreams were left to cool on the windowsill. While he helped his comely companion with her wrap, the unidentified man caught Phryné's inquiring glance just as she was attempting to look away. She was momentarily seized by his deep brown eyes and steely smile. He boldly dared to send a miniscule nod in her direction. Phryné felt a flush at her brief embarrassment and helplessly watched as he placed his hand gently onto his partner's lower back. It was a gentlemanly gesture, one of tenderness and endearment. Regardless, Phryné was secretly envious and imagined the feel of his hand, the warmth of his touch and the tickle of his pencil mustache on her cheek. She felt a tingle running up her back that switched on a wave of electricity across her shoulders and sent charged ripples racing along her loins.

Phryné's eyes followed the pair toward the forward vestibule and out of the dining car toward their roomette on the *Centgarde*. She then needed to force her attention back to Hugo and the attractive, colorized Union Pacific menu with Bryce Canyon on the cover. Her eyes danced blindly across the pages without reading and scarcely recognized the printed words. She saw only the black hair and square shoulders of her mystery man.

She anticipated that she would have the opportunity to meet him again and convinced herself that she could continue her fantasy tête-à-tête the next day at breakfast, lunch or dinner. Hopefully, her chance would come sometime sooner rather than later.

When they had finished their dinner, the steward announced that they were in Green River, Wyoming and The Limited had cleared the tedious haul through the Rocky Mountains. A fresh driving team arrived and the train switched power to a Baldwin 4-8-2[**] locomotive for the remaining miles across the Great Plains to Chicago. That night, Phryné and Hugo managed to make love rolling to the rocking rhythm of the rails in the double bed of their First Class Drawing Room in the *Glen Dee*.

The session was awkward and brief, leaving Phryné's libido unsatiated and her ego bruised. Hugo fell asleep fulfilled but vanquished. Phryné initially scolded her selfish fantasies, but went on to dream of her broad-shouldered stranger throughout the night.

Pennsylvania 6-5000

1 PM, Friday, October 11.
Chicago, Illinois

Phryné didn't lay eyes on the mystifying couple at any time during the remainder of their sixty-hour trip from Los Angeles to Chicago. She tempted the Fates[**] and tried everything short of camping out in the *Centgarde* walkway, but her efforts were unsuccessful. An attempted five-dollar bribe of the Pullman Porter was also fruitless. His stoic reply was, "I'm sorry, Miss. I cannot disclose compartment numbers. The privacy of Union Pacific's passengers is a primary bulwark of Pullman service."

Additionally, she took numerous extra trips to the lounge car, explaining to Hugo that she felt cramped in their drawing-room and simply needed to move about a bit, if only to have a king size Pall Mall in a drafty vestibule. Twice she traversed through the narrow walkways of the Lounge Car and all ten Pullman sleepers on the odd chance that she could bump into the leading man of her erotic dreams. Frustrated at her efforts, she went so far as to admonish herself for trying to force a "chance" meeting, and dressed-down such school-girl antics.

But, when she and Hugo switched trains in Chicago and boarded Pennsylvania Railroad's *Broadway Limited*[**] for the overnight trip to New York, she resumed her fruitless scrutiny of the station and its platforms. The unknown traveler and his companion were nowhere to be seen and yet again, Phryné's untethered, high hopes for a meaningful meeting were deflated. Their paths didn't cross and a clandestine romantic rendezvous appeared to be highly unlikely.

Her disappointment however, was tempered by the thrill of their ultimate destination. A night on the town, Times Square and a Broadway show trumped her blues. Hollywood had its shining stars and night clubs, but Broadway had far more sparkling lights. New York City was a mere sixteen hours and nine hundred miles of steel track away.

Puttin' on the Ritz

9 AM, Saturday, October 12.
The lobby of the Hotel Belvedere,
West 48th Street, New York, New York

The Broadway Limited delivered them to Pennsylvania Station** on schedule, just as advertised, at eight-thirty in the morning. They were welcomed by masses of humanity.

The efficiency of the railroad's baggage service impressed Hugo despite the station's daunting aura of ordered metropolitan chaos. Porters and Red Caps scurried through the swarming crowds from the platforms to the baggage carts and out to the sidewalks. A few moments after they stepped off the railcar and their feet touched terra firma in New York, Phryné and Hugo climbed aboard a much smaller cocoon of steel and glass: a bumblebee-yellow Checker** taxicab on the way to their hotel on West 48th Street.

The Hotel Belvedere was everything that Agnes at Starr Travel had promised. Phryné and Hugo were surrounded by experiences that thrilled the senses, fulfilled their expectations and ignited dreams. Phryné's first impression of New York City was that unlike Hollywood, the city's life-blood wasn't the film industry; it was people. People were everywhere.

The streets and sidewalks throbbed. The lifeblood of the city moved on rubber tires and shoe leather.

Throughout the hotel's expansive domed lobby, potted palms and figs were tucked into corner niches and tiled, terra cotta grottos. Hand-carved, six-foot, polished wooden statues of Nubian servants covered in only white loincloths and red turbans stood tall at each end of the balcony stairway. In the center of the atrium was a gurgling water fixture featuring a circular trio of sculpted bronze Roman maidens spilling water from earthen urns. The statues were artfully presented in varying stages of nudity, and displayed a varied spectrum of emotional and physical expression. The verdigris figures were prominently featured as the focal point of a tranquil pond that was surrounded with plantings of philodendrons, colorful caladiums, ferns and pink angel-wing begonias. Queen Anne chairs and settees upholstered in richly-colored embroidered brocade were smartly positioned to present a cultured Victorian, turn-of-the-century ambiance. Overhead, a second-story balcony embraced the lobby in a swooping half-circle. Behind the black iron and polished brass railing was a panoramic gas-light walkway with all the commerce of a small village: newsstands, beauty parlors, barbers, clothiers, tinkers, tailors, cafés, and curiosity shops. An eight-foot diameter, ten-foot long crystal chandelier hung from the two-story vaulted ceiling. Its dangling, ten-inch rectangular prisms created an indoor, daylight Milky Way of dancing, twinkling stars.

Agnes had secured an exclusive first class, two-day reservation a month earlier to accommodate Phryné and Hugo's early morning arrival from Chicago. To their left, right and rear, the reception area was bustling with guests and clientele either waiting to check out or attempting to traverse the polished pink marble floor out toward the street for sight-seeing, casual appointments or further travel to destinations far and wide.

Phryné and Hugo were standing at the Reception Desk across from a waxy-faced clerk with slicked hair and delicately colored lips. He was wearing a stiffly starched white shirt, a black bow tie and a tailored chartreuse jacket with a gold crest on the breast pocket.

A bellhop in a red and black pillbox hat was waiting patiently for them near the elevators. He was positioned at parade rest; his hands folded in front at the beltline and his eyes locked on Phryné with barely a hint of an emotionless smile. He was standing guard at his rolling brass luggage rack in charge of Phryné and Hugo's three suitcases, two Pullmans, two hatboxes and Phryné's overnight and personals case.

The clerk behind the reception counter passed Hugo the key for the fifteenth-floor Stuyvesant Suite and spoke in a banal monotone, "I hope you enjoy your stay here at the Belvedere, Monsieur Grétillat. Please remember that we at the Belvedere are here to make your stay as comfortable as possible."

It was immediately apparent that the fellow knew enough French to at least pronounce Hugo's name correctly.

Hugo asked, "Breakfast is still being served?"

"Yes, sir, it's available until ten in the Olde Amsterdam Room. Then it's brunch until one, and closed until dinner at six o'clock, sir."

Phryné couldn't help herself. She purred, "How about a Hollywood breakfast? A breakfast in bed?"

Hugo knew what she was doing and smiled. He loved it.

The clerk didn't cast a blink, having heard countless such open-ended remarks over the course of his employment. He looked to the registry to confirm the name of his feisty female guest and offered with a devious smile, "Room service is available for each of the twenty-four hours in a day, Miss Truffaut."

Again, the clerk affirmed his knowledge of Continental pronunciation and professional etiquette.

Phryné wasn't about to be out-done. "Wonderful. Sometimes my appetite is simply insatiable."

Hugo chortled, "Don't I know it."

The clerk tried his best to choose decorum over gaucherie[*] with his comment, "I know you will find all of our menu selections deliciously tasty, our amenities luxuriously tempting, and every one of our concierge services to be top-notch. At any rate, I hope you enjoy your stay."

Phryné nodded and sent a demure smile across the counter, "Thank you."

Hugo offered her his arm, she shifted her handbag from one hand to the other, took Hugo's elbow, and they started toward the elevators. Phryné's heels had clicked twice on the stone floor before she heard the clerk add, "Bon appétit, Miss."

She decided not to turn around just then, but rather let her hand slip from Hugo's arm and drop to his right buttock just as they arrived at the elevators. It rested there until the bellhop pushed the luggage rack onto the hoist and she and Hugo walked aboard. Inside the lift, she turned and noticed that the reception clerk was indeed looking her way, ignoring the gentlemen at the counter and smiling like the cat that licked the sardine can.

Phryné boldly aggrandized into Hugo's ear, "I enjoyed that!"

The bellhop remained silent, unmoved, and dutifully pushed the button marked "15". The doors closed from top to bottom with a mechanical, muffled whoosh and the Otis elevator jerked upward toward the fifteenth floor.

Inside the double doors of the Stuyvesant Suite, Hugo passed a silver dollar into the bellhop's palm as he finished unloading their cases and bags. Before the room steward was completely out the door, Phryne had kicked off her pumps and was standing bedside in her stocking feet, removing her shoulder wrap and tapered-brim, soft camel bonnet. She sighed, ran a finger through the ends of her cocoa-brown curls and sat on the bed. She looked around the room and acknowledged that it was a first-class suite. The room alone was nearly half the size of Hugo's five-room accommodation at the Garden of Allah.

Phryné reached into her handbag, took a cigarette out of its silver case and lit it with her Ronson^{**} all-in-one. She expelled a sigh of relaxation and said, "My darling, I'm going to take a long, hot, soapy shower ... a shower without swaying back and forth and hanging onto a railing or hand grip and watching the waste water drain down and out and onto the tracks and ties beneath me ... a long hot shower. And then I'm going between the sheets. And I will go to sleep."

She drew deeply on her cigarette, closed her eyes and paused for a moment before she exhaled. She reached for the cut crystal ashtray on the bedside table and explained, "I feel like I'm still moving, for God's sake. I still hear the noise, smell the smoke and taste the coal soot and all that stale air inside the railcar."

Hugo stepped to the bedside and sat next to her. His hand went to her thigh. "A nap is a superb idea, ma chérie. We have been traveling for a full three days, now. We have reached New York and now we may rest and relax. Tonight we'll enjoy Cole Porter's *Jubilee* and we sail tomorrow. I'll call room service."

She took one last puff and crushed out her Pall Mall. Fading grey wisps of smoke drifted up and away.

She kissed his cheek and said, "I need to take that shower and take a rest from our travel, my darling. Order some hot chocolate and a pastry or croissant or something for me, please. That's all I want. A shower, a nibble and a good, long nap." She briefly drifted in thought, and then added, "I need to rest up. Tonight we're doing the town big time. You're right. We're in New York! I'm going to ditch these dowdy railroad dresses of mine and glam it up!"

Lovely to Look At

4:30 PM, Saturday, October 12.
The Stuyvesant Suite, 15ᵗʰ Floor, the Hotel Belvedere

Phryné awoke from her nap about four o'clock after nearly sleeping the afternoon away. She reached to the bedside table, checked her Longines wristwatch, set it down, found her pillow again and closed her eyes. She felt refreshed, reborn.

Her body and mind had demanded that nap. The slate needed to be wiped clean. Her deep sleep allowed the persistent rattle of the rails beneath her to drift away with the wind. The monotonous vision of whisking across the landscape at fifty miles an hour disappeared from her mind's eye like the last mile post of a dream.

But it was unavoidable. The three-day trip from Los Angeles to New York brought back memories of another marathon railway excursion that Phryné had taken eight years earlier in 1927. At the time, she and her fiancé were on the run and fleeing Buffalo, New York, trying to escape the Black Hand Mafia and its vindictive violence. They were on the lam and dodging the FBI following a badly botched Canadian bootlegging scheme. After an impromptu wedding in Chicago, she found herself a week later in Los Angeles, twenty-two years young, abandoned, pregnant and alone. It was then that she met Abner Mandelbaum, who took her under his wing and introduced her to Hollywood. They were married a few months later at Christmas.

Her pregnancy ended four months later with the premature birth of a baby girl, who died the next day from respiratory failure.   There were more bumps in the road, and it was necessarily to take a few detours, but all things considered, Abner steadied the wheel and tried his best to smooth the ride. Unfortunately, five years of philandering drove their relationship into the ditch and put their marriage on the rocks.

Phryné had thought once or twice about telling Hugo about her youthful missteps but believed that her story would just cloud otherwise clear waters.   She reasoned that it served no purpose to re-shoot a black and white melodrama in three-reel Technicolor.

Phryné shoved her maudlin memories aside and took a deep breath, filling her lungs with air.   Fantastic new ideas were fluttering like butterflies on gossamer wings, and searching for a field of daisies; somewhere to sip at all the nectars of life that New York City had to offer.   She was quickly developing a flight plan and needed to tell Hugo all about it.   There wasn't much time before they sailed, and knew that she needed to get out of bed.

She wasn't wearing a stitch, and was covered only by the snow-white bed sheet.   Looking around the expansive room, she spotted Hugo: asleep, sprawled on the settee next to the midget-bar and lounge, and still in his silk shirt, slacks and stocking feet.   The barely audible, sleepy music of Eddy Duchin and his Orchestra was coming from a Philco table radio on the counter top.

Again, she fought the temptation to languish under the cool sheet and rolled onto her back, spread her arms wide, flexed, tightened and relaxed every muscle she could from fingers to toes.   Phryné repeated her stretching regimen to discover that much like an Olympic runner can catch a 'second wind', she found renewed vigor and excitement after her nod on the Stuyvesant Suite's king-size bed.

She slid out from under the sheet, donned the white terry bathrobe that she had left lying at the foot of the bed and walked across to her sleeping Hugo.

She silently went to her knees next to the small sofa, leaned in and placed a gentle kiss on his lips. Only the least bit startled, he smiled and whispered, "Allo[*], ma chérie," and took her hand.

Phryné kissed him once again on the lips. "Please wipe the sleep from your eyes, my darling. I had the most spectacularly marvelous dream that I was wearing a dress so wonderful that the traffic on Fifth Avenue was jammed. Imagine that! Dreams can come true!

"I think it's time to get dressed and go shopping. We need to get our wiggle on.[*] I need to get that dress ... a gown for the theater ... a proper gown ... and of course, I can wear it on the ship, too ... in the ballroom, certainly. And I know just the place. I absolutely have to go shopping at Saks^{**} ... just like my dream ... Saks on Fifth Avenue. We're in New York and there's no excuse not to ... no excuse at all. I want a lamé dress ... of any color, and possibly with spangles or sequins."

Hugo sat up and affirmed, "Magnifique. You are always lovely to look at."

"We can go shop at Saks and then to Sardi's^{**} for dinner afterwards. I've heard so much about both places, we absolutely have to go there tonight."

He asked, "Sardi's?"

"Yes. Everybody who is anybody goes to Sardi's. And they usually get their picture on the wall. There's one in Hollywood, too ... I know that you've been there ... but the New York restaurant is the original ... and the best. I would love to have either your portrait or mine on Sardi's wall! We may even meet Cole Porter or that young Montgomery Clift of his there between shows! Who knows? According to Cole, anything goes."

Oh! Look at Me Now ....

7:45 PM, Saturday, October 12.
Le Chic Salon, Hotel Belvedere, West 48ᵗʰ Street

After surviving a hellish half hour under assault by brushes, combs and steam-heated curling irons, Phryné left a hefty twenty-dollar tip for the stylist and beautician. She met Hugo in the lobby and they scampered out of The Hotel Belvedere into a waiting cab. The salon had set waves galore into the long dark tresses that framed her oval face and fell gently onto her shoulders. Her hair was parted on the left, pulled and pinned back. The styling left a slight hint of pouf bangs on the right, softly falling over her forehead to the corner of her eye.

The Belvedere's laundry service steamed and brushed Hugo's black, three-piece, silk suit while Phryné was in the salon. He would step out in white-on-black wingtips, a jet-black fedora with a red band and a matching crimson silk ascot inside a ruffled white shirt.

Phryné selected a crushed silk, champagne-pink and silver lamé gown mere minutes after she had entered the Saks sales floor, but regardless of Phryné's words of encouragement and Hugo's pleas for expediency, the fitting and resulting nip and tuck alterations took nearly an hour. While they were leaving Saks, Phryné and Hugo agreed that they unanimously shared the opinion that the end result was worth the time, effort and stress.

It was a form-hugging, ankle-length gown, with a semi-sheer fitted bodice, a small collar, soft lapels and a sweetheart neckline. Small, fabric-covered buttons were in front from the collar to below the waist. For her feet, Phryné indulged in a pair of two-inch, ivory T-strap heels with silver toe, heel and instep. A creamy white, lace wrap covered her shoulders.

Hugo had arranged for a ride from the Belvedere to the theater at seven-thirty for the eight o'clock show. As if she were testing his nerves, Phryné's personal preparations had pushed the clock precariously close to show time. When they boarded the jet-black Cadillac limousine at quarter-to-eight, curtains-up at the Imperial Theater was only five minutes, three blocks, and a mere quarter-mile away on West 45th.

New York City was aglow. That evening set the city forever into Phryné's memory. Life coursed through every imaginable thoroughfare, giving the concrete and steel a breath of its own, interdependent on every man, woman and child within its bounds. All were exactly in their places, synchronized and dancing as one on Life's stage.

Every light in every socket, either hanging or fixed, twinkled like the brightest star on the darkest of nights. Countless neon tubes blushed warmly in the brightest colors of a man-made phosphorescent rainbow. Streets overflowed with trolleys, busses, taxis and hired cars of all makes and sizes. Sidewalks were flooded with ambulatory traffic representing every slice of life from tourist, piker, prostitute, panhandler or professional.

Their chauffeur stopped at the curb, in queue behind two other cars waiting for the Imperial Theater's crew of doormen to open car doors for exiting theater-goers. *Jubilee* had opened the previous evening, but the excitement and anticipation of a new Cole Porter musical remained fresh. To keep zealous photographers and autograph seekers at bay, The Imperial had placed theater ropes along both sides of the entryway. As at the Trocadero in Los Angeles, cameras took photographs of every passing gown as if it were a fancy dress ball. Flashbulbs popped and crackled as Phryné and Hugo walked along the short-pile red carpet. Just as he did in

Hollywood, Hugo tried to position either his hat or the back of his hand between his face and the camera lens. Phryné didn't understand Hugo's timidity with photographers. She, on the other hand, never gave protest or fretted. She believed that her jazzy behavior affirmed her cosmopolitan presence and that Hugo's timidity only added mystique.

There was no way to know for sure, but Phryné suspected that Agnes at Starr Travel had arranged their theater seating on the sly. It was after the usher escorted them to their seats that they discovered that Maurice Chevalier and Jeanette MacDonald shared their reserved box in the elevated section of the left orchestra. They were in gracious company.

The musical and its cast were received with overwhelming approval and applause. Chevalier and MacDonald were charmed by Phryné and Hugo's personal history and impending adventure; so much so that Maurice and Jeanette invited them to return with them to their hotel, The Algonquin on 44th Street, for drinks and hors d'oeuvres[*]. However, Phryné and Hugo's 8 to 9 AM boarding window for the Normandie however precluded their accepting the invitation and initiated an apologetic, cordial decline. Alternatively, Phryné presented an open-ended, empty proposition to Maurice and Jeanette that they visit the next time they were in Paris.

While waiting in the Imperial lobby for their ride back to the Belvedere, Phryné offered Hugo another suggestion. She convinced him that a small detour on their way back to their hotel would enable them to see all the lights of Times Square up close and comfortably from inside their limousine. Hugo agreed, and once they were in the car and seated, their driver cheerfully obliged.

It was America on parade with colorful neon and incandescent accents. The flashing lights of the tall, thirty-foot marquee above the doors of Paramount Central Theater declared that *The Devil Is a Woman,* and co-stars Marlene Dietrich and Lionel Atwill would prove it. Illuminated neon advertising assured the wide-eyed public that *Camels never get on your nerves, Coca Cola is ice cold sunshine that soothes, Lucky Strike is the clean smoke,* and *you should be a member of Canadian Club.*

Phryné's pulse hastened as the limousine took the corner at 47th Street and 8th Avenue, outside the Ritz Carlton and just a half mile from their suite at the Belvedere. A well-dressed, flashy couple stood near the curb and barely five feet away, under the subdued, yellow light of a lamppost. Because of the tilt of his hat, the scarf over her head and the speed of the car, it was impossible for Phryné to positively identify them as her the fantasy pair from the train.

She chose to believe that it was.

4. The "SS Normandie" to Le Havre, France ~ 1935 ~

Begin the Beguine[*]

8 AM, Sunday, October 13, Port of New York,
Pier 88, Hudson River at 48th Street.

High tide would occur at ten o'clock, and at quarter past, the SS Normandie[**] would steam south out of the Hudson River into the Atlantic Ocean on the way back to her home port in Le Havre, Normandy, France.

The collection of travelers arriving and awaiting passage on the new 'Liner of Legend', the SS Normandie, was kissed by the fresh air of autumn. It was a clear, crisp, fifty-degree morning with a calm breeze from the southeast. The sun had risen an hour earlier and had begun to clear the New York skyline over Hell's Kitchen and the Theater District. Moored motionless at Pier 88, the 'Ship of Light' beamed brighter than the sun and loomed larger than the morning.

Notwithstanding the preeminence of the Empire State Building[**] and New York's other skyscrapers, the 'Pride of the French Line' presented a majestic, daunting and lasting impression with its nearly quarter-mile length and eighteen-story height. The ocean liner consumed the entire span of the pier; as long as the Chrysler Building stood tall.

A Yellow Cab delivered Phryné and Hugo to the Première Classe (First Class) Embarkation building at Pier 88, New York Harbor at exactly eight o'clock. The smaller, austere Second and Tourist Class boarding facilities were much further down the dock, seven-hundred feet away at the ocean liner's stern[*], downwind and distanced from the more privileged passengers. The inanimate, grey steel hulk awaited and welcomed them all, either entitled, endowed, or of meager means. Whether they were warmed and adorned in sable, silk, cotton, fox or flax, the Normandie stood ready to swallow every paying passenger up and inside its welded, riveted and bolted hull. Baggage, pets, freight, foodstuffs, automobiles and bits of humanity's upper crust were welcomed and given their specific place aboard.

The Première Classe welcoming hall was a buzzing, bubbling stew of French and English conversation within a simmering cauldron of refined, civilized chaos.

Hugo presented their boarding ticket to one of the dozen-plus purser's mates working behind polished teak counters and brass railings. Further along the counter, French Immigration clerks in blue, stiff-brimmed, short, round-topped kepi** hats, performed cursory identification and passport checks at the entrance to the covered gangway.

As she and Hugo exited the departures building to board the ship, Phryné stepped along the center of the walkway, slightly intimidated by its seemingly precarious course, incline and height above the dock. Relief came as her timidity dimmed once she had passed completely through the portico, into the hull, onto the elevator and was standing safely inside the opulent Main Entrance Hall and Grand Salon of the Ship of Light.

Phryné was then overwhelmed by spectacle, but she was not alone. Every first-time passenger boarding the Normandie experienced awe. Five months earlier in May, on the occasion of the ship's maiden voyage, the prominent French newspaper, *Paris-Soir*** boasted editorially that 'even a blind man could see' how grandiose the opulent ocean liner was fitted out.

Stamped with the French Line logo, an otherwise nondescript brass key opened the door to Stateroom 162. Their suite was on the Main Deck; portside* and midship*.

When Phryné and Hugo stepped inside their quarters, their sensual wonderment grew. From vases to tables to mirrors, art deco accents of bronze and stainless steel teamed with colorful tapestries, tucked upholstery and crafted fabrics.

Louvered glass double-doors opened to a private balcony with furniture of burnished Burmese teak.

The lavatory, bath, showers and adjoining powder room were marble tile with heated floors and woven area rugs.

In the bedroom were two beds; one twin and an oversized double situated directly beneath a mirrored and textured plaster tray ceiling. The adjoining lounge had a wet bar, refrigerator and wine cabinet with a carmine and gold Persian carpet that matched the one in the bedroom.

In the smaller sitting room, on a round side table, nestled between a settee and two lounge chairs, was a bottle of *Champagne Salon* in a sterling silver bucket icing under a linen towel. Alongside the bottle of bubbly was a cheese plate with chunked gouda, sliced chèvre[*], apples, apricots and fruity puffed pastries. Also on the table were two fluted glasses and a vase of fragrant yellow daffodils and white freesia from the ship's temperate greenhouse.

An international cablegram stood tucked between the champagne glasses.

Hugo appeared annoyed, picked it up and granted the transatlantic dispatch from Pathé Frères Productions only a cursory study before he tore the envelope open and quickly read the teletype message. He then stuck the letter back inside the envelope and placed them inside his breast pocket. Phryné had never understood the hot and cold relationship Hugo had with his bosses back at Pathé. He hadn't ever volunteered any reasons and she decided to leave those stones unturned. And of course, because she couldn't read French, she could only rely on his brief, offhanded explanations of the occasional transatlantic correspondence. She trusted him, and tried unsuccessfully to understand his detached attitude toward his home studios and his temperamental reaction to the surprise recall back to France.

She asked, "Is there anything new from your boss in Paris? Anything wrong?"

It was obvious that Hugo was annoyed, but he forced optimism and declared, "I will not allow those capitalist alley dogs at Pathé to ruin this day for us, ma chérie. We are free to write our own history!"

Phryné noticed that the artificial smile glued to his face looked like the cracked, peeling veneer of an old rummage-sale coffee table: nothing but a failing façade. He was clearly upset.

He continued, "You recall that I sent my boss at Pathé, a telegram from Hollywood, and advised him of our travel plans after we had our itinerary completely worked out."

"Of course, I do. I remember that Lenard asked you to forward the details to them."

"This radio cablegram was his reply to that message. He has now cast deep insults at you and me. Foolishly, Lenard the worm, the Studio Chairman and Direction President asked if I alone was paying for the transport of my American lover and if I had informed you that the streets of Paris are not lined with gold as they are in Hollywood."

Her light-hearted laughter brightened the room and his disposition.

While she couldn't understand the off-putting opinions of his boss and the Pathé patriarchs, Phryné was willing to sympathize with Hugo and rationalized that the glitz and glamour of Hollywood could certainly be confusing to foreigners, particularly to those artistic, aristocratic and finicky French.

She turned to Hugo and held him, giving him encouragement and support, "This time is ours. It belongs to us. Together we own this time. Nobody can spoil it. Not even the Pathé brothers, their President, Lenard, or the Chairman."

Her embrace cooled his anger.

He merely smiled and nodded in agreement. Then he picked up the chilled Salon champagne, peeled off the foil, opened the wire cage and carefully let the cork pop into the palm of his hand.

Phryné held the glasses as he filled them. It was indeed a special time. He was returning to his homeland. She was chasing a revived romantic dream and embarking on a voyage of a lifetime.

"After we arrive in Paris, and I escort you to the offices of Pathé, you will stand close to me, Phryné. I will show those dogs the real beauty and talent that I will have on my arm."

Phryné wasn't certain if Hugo's statement was purely braggadocio or honest opinion. However, she realized that it wasn't that long ago that their roles were reversed and it was she who held a prize at her side.

They finished the last bites of the hors d'oeuvres and poured the remaining ounces of champagne just as the steward knocked on the oak and brass door of their stateroom with their luggage.

Two decks above Main Deck Suite 162, a steam-powered announcement split the air. The luxury liner gave empirical notice of her impending departure from the docks of New York.

Mounted on the Normandie's forward funnel, behind the radio masts and the wheelhouse weather station, a gleaming set of three polished brass air horns (18, 24 and 36-inches high) released a massive cloud of white vapor and an explosion of sound that blew a hole as big as New Jersey into the sky above.

Let's Sail to Dreamland

It was absolutely necessary for them to stand at the balcony rail and wave goodbye to the celebratory, enthusiastic crowd standing on the dock one hundred and fifty feet below their balcony. Everyone was living in the moment and sharing the excitement.

The sun had begun to warm away the October morning chill, but still Phryné and Hugo snuggled. They stood close to one another, sharing the warmth of a crimson red wool deck blanket, and watched six New York Harbor tugs nudge and push the Normandie out from its moorings to navigate the lower Hudson River.

Soon, the island of Manhattan began falling away to the East, and when Battery Park came into view, they took the stairs to the Boat Deck and witnessed Lady Liberty and Ellis Island disappear from sight. Fifteen minutes later, the premier ship of The French Line passed through the mouth of the Hudson and into the Atlantic.

The departure from New York didn't turn out to be as exciting as she had originally expected, but Phryné's first ocean voyage had begun. She heard plenty of ships' horns, bells and whistles coming from the farewell parties on the pier and saw hundreds of seagulls, terns, harbor herons and cormorants calling noisily for their supper and winging goodbye. The raucous hoopla and noisy, boisterous sendoff heightened the anxious anticipation she held for their impending crossing and ultimate arrival on the Continent.

The magic and romance of France awaited her. Her future was about to open up like the pages of a long-awaited first edition from a Pulitzer laureate. She could not recall ever carrying so much bubbling excitement within her bosom and decided that nothing would spoil her first evening aboard the Normandie.

Hugo and Phryné spent the rest of the morning and the first portion of the afternoon in their stateroom. Hugo donned his black silk smoking jacket and doeskin slippers. Phryné kept busy and spread her best dresses across one of the beds, studying and arranging outfits for the upcoming four nights of dining, dancing and entertainment. She paid meticulous attention to them all, wrote down her instructions and summoned the cabin steward when her dry cleaning, ironing, steaming and brushing list was complete.

While Phryné worked on her wardrobe, Hugo kept his right hand around a snifter of cognac and his nose inside day-old copies of the *Paris Herald Tribune* and the French language *Je suis partout*** newspapers.

At about five o'clock, Hugo complained of a looming headache and took a Luminal** tablet from its paper packet in his coat pocket. He swallowed the little white pill with a gulp of cognac and explained that he felt fatigued from travel and thought it best if he took a nap. It was still a bit more than three hours until dinner and twilight was just beginning to settle a blanket of dim over the Atlantic coastline of Long Island. Phryné gave him a soft kiss and promised to wake him about seven.

Dinner for all Premier Class passengers was at eight o'clock in the First Class Dining Hall, directly above their stateroom on the Main Deck. Their tickets assigned them to Table 64.

Earlier, Phryné had studied the deck plan inside the ocean liner's Welcome Packet and decided to explore the Grand Salon, Lounge, Smoking Room, Theater, Entrance Hall, Gymnasium, Olympic Pool and Winter Garden while her lover napped. She decided on a casual, chic look and dressed in a pair of wide-bottomed, burgundy corduroy slacks, a bulky knit, cream turtle neck sweater, an offset, soft yellow felt cloche hat and brown-over-white saddle shoes. She added over-the-calf, orange and burnt sienna argyle socks should she need or want to flash a bit of leg.

Anything Goes

Everything aboard the ocean liner was refined: from chandeliers to candelabras and from purser to passenger. Phryné was accustomed to the flamboyant, extravagant lifestyles and amenities of Hollywood, and so she wasn't a complete stranger in paradise. The overflowing, grandiose decor of the SS Normandie, however, overshadowed Hollywood to an astonishing degree. It lifted her emotions and filled her sails. The ship was a luxurious iron crucible adorned with fashions of gold, silver and crystal steaming across a glistening sapphire sea.

The Normandie was a stage. The romantic drama being played onboard may have well been a live performance of a bawdy Cole Porter musical, and each stagehand and every player knew the lyrics and sang along to the title song *Anything Goes*. Temptation was the opening act. Hedonism was the main attraction.

Phryné loved it. From the moment the soles of her shoes left Pier 88 and came aboard, she was awestruck. She certainly wasn't the only passenger amazed by the lavish ocean liner, but still, she fought feelings of isolation and disappointment. Hugo largely ignored her comments about the luxury around them and didn't share her exuberance. She blamed his lack of enthusiasm on familiarity, considering that he had experienced First Class transatlantic travel earlier in March aboard the Île de France. Still, she would have like him to share her excitement.

Walking aft* from the Main Entrance Hall, Phryné discovered that the atmosphere aboard ship was like that of an ostentatious opening-night ceremony and red-carpet movie premier at Grauman's Chinese Theatre** on Hollywood Boulevard. There were a few reporters and cameramen aboard, but the Hollywood hoard of obnoxious photographers, their cameras and flashbulbs were the only missing ingredient within the churning mix of humanity on the Normandie.

The French Line only allowed the upper-crust travelers access to grace the upper decks of the SS Normandie. The ocean liner was filled to capacity by urbane, polished patrons from both sides of the Atlantic. First Class passengers paid not only for transportation, meals and accommodation aboard the world's first-class transatlantic ocean liner, but also to be seen aboard the ship.

Phryné happily accepted her lot and willingly partook in the display, all the while recognizing what her circle of Hollywood associates actually was: a mutual glorification clique. And as long as she could maintain her good looks, seven-inch ankles, thirteen-inch calves and nineteen-inch thighs, she could continue to dance and mingle with a troupe of beautiful people. She recognized the shallow nature of these connections, but embraced them nonetheless.

The staircase leading one deck up from the Grand Salon, through the Smoking Room and to the Café Grill was twenty feet wide, with five sets of five steps passing through alternating walls of fresco murals and mirrored marble tiles. Potted palms, philodendrons and flowering calla lilies were nestled against the walls at each of the six landings.

A large chrome easel at the Café entrance displayed a full-color poster of the evening's scheduled entertainment, announcing the exotic new Gypsy Jazz** stylized by Stephane Grappelli, Django Reinhardt and The Hot Five Quintet, direct from an engagement at the Hot Club in Paris.

The celebrated string-and-brass quartet was to take the stage after dinner service ended and more floor space became available. Admittedly, music and dancing primed her pump and enlivened her spirit, but the words *Gypsy Jazz* sounded temptingly erotic. Phryné resolved that the Café Grill would definitely be part of her and Hugo's evening entertainment lineup.

But the Café Grill wasn't the only entertainment venue available. Another, larger three by four-foot poster promoted the dance music of Argentine orchestra leader Rodolfo Biagi in the Lounge Ballroom at the forward end of the Grand Salon.

Further along the Entry Hall, at the fifteen-foot high, six-foot wide embossed brass doors of the Grand Lounge, Phryné spotted actor and long-time friend, Lew Ayres. He was looking her way, smiling and waving from about thirty feet inside the crowded club room. Theirs was one of her longest and closest friendships; they had known one another since her very first days as a line dancer at Paramount Famous Players back in 1929.

She acknowledged Lew, returned his smile and began to weave her way through the undulating blanket of humanity toward the actor and his party. Halfway to her destination, a handsome young waiter took a glass of champagne from his tray and simply placed it in her hand without uttering a word. Just as she had started to make her way nearer to Lew, she noticed that he and his new wife, Ginger Rogers, were in the company of the blonde bombshell, Joan Blondell and her current co-star and companion, Dick Powell. Unfortunately, Phryné was beyond the point of turning back and too deep into the crowd to retrace her steps. She had reasons to believe that Miss Blondell was Abner's first extramarital fling and although Joanie could be considered faultless in the affair, Phryné found it hard to forgive the perky actress.

Lew exclaimed, "Phryne! What a surprise! We're steaming to the Continent with half of Hollywood and Broadway on our coattails! Come and join us! Let's park our backsides and sip and gossip." Phryné then noticed that fellow dancer Ruby Keeler and actor Warren William were also in the troupe.

Ruby asked, "Are you travelling alone, Phryne? Where's your final port of call? Southampton? Le Havre?"

Brief hugs and nuzzles ensued and Lew quickly laid claim to a nearby half-round sofa. Instantly, a waiter appeared and took their drink orders. Phryné momentarily ignored Ruby's question, and began thinking of an apropos response. She crossed her legs, sipped her champagne and was thankful for her choice of slacks, sweater and hosiery. So many other women in the lounge seemed over-dressed, stressed and totally uncomfortable. Phryné's nonchalance gave the impression that she'd cruised to Europe more frequently than they.

The Grand Lounge was a gigantic parlor, a sitting room of Jack-in-the-Beanstalk proportions, full of upholstered Queen Anne armchairs, leather sofas, Morris chairs, love seats and long, back-to-back divans in tufted brocade. Side tables and large, flat-topped ottomans were tucked between the seating. Full service, room-length bars lined the opposing walls and one-hundred-fifty feet deep into the room, a bandstand occupied the far wall of the lounge. Twenty-foot tall painted murals and woven tapestries adorned the walls with historic themes depicting the connection between man and the sea from Biblical to modern times.

Ginger pushed Ruby's question further and pressed for tasty gossip, "I heard that you left Abner, Phryne. Is that right? What will you do now? Is there anything I can do to help?"

Perhaps to disguise her search for dirty laundry, Ginger continued, "We're on our way to England, for the release of the British cut of *Gold Diggers*^{**}, so we'll be jumping ship in Southampton and going on to London."

Ginger watched for Phryné's reaction while taking the time to put a cigarette into her black Bakelite holder and light it. Her comment was as subtle as dropping bricks into a teapot. She watched Phryné closely through the smoke of her Chesterfield, looking for an expression of emotion.

Phryné called the women's collective, inquisitive bluff, laid her cards on the table, and calmly replied, "Oh, I didn't leave Abner. I'm starting over. We were officially separated months ago and now we're finally divorced and split for good. My attorney secured an excellent settlement for me and to put it bluntly, I'm not leaving ... I'm moving on ... moving far beyond Hollywood's snobbery, slanted views and phony moral codes."

In a haughty, nasal tone, Ruby pressed for more, "What will you be doing in Europe, then? Taking some time off work or vacationing?"

Phryné answered, "You know me, Ruby. I'm not hanging up my dancing slippers just yet. I'll continue working, of course, just like hundreds of other highly capable, uncredited talent. I had six big, high-stepping scenes in *The Gilded Lily* with Claudette Colbert and Fred MacMurray earlier this year and I intend to keep dancing and working in France as long as my gams[*] can take it. I'm so serious about this move that I've gone so far as to change my given name so it sounds a bit more French, with a little accent on the last vowel. I've packed my bags, pulled up stakes and folded my tent, and I'm moving to Paris with Hugo Grétillat, a director with a solid, Pathé Brothers contract. I'll be kicking up my heels for them, I'm sure.

"My Hugo isn't here with me now because he's napping in our stateroom on the Main Deck ... enjoying a well-deserved and hard-earned rest. You know that a director's work is never done. And together, we have been travelling hard, but we are on our way to a beautiful, bright new future in Paris. For days, we were aboard the Los Angeles Limited to Chicago, then the Broadway Limited to New York and immediately came aboard this wonderful ship, the Normandie, so my poor Hugo is travel weary for sure. And the truth is that I am partly to blame, without a doubt. The steel rails had us rocking and rolling across the prairie and then we did up New York ... Sardi's and shopping at Saks ... and we had box seats for *Jubilee,* the latest Cole Porter show on Broadway at the Imperial Theater. And then, yes, it's my fault, I must admit ... we stirred it up at the Ritz with Maurice Chevalier and Jeanette MacDonald until the wee morning hours, so my Hugo is understandably wiped out. Even first class nights on the town can take the wind out of your sails."

She sent a wink and a little smile their way and continued, "You may very well get the opportunity to meet Hugo tonight. We'll likely be in the Café after dinner and we'll certainly be dancing in the ballroom afterwards, until the very early hours."

She had stretched the truth ever so slightly, but got her point across. The churning waves of questions from Ginger and Ruby had washed ashore and evaporated like the salty brine they were. After Phryné's impromptu storyline of white lies and embellished truths, the pointed queries and were replaced with empty cocktail chatter and scripted smiles. She believed that her somewhat sympathetic replies had quenched the women's thirst for gossip, at least temporarily. At any rate, she decided to attempt to avoid the 'Gold Digger girls' for the duration of the crossing.

She took her cigarette case from her clutch, lit a Chesterfield and finished her gin and tonic. She was glad to have the impromptu interrogation over, and cordially excused herself.

Phryné could dawdle no longer. It was half past six, and time to return to Stateroom 162. She needed not only to shower and dress for the evening, but also make certain that Hugo was awake after his nap.

Si j'aime Phryné (If I like Phryné)

Phryné unlocked the door to their chambers, entered the foyer and stood beside the sideboard. She was met with a silence that was abruptly broken with the muffled thump and clatter of her clutch and room key dropping into the rosewood compote.

The dust settled and the silence returned. She walked to the sitting room and stood alongside the plush, carmine loveseat. It was absolutely necessary to wake him.

"Hugo ... Hugo ... Hugo!"

A new cablegram from Paris was on the end table. It had been opened and its contents stuffed back inside the abused, tawny envelope. Phryné assumed it was another troublesome, trivial dispatch from the Head of Production, Lenard, at Pathé.

Hugo's face strained and a yawn escaped. He fought back at his drug-induced, drowsy twilight and forced his eyes to open.

She bent at the waist, softly placed a hand on his shoulder, kissed his cheek and said, "Hugo, I hope that you're feeling better and rested. It's time we get ready for dinner, because time stops for no one."

While she felt concern for Hugo's well-being, other priorities stood center stage. Preparation and primping for dinner and the evening's entertainment were in the spotlight.

Hugo stretched his frame, sat up, and looked around the room, rediscovering his surroundings. He made an attempt to wipe away the stagnant fog of sleep with an open palm across his face and murmured, "Oui ... oui ... yes ... of course."

Phryné didn't wait for a reply, and expressed a sense of urgency, "You must get ready for the evening, Hugo! Tonight we must ignore your tyrant boss in Paris. Please don't allow him or the business to trouble you ... gather yourself ... the rest of our lives awaits us! Let this night be ours!"

As she turned toward the bath and powder room, she added, "I'm going to shower and dress. Remember, our reservation is set at eight."

Hugo could dawdle on occasion, and Phryné hoped that her comment was enough to motivate him, without sounding like she was handing out an ultimatum. Although Hugo had managed to mesh some of his gears deep into the machinery of her life, it was not yet the time to throw a monkey wrench into the works or leap into uncharted waters without a life jacket. It was their first night aboard, and she secretly hoped that leaving California for France would swing the pendulum from unpredictably volatile to romantically feasible. She was excitedly anticipating that their Atlantic Crossing aboard the Normandie was not only the launch of a new life together, but also the champagne christening of their future.

In the powder and shower room, Phryné stripped to the soft pink and stood barefoot, studying herself at the twin wash basins in front of the mirrored wall. The steam-heated tiles beneath her feet radiated their warmth upward through her body and quickly banished the chill. The image in the mirror strengthened her innate, private pride, purpose and self confidence.

She allowed her thoughts to spring from her lips, "Not bad for thirty," and she winked at her reflection.

Whether as a curtain call at the end of the day or the first act of a night on the town, a refreshing shower was part of Phryné's regimen. She languished in the embracing warmth and massage of the water. During her marriage to Abner, she had clung to simple personal routines in an attempt to maintain a sense of order in Hollywood's chaotic lifestyle.

The steamy mist of the shower immediately fogged the glass door before she stepped inside to become completely wrapped within its intimate cascade of warmth. For Phryné, it was a private, personal whirlpool of serenity. Standing under a warm, gentle patter of water with a soft washcloth and a snow-white bar of Camay[**] soap was a ritual to relish, and the accommodations on the premier ship of the French Line did not disappoint. She languished in Camay's scent and sleek softness; lingering under the calming cascade for a quarter hour. To finish, she lathered generously and carefully, gently used her gold-plated Gillette Décolleté Milady razor[**] to touch-up her intimate grooming. Finally, she disposed of the blade and dried the delicate instrument before returning it to its compartmented, mother-of-pearl folding case.

Nearly twenty minutes after the bright chrome shower fixture began spewing its warmth, the last drops of soapy water swirled rhythmically clockwise around, down and through the polished drain cover on its way below decks to the bilges[***] and the bottomless Atlantic Ocean.

After drying and slipping into her bathrobe, Phryné sat at the vanity for the methodical application of her personal beauty products. She carefully removed her silk-knit shower cap, folded it over the counter's edge, ran her fingers through her hair and tousled her deep brown tresses.

Her private makeup regimen had evolved into a disciplined procedure that consumed no more than a few minutes of precious time. She was purpose-driven and didn't sit at a vanity simply to warm the chair. When Abner Mandelbaum first hired her as a beautician to the stars at Famous Players Paramount, Phryné began sharpening her skills and mastering the art of personal cosmetology. She discovered the most stable fragrances, lasting foundations, non-smear paints, lipsticks and chalk-free powders.

Phryné promptly finished her artistry, set her brushes down and allowed the reflection in the mirror to commingle with her romantic expectations for dining, dancing and dallying. Soft purple Max Factor eye shadow, deep lavender eyeliner and Revlon Deep Magenta lipstick created her mystic façade for the evening. She envisioned Hugo gently holding her in a soft embrace, gliding across the ballroom floor into a land of promise, fortune and starry-eyed bliss. France was only three days away. With a dusting of Lenthéric bath powder and a drop of Lancôme Conquête Parfum on her wrists and behind her ears, she was nearly ready. She glanced at her wristwatch lying on the vanity. It was twenty past seven.

She turned her head toward the hall and called out to Hugo, "I am nearly finished!"

There was no reply. She stood, holding her bathrobe closed at the waist and stepped to the living area where she found Hugo on the settee, holding a snifter with an inch of cognac in his left hand and a cigarette with a half-inch of ash in his right. He was staring far beyond the sliding glass doors of the patio, out into the darkness of the sea and the blackness of night.

He had changed out of his smoking jacket, pajamas and slippers, and was dressed in a shirt, slacks and dress oxfords. His jacket and tie were lying across the back of the curved, vis-à-vis[*] settee. He may not have been jubilant, but it appeared that he had beaten back the deep indigo of his blue mood and was, at the least, willing to leave the stateroom.

He didn't acknowledge her presence, move a muscle or cast a glance her way, but asked, "Have you ever been afraid, ma chérie? I mean, not afraid for your safety, but unsure of your future or that you could be walking down the wrong path of life?"

She didn't hesitate, "No. Maybe I was once ... or twice. But one thing that life has taught me is that there's nothing that I can't handle. But I believe that if you waste your time second-guessing the decisions you've made, you will lose the life that you could have lived ... so gather yourself, get ready and let's get to the upper decks for the night."

Phryné needed Hugo to get out of his doldrums. She was looking forward to a lively evening and realized that he needed some encouragement and a persuasive nudge to lift his spirits. She was looking forward to some Gypsy Jazz.

She prodded him further with a tease, "You desperately need a shave and it's closing in on the eight o'clock hour, so get up off your ass and get ready for dinner. I need to dress. And I'm hungry."

He gulped the last of his cognac, stood and turned to face her, "That's what I like about you, Phryné. There's no nonsense."

Fidgety Feet

The Dining Salon, SS Normandie
Sunday, October 14, 8 PM

The inducement that Phryné delivered to Hugo seemed to do the trick. He answered her trumpet call and in just a few minutes they left their stateroom for the entertainment, opulence and pomp of the upper decks. Phryné hoped that she could continue to buoy his spirits enough to keep the evening afloat. She could not, however, totally ignore a slight resentment of Hugo's self-absorption.

The dining salon was a three-hundred-foot hall of chrome, brass, mirrors and glass illuminated by twelve tall pillars of Lalique** glass. Forty matching columns of light flanked the pillars along the walls. Massive chandeliers hung at each end of the room, casting additional rays of incandescent light onto the sparkling gemstones, gleaming jewelry and twinkling sequins of society's upper crust. Overhead, the coffered ceiling of inlaid mirrors softly, gently reflected subdued light back onto the dining room below.

A larger-than-life bronze statue of a robed woman dominated the center of the dining hall. At thirteen feet and standing on a six-foot-high mahogany pedestal, she offered an olive branch to everyone who gazed upon her. Named 'La Paix', she was the work of French sculptor Louis Dejean. The lady was a work of cultured refinement and depicted 'Peace'; the illusive political and social ideal of civilized man.

Phryné's soft lilac cocktail dress of multi-layered, semi-sheer silk and Hugo's three-piece suit were modest, compared to the evening gowns and tuxedos throughout the dining hall. Theatricals were figuratively tripping over one another, oblivious to the concept that those who flaunt status and dress over the top overstate their social standing, and invariably display themselves as insatiable, self-aggrandizing exhibitions of fashion.

Nearly one-hundred young men in black slacks and white jackets provided refined, precise service to the dining passengers. The wait staff moved as if choreographed, with serving trays balanced one-handed and over-the-shoulder among the one-hundred-fifty tables in the First Class Dining Salon. Shrimp bisque, breads, cheese and salad preceded the main course of foie gras** and filet mignon.

Hugo's state of mind cast a cold, wet blanket over dinner. Although she recognized it as unintentional, and it could not be contributed to him alone, his dark-blue funk irritated Phryné. She feared that the evening was doomed from the start. It was difficult, but she tried to show empathy and made several futile attempts to throw an unresponsive Hugo a life line with her lopsided conversation. Halfway through the meal, it was apparent that he was too deeply mired in Pathé's muck to be either rescued or resuscitated.

Phryné allowed her eyes to rest momentarily on the bronze statue of peace on proud display in the center of the hall. Although Lady Peace and Phryné held different aspirations, she believed that they shared the same level of frustration.

No more than two dozen words passed between Phryné and Hugo during the first four courses. They each realized that nothing could be said to ease the awkward tension or remove the poisonous pins and needles that Pathé's brusque cablegrams had injected into their lives.

Hugo struggled through dessert, barely tasting the crème brûlée[*] and timidly sipping at his coffee. Finally, the digestif[*] course of Cointreau[***] liqueur arrived in short-stemmed tulip glasses, signaling the end of a six-course meal that had evolved into a torturous, one-hour ordeal.

The Dining Salon began to empty. The din of human chatter, silverware clangor and porcelain clatter began to subside. Phryné's celebratory hopes were torpedoed early on, and she secretly plotted a new course for her evening.

Hugo brought his cigarette case out of his jacket pocket, lit an Old Gold and offered it to her. She accepted, and waited as he lit another for himself.

She had an elbow on the table, holding the cigarette between her fingers. She exhaled a blend of smoke and frustration from the corner of her mouth and began, "It's obvious that you're not feeling well, Hugo, and somehow your job has continued to upset you, but I'm not going to sit in our cabin all night long and stare at the walls and patio windows. I'll escort you back to our stateroom, my darling, but I'm not staying in. You know that I have been looking forward to this evening. There's jazz and Latin music playing tonight in the Lounge and Café that I don't want to miss."

Hugo pled his case, "Certainly, I understand. I apologize and am sorry to disappoint you, but I can be nobody's company tonight. Perhaps I have a touch of the sea-sickness, but I'll be fine by morning and of course, please, you may go and enjoy the entertainment."

Phryné accepted Hugo's apology and explained her intent without an ounce of guilt, "If someone asks me to dance, I believe I will. I've got jumpy legs, fidgety feet and tickling toes. I'm going to dance tonight."

Hugo's reply was painted with an apologetic brush, "You know I have no chains on you, ma chérie. Yes, of course you should dance and celebrate and enjoy yourself. I will take some sleeping salts and retire. I am sure that I'll be refreshed in the morning."

Her spirits rose. The evening once again held promise.

They left the Dining Hall in the company of hundreds of fellow passengers moving in all directions out of the Grand Salon. Once they were back inside Suite 162, Hugo peeled off his shoes, suit, shirt and tie and stepped into his combed silk pajamas. He paid no attention as Phryné returned to the bath, freshened herself, powdered her nose, primped her hair and checked her makeup. After two little Secobarbital[**] pills, a half bottle of Evian[**] water and ten minutes off the clock, Hugo was asleep between the sheets of a King bed.

I've Got My Fingers Crossed

The Café Grill, SS Normandie, 9:30 PM

Phryné left the stateroom in high spirits. She had confidence that it would be a fun evening. She would do everything within her power to ensure it.

The fifteen-foot tall, brass medallion-adorned doors between the Grand Salon and the Café Grill stood wide open, as if awaiting her arrival. Inside, scores of First-Class patrons were seated at round tables of all sizes to accommodate parties of any number. In the far corner was a large candlelit grotto, separated from the rest of the floor with a circular philodendron-covered trellis that concealed its occupants in shadowy intimacy.

Phryné spotted a half-dozen scattered empty, spots at the imposing, semi-circular bar when she entered the Café. She stepped inside, walked along the bar to its far end, and stood next to an unoccupied stool, claiming possession. Her eyes quickly surveyed the room and those patrons nearest to her.

A polished brass plaque at the end of the bar proclaimed that the thirty-foot, hand-crafted woodwork was fashioned of mahogany harvested from Upper Volta in French West Africa[**]. Like many other amenities aboard the Normandie, brass plaques honored the craftsmen who created the work, the materials used and their origin. Four impeccably-dressed barmen were on duty serving the fifty-odd customers seated along the bar. The bar staff consisted of young men wearing white shirts, black string ties and cropped black jackets.

Phryné was welcomed by a tall, eager bar-back with a pencil-thin mustache, "Bonsoir[*], Madame. I am Félix ... what may I prepare for you?"

Phryné smiled back, mirroring the young man's charm. "A Mary Pickford[**], if you please."

She set her clutch onto the bar and wriggled her form onto the stool. On her immediate right sat a ginger-haired man of perhaps forty in a brown tweed suit, white cotton shirt and a red woolen tie. There was an odor of gin about him and his eyes were out of focus. He clearly was under the influence.

He managed an inebriated grin and welcomed her in a slurred, sticky, cotton-candy mumble, "Good evening. I'm Nelson McIver; an exporter for Morgan Motorcar Company on my way back home to England from Detroit, in the State of Michigan. I'm traveling to Southampton, and then back to my family in Kidderminster ... in the West Midlands,

Worcestershire County. I've been on a business trip, of course. And I'm guessing that you must be from Hollywood, like so many others aboard. Because of your drink order, I mean. Oh, and of course, you're beautiful. You're as lovely as a cinema star should be, and you're simply charming."

She said, "Thank you," and did a quick study of this fellow. His nose was rosy pink, his cheeks were flushed and his gaze was vacant.

Phryné recognized that she needed to lay the foundation for a quick exit away from this man. She continued, "It's nice to meet you ... Nelson. I ordered a Mary Pickford because I enjoy them and they taste good. I'm not from Hollywood, but I am leaving Hollywood for Paris ... my name is Phryné and I'm waiting for ... rather ... I meant to say that I'm expecting someone. We have arranged a meeting."

She moved her head slightly to the left, then right, and feigned looking out over the crowd for a familiar face. For a moment, she wondered if Nelson was jumping class and had snuck into the Café merely guised as a reputable passenger. He seemed innocuous, but Phryné was in no mood for chit-chat with a tipsy Nelson. He had the growling voice, sandpaper persona and sobriety level of W.C. Fields.

The barman mixed, iced, shook and poured Phryné's drink, set it down in front of her and offered, "I remain at your service, Madame."

Phryné realized she could have an unexpected ally and thanked the French mixologist. He had remained within earshot while he prepared the drink and likely heard the entire conversation with Nelson.

At half-past nine, the SS Normandie was 93 nautical miles[**] south south-east of St. Johns, Newfoundland. The seas were calm, the skies clear and the stars had aligned perfectly.

To Phryné's right, twenty-five feet away, backlit by the lights of the Grand Salon, a tall, tan, familiar stranger appeared at the Café doorway. Her heart jumped. To err on the side of caution, she studied him closely to be certain. Phryné had confidence in her identification, and this time she wouldn't allow her incidental stranger to escape. She was ready to pounce like a cat on a ball of yarn. She was confident that the handsome stranger aboard the Los Angeles Limited was again in sight.

Phryné didn't want this chance to slip away and wasn't about to dillydally. She left her drink sitting untouched on the bar and slid off the barstool, both feet hitting the floor simultaneously. Nelson was briefly bewildered and disappointed, but assumed that Phryné's awaited date had arrived.

She grabbed her clutch off the polished mahogany, stepped away from the bar, moved rhythmically across the floor, and made a beeline toward the stranger. She raised her arm and waved energetically. She was smiling, beaming at him, as she were greeting a long-lost friend, or welcoming home a soldier from war.

The handsome stranger noticed this wondrous woman coming closer, tried to imagine who she could be and why she would be making such a bold and determined approach. His eyes surveyed the Café from side to side, as if he were about to climb out from the trenches and into no man's land. He searched his memory for her image and discovered naught. The thought crossed his mind that perhaps she had mistaken him for someone else, or for whatever bizarre reason, she was offering him an evening of casual female companionship or simply a complimentary cocktail. He allowed the mystery to deepen.

The tap-tap of her heels kept time like the metered beats of a metronome sitting atop a music student's piano. Her hips moved in a rhythmic, hypnotic sway that set the hemline of her soft lavender dress dancing side to side. The layered silk of the gown mimicked soft ripples across a lilac-colored lake. Her coifed curls kissed her shoulders.

Phryné's derring-do had stopped the stranger at the doorway in his tracks. He was captivated, frozen in time and assumed that any effort to escape would be fruitless and was resigned to accept the oncoming, impetuous challenge. He was willing to take a chance and ready to face his fate.

In this case, Fate was quickly approaching in the form of Phryné. She stopped no more that two feet in front of him and performed her first assessment.

His appearance was unmistakably Continental. His steel-blue, double-breasted suit jacket had strong, squared shoulders and wide, V-shape lapels that tapered down not to the second set of buttons, but the third. The jacket angled to the waist and the sleeves narrowed at the cuff. Tucked inside his ruffled white silk shirt was a crimson ascot.

His complexion betrayed Mediterranean heritage along with pitch-black, curly hair, a pencil mustache and eyes of midnight brown. He was standing inside white-on-black wing tips.

Several times during her twenty-nine years Phryné found herself in situations that required unscripted decisions. She had years of experience thinking on her feet and performing improvisations in unfamiliar surroundings.

She began her plea, "Hello. I'm in a pickle and I hope you can help me. Sir, I require a knight in shining armor to rescue me, so I will quickly lay all my cards on the table. There's a man at the bar who has been pestering me, and I needed a reason to walk away, so I told him that I was expecting someone ... and when I saw you in the doorway, I took a chance and walked over here."

She smiled and extended her free hand.

He appeared a bit uncertain but took her hand in his, placed the other on top and accepted her invitation, "Consider yourself rescued from your pickle, my dear lady. My name is Guilermo Gaeta."

His name rolled off his tongue and surrounded her thoughts. The melodious, romantic accent seemed Spanish. She glanced down at the left hand that had completely covered hers and imagined its brawny strength. She surrendered to his touch and sensed his deep, dark eyes capturing her soul.

"Oh, thank you ever so much for understanding. I'm Phryné Truffaut ... and I'm traveling to Paris." She felt a passing flutter deep within.

He released her hand. "Wonderful! It must be so exciting for you."

"It's an exhilarating new beginning for me."

"Perhaps I should embrace you, Señorita, like we are old friends? That man back at the bar is watching you. If only we do it for his benefit?"

His comment unmasked his native language and pinned down his accent.

Phryné brightened, "Great idea!"

It only lasted a few seconds, but his embrace secured her salvation from Nelson McIver and was the culmination of a days-old fantasy. She tingled from head to toe. Her imagination didn't fail. Her senses were electrified. She detected the rare, subtle scent of Fougère Royale[**] men's cologne.

Her cryptic sightings of him on the train platform of Central Station, in the dining car of the Los Angeles Limited, and on the street corner in New York were affirmed. She was confident that he was her mystery man. There was no doubt; his shoulders swallowed her. Serendipity prevailed.

"Help me with your name ... Guilermo? Did I say it right? Is it South American or Spanish? It must be."

"Yes. You said it correctly, and I am Catalonian, from Barcelona, Spain."

He then offered his arm, and she accepted. With confidence, he suggested, "Let's find a table, my dear, long-lost-friend, Phryné!"

"Yes, please," was her reply. She glanced toward the bar and noticed Nelson intensely watching their every move. She sent a meek wave and a tepid wink in Nelson's direction, believing that she would never see him again.

Phryné and her new escort walked further into the Café and she suggested, "Let's find a spot near the band and dance floor ... I'm in the mood ... in the mood for dancing." She hesitated, and added, "Let me try your name again ... Guilermo?"

"Perfecto! Perfect."

He stopped at a small round table against the wall near the raised stage and asked, "How is this? Good?"

Phryné beamed and echoed, "Perfecto! Perfect."

La mer (The Sea)

The Café Grill, SS Normandie, 10:15PM

Exactly one week earlier, at Central Station in Los Angeles, Phryné first laid eyes upon the man she came to know as Guilermo Gaeta. She could not have imagined that eight days and seven nights later she would be about to begin a tête-à-tête* with a random stranger she noticed on the Union Pacific platform.

She was experiencing an untargeted rapid-fire, unpredictable series of events that jolted her senses with every burst. Everything was charged with electricity. From the moment she first laid eyes on Guilermo, her imagination sailed away into uncharted waters, and try as she might, she was unable to pinpoint the exact reason behind her infatuation with him. During her years in Hollywood she'd certainly had contact with attractive men, but none had lit the slow smoldering fire of fantasy like the Spaniard. Even from a distance, she felt drawn to him. Like a meadowlark migrating north in spring, she allowed herself to be captivated by inexplicable forces of nature and fly a beeline to her vibrant Spanish flame. She hadn't felt so giddy in years and it felt fantastic.

Additionally, Phryné didn't give much thought to where Guilermo could fit into the puzzle of her life. She realized early on that there were so many obtuse angles and sharp curves already cut onto the pieces, it would be impossible to come up with a fitting explanation. It was much easier to visualize the picture on the box and simply imagine the puzzle's ultimate solution.

For Guilermo, Phryné was a passing ship in the night and a good-looking, if not baffling, curious distraction.

They had no sooner taken their seats at their table, than a waiter appeared and took their drink orders; a replacement Mary Pickford for Phryné and a brandy and soda highball for Guilermo.

He offered Phryné a Marlboro. She accepted; he lit one for her and another for himself.

She couldn't resist, "Do you know that these are advertised for ladies? *Mild as May* is their slogan."

He grinned and said, "Good. I'm mild also." He inhaled, studied her, and wondered what drove her actions. Seconds passed and he expelled the smoke, "Do you feel safe, now? I mean, after I saved you from the clutches of that man at the bar?"

She lifted her glass, as if she were offering a toast. "Yes, thank you very much!"

"Do you often find the need to be rescued, Phryné?"

She smiled broadly, telegraphing a joke, "It seems it only happens on Sunday nights ... when I'm sailing to France."

He teased back, "I think you're safe for now."

Phryné relaxed back into her chair and endeavored to explain her ploy, "I really needed someone to keep me from that obnoxious man. It's not that I couldn't simply get up and walk away; I was looking for an excuse ... maybe I didn't want to appear rude. I don't know. It was fortunate for me that you appeared ... in ways I'll probably never know or understand.

"When I saw you at the Café entrance, I almost did think of you as a long-lost friend. That part is a little complicated and hard to explain, but I'll try.

"Actually, I first saw you when I was leaving Hollywood, and to me, deep down, I felt that somewhere, somehow we had met before. You were a stranger, but I felt that I already knew you. Don't misunderstand. We were never directly introduced or even connected personally, but it sure felt to me like we were. I heard once that people who get that feeling actually knew the other person in a previous life or dream or something.

"I remember seeing you last Monday at Central Station in Los Angeles boarding the same train as me, and later that day in the dining car aboard the Los Angeles Limited on the way to Chicago. And I'm not one hundred percent certain, but I believe that I saw you one other time ... standing on a sidewalk in New York City just last night ... yesterday evening. So I've seen you three times so far. Tonight makes four. When I think about it, my head spins.

"In Los Angeles and on the train to Chicago, and in New York I believe that I saw you in the company of a woman, a blonde.

"Just now, when I saw you at the Café doorway, I felt some sort of irresistible force. I can't explain it. I was being drawn toward you when I left that pest of a man at the bar and approached you. I needed to meet you. I somehow believe that such chance meetings are written in the stars and because the heavens went to such lengths to make our paths cross, that we must simply oblige and dare to accept the weird serendipity of it all. And that's what I did just now. I know it must sound silly. I hope I didn't step over a line.

"What I'm trying to say is: for one reason or another, we were very close on the train platform in Los Angeles, on the train, and when we were in New York. We were just a few feet apart. Now we're closer than we ever were. We're on the same boat ... and maybe in the same boat, so to speak, or whatever our situation really is. But, it doesn't really matter, does it? We are two people from completely different parts of the world and we've been here, there and God knows where and now here we are sitting across from each other.

"My name is Phryné Truffaut and I'm traveling to Paris and I'm glad I'm here."

The corners of his eyes wrinkled ever so slightly. He studied her and asked, "You haven't been following me, have you?"

"Heavens, no! Why would I do that? I'm not a gumshoe*! Do I look like Dick Tracy!?"

Signaling she was perturbed, she took a swallow of her drink, then asked, "Are you poking fun at me?"

The Spaniard was caught in a cultural faux pas*, "Who is Dick Tracy?"

"He's a detective, you silly ... a comic strip detective. And why would I be following you? Think about it ... Why would I follow you all the way from Hollywood to Chicago to New York and all the way out here on a boat in the middle of the sea, just to sit at a table and share a drink? That's just foolishness."

He was apologetic, "You're right. I was only joking, but perhaps it was a bad joke. Forgive me. It meant nothing."

Somehow his words triggered one of those magic moments when two souls connect. They dove into one another's eyes and swam into the deep end of intimate thoughts and private dreams. The chatter and bustle of the Café was silenced. Together yet separate, Guilermo and Phryné began surfing on perfect waves of what could or would become of their evening.

Their daydreams ended some moments later when the jazz band began taking the stage and the cymbal stand fell to the floor.

The racket jolted them back into real time. Each awoke to the warm smile of the other. Their expressions signaled the longing gullible gaze of lovers who had quietly shared secret fantasies of what was yet to come.

Guilermo boldly removed the covers from dreamland, "Please, you must tell me about yourself. Who is Phryné?"

She played coy, placed an elbow on the table and barely set her chin on the back of her hand, "I've spent the last seven years as a dancer, studio extra and chorus girl for Paramount Studios in Hollywood, and now I'm traveling to France for a fresh start and a new life. How about you?"

He ignored the question temporarily. He believed his to be more pressing, "I cannot believe that you are traveling alone. Are you?"

"No, I'm not alone. I'm traveling with a French film director, Hugo-Henri Grétillat. He works for Pathé Frères in Paris."

"He is your friend, this director, this Frenchman Hugo?"

"Yes. And to be honest, he's more than a friend. He's my paramour*."

Phryné had purposely baited him and awaited his reaction. By design, she was testing him on a level generally reserved for serious relationships and sat ready to judge his response.

He offered his opinion, "Intimate friendship is a gift to be shared by lovers. I think it's important to trust someone on more than on a level of conventional convenience. It needs to be honest or it's not worth the effort. You cannot argue with genuine honesty if you are honest with your conscience."

To Phryné, his reply sounded like her ex-husband Abner spewing Yiddish, but it passed the test. She decided to press him, "Who was the blonde?"

He smiled, "Touché*!"

After a short swallow from his highball, he answered, "I met the young woman at the Union Pacific ticket office in Los Angeles while I was arranging my train back to New York. Her name is Nancy Kenyon, an actress from Toledo ... not the city in Spain, but the one in your American state of Ohio. She was traveling from Hollywood, like you, but to Broadway, in New York City to try her luck finding work on the stage. When we arrived, her agent had left a message at our hotel that she should return to Hollywood immediately for a part in a new production. Peter Ibbet-something, I think."

Phryné was overwhelmed by the coincidence and answered in disbelief, "*Peter Ibbetson!* Unbelievable! And you were at the Ritz with her?"

"Yes, that's correct! How did you know?"

"That's amazing. How strange is that? *Peter Ibbetson!* That's the film that Hugo was scheduled to start shooting at Paramount before Pathé cancelled the exchange program and they recalled him back to Paris! How strange is this world that we live in?"

She continued, "The Ritz: that's where I saw you last night in New York; under a streetlight on the sidewalk outside the Ritz Carlton with your friend Nancy, the budding actress. Our meeting, us finally finding each other, and this whole thing is like a fairytale."

Phryné took a sip of her drink and studied him over the rim of her glass, "And now it's your turn to tell me who you are."

"As I said, I am from Catalonia. My family owns the Roca Pintada vineyards and winery in Alella, twenty kilometers[*] northeast of Barcelona; a very beautiful part of the world.

"I am returning from a two-week trip to San Francisco, California, where I was meeting new contacts, making new friends and selling and trading and purchasing vine cuttings[**] of Cava grape varieties from vintners growers from wineries in Sonoma and Napa. My new American friends bought some of my cuttings and I bought some of theirs and we traded some new varieties to see if they grow in our different soils and climates. And I introduced them to the fine cork bark that is available for import from the Maresme district in Catalonia.

"It truly was much more business than a holiday. I sold triple what I purchased, but still, I am returning to Alella with a trunk full of wood shavings and five hundred vine cuttings from California. And I have a folio full of orders for the

Catalonian Cork Company. It was all about the vine, the grape, the wine, the bottle, the stopper and the money.

"But so much of the money always goes into the sticky hands of the political class and the ironclad vaults of the bankers in Madrid. The struggle is to get all the money back into the hands of the people who earn it. Someday soon I hope that things will change. I know that there are people trying to change things.

"But I am boring you and making my story longer than it needs to be! My trip has given me many memories of America. People are friendly and there is so much room everywhere and it's so far between places.

"And now I will stop talking. I have used too many words."

Guilermo grinned and swallowed the last of his drink. Phryné was amused and smiled back.

The activity on stage could no longer be ignored. The distraction had become an attraction. The ambient noise inside the Café was growing in anticipation of the showcased new jazz style.

The Paris Hot Club Quintet*** had worked behind the footlights for a few minutes setting up three waist-level microphone stands, a few stools, the upright bass and the drum set. Intermittently, a musician would pluck a guitar or banjo string, change out a saxophone or clarinet reed, rosin the bow or tighten the gut string** of a violin.

Their waiter arrived with fresh drinks as the quintet finished their 'who's who' introductions and performed their opening number, *Swing de Paris*. Phryné moved her chair to the right, sat closer to Guilermo and asked, "You will have enough wind in your sails to dance with me tonight, won't you?"

"You Americans! Your expressions sometimes make no sense at all! Of course I have enough wind to dance with you.

You remember that I am that knight in shining armor that you were looking for."

He stood, mimicked a bow, gestured toward the quintet and offered his hand. Seconds later, they were on the dance floor, where they remained for a full thirty minutes, when the band took a ten minute break. Bit by bit, touch by touch, they became familiar dance partners.

They returned slowly to their table, reluctant to separate their bodies.

Phryné was delightedly surprised at how well Guilermo moved across the floor and commended him, "You are a very good dancer."

"As a boy, during my summers at the vineyards, I was pushed into fencing lessons by my maternal grandmother, Margarida. Unfortunately, the dear lady passed away when I was fifteen, and she never had the chance to see me become the next great swordsman or d'Artagnan**. I stopped taking lessons and never appreciated the footwork and grace until many years later."

"I'm sorry ... it seems that too often we miss the opportunity to thank people."

Guilermo grasped a memory and said, "The most important thing I learned about dance is that it is much like the fencing. You should watch your partner's eyes. If you follow your partner's eyes, you cannot take a misstep.

"And you! You can certainly dance circles around me. You move on the dance floor like warmed olive oil on a griddle."

With a dual pluck of a single string, bandleader and jazz violinist Stephane Grappelli signaled that Gypsy Jazz was about to flow through the Café again.

After holding each other with their eyes and arms during the prelude to the up-beat *Love Notes,* Phryné stood, smiled and asked a selfishly curious question, "Do you have someone waiting for you in Catalonia?"

He didn't flinch, but took her by the hand and stepped to the dance floor.

He answered, "Yes, several people await my return for one reason or another; either personal, monetary, or whatever the arrangement is. But there is no intimate relationship etched onto a cameo brooch or a promise engraved onto a gold band, if that is what you mean."

Phryné had asked an open-ended question without demanding details and Guilermo gave an answer without a commitment. Things were progressing. The music resumed.

Well into the band's second set, it was apparent that drummer Alain Welloph was totally consumed by the overflowing enthusiasm in the Café and had either caught his second wind or was tipping spirits between numbers. He began hitting rim shots on the downbeat shuffles and swishing brushes on the triplets.

It was time to pick up the tempo. Phryné and Guilermo decided to trade the Café and the Hot Club's moody Gypsy Jazz for the Lounge and the passionate Latin beats of the Argentine tango. Each knew what the other was anticipating.

Tango Negro (Black Tango)

The Grand Lounge and Ballroom, SS Normandie

Monday, October 15, 1:55 AM (West Atlantic Time Zone)

They left the Café side-by-side, arms around each other; as if poured into a mold, conjoined and inseparable.

He held her close, his hip fitting perfectly into the contour of her waistline. Her entire body swayed with a degree of exaggeration to compensate for the length of his stride.

Guilermo held his jacket over his left shoulder, hooked onto two curled fingers of his left hand and Phryné carried her lace evening wrap draped over her right forearm. They had cast off their separate identities had become oblivious to anything but the other. For all it mattered, they may as well have been strolling along any street in any city in the world. In a mere two hours, they had formed an intimate, private alliance with the unspoken goal of living in the moment and swimming in a pool of passion.

A few dozen steps along the Grand Salon, the milieu changed from Paris coffeehouse to Buenos Aires cabaret. Latin music pulsed from the Lounge and coursed through the Salon. Inside, the seating was predominately intimate tables for two and lighting was subdued. The closer quarters allowed the dance floor to triple in size, but it wasn't the singular variance between continental French and colonial Spanish. Drums were changed out for bandoneóns[*], guitars for a piano, trumpets for a flute and double bass, and saxophones for castanets.

They entered the Lounge and were met by one of a dozen or so young men in impeccable black silk uniforms. The steward flawlessly piloted them through a sea of clinking glasses, carousing patrons and jutting chairs to an empty table about halfway into the room. As soon as they took their seats, a waiter took their drink orders.

Phryné recognized Charles Boyer, his wife Pat and celebrated couple Lupe Vélez and Johnny Weissmuller[**] at nearby tables. With relief, she noticed that the 'Gold Digger girls', Joan Blondell and Ginger Rogers, along with Dick Powell and Lew Ayres were seated further away, on the far side of the room at a VIP table with Vivien Leigh, Laurence Olivier, Merle Oberon and her current flame, Douglas Fairbanks Jr. They were far enough away not to prod, pry or pester Phryné with gossip. Phryné and Guilermo enjoyed a cushion of at least fifty feet, and were securely wrapped in a collective cocoon of festive anonymity with other partying passengers in the Lounge.

The entire ballroom was expecting the emotional Latin beat of Rodolfo Biagi's orchestra and the steamy voice of vocalist Libertad Lamarque to ignite a fiery mood that would burn through the night.

After the waiter brought Phryné's rum concoction and Guilermo's brandy, they were left to their resources; alone in a crowd of pleasure seekers. They inevitably sensed their isolation, and sank into the warm depths of each other's eyes.

Phryné smiled. "I think I now understand why you mystified me when I first laid eyes on you. You said that you're Catalonian, but you look like an Argentine. You certainly look Latin, and I believe that you know how to tango and can do the dance justice."

He needed to prod her humor and asked a pointed question of his own, "Yes indeed, I tango. And you say you are a dancer. And you know the tango well enough?"

She gave him a teasing reply, "Of course. Some people devote all their time to the dance and study every move over and over. I'm not one of those people, but I believe that I can dance circles around many of those who think that they are experts. The tango is my favorite because emotion is not only in the music, but the dance as well. I think you will be pleased with what I can do."

She was smiling, revealing that she was about to play the hidden ace she was secretly holding. She asked, "Have you heard of the late Carlos Gardel**; the Argentine tango band leader and actor?"

"Of course. He is a legend in his time and known all over the world. Why?"

"I made three musical films for Paramount Pictures last year in uncredited roles as a dancer. Each starred Señor Gardel and Rosita Morino: *The Day You Love Me, Tango Bar* and *Tango on Broadway.*

"So, now you know. I know tango and I hope to prove it to you."

He smiled across the table at her and said, "It seems that I will be dancing tonight."

As if on cue, the lead violinist drew his bow across the instrument's four tight strings and filled the ballroom with the first notes of *Viejo porton.* The piano and a concertina joined in as Guilermo took her hand with the mischievous smile of a sixteen-year-old. He made direct eye contact, nodded and politely expressed his cabeceó* with the words, "Let's dance."

In mere moments he recognized that Phryné did, in the least, know the protocol of tango. She accepted his invitation with a smile and a nod of her own. In short order he would discover that Phryné could, indeed, dance the tango.

They were the first on the floor and without hesitation Phryné made it her stage. She intended to test the waters and politely left Guilermo to control the action. For the first two dances they were alone and telegraphed their enthusiasm to the rest of the room. Gradually, one at a time, several more pairs left the sanctuary of their tables and joined them on the polished parquet. The crowd sensed the festive mood that was pulsing through the room with a throbbing, resolute emotion.

Perhaps it was the music that charged Phryné's passion and fueled her imagination; or maybe it was Guilermo's touch, moves and expressions. Halfway into the second dance, she got her sea legs. Phryné felt that she was dancing among the stars, not aboard the Normandie or in Hollywood, but somewhere beyond the moon and in the Milky Way. She could not pinpoint the last time she enjoyed herself so much.

During the orchestra's fourth number, *Flor de Monserrat*, Johnny Weissmuller's athleticism and his wife Lupe's enthusiasm captured the crowd's attention and took emotional control of the ballroom. They became the focus on the dance floor. Lupe's high kicks and bawdy gesticulations between her partner's dips and lifts enraptured the room with her spicy Mexican sauciness.

Biagi's band took a pause after the second tanda[*] and received rousing applause.

Guilermo gently took Phryné's hand, walked her back to their table, kissed her on the lips and moved her chair next to his. He moved close and proclaimed, "You surprise and amaze me. An American who knows tango is as rare as snow on the streets of Barcelona! An American who can dance the tango is a gift from the Saints themselves."

Phryné feigned modesty and sipped at her drink, "It has been a passion of mine for years. I told you I was a dancer."

"But, oh, you are so much more. You are beauty and grace moving across the floor. And you are not just a vision in that lavender gown ... the softness befits you and flatters your presence ... your scent mimics the sweetness of lilac blooms in March ... and you carry a sophisticated elegance with your white pearl necklace. And your legs, Phryné ... your legs go from your wonderful ankles straight up to Heaven."

Affected, she gingerly placed a hand on his thigh, leaned in and spoke softly, "Thank you, I love to wear satiny things. I love the feel of silk gliding over my body. And my single strand of pearls ... you're correct ... they're so simple yet so exciting ... I love pearls ... so smooth, slinky, and sensuous ... touching my skin like tiny, soft little fingers dancing in a circle around my neck. It feels like the little round things are kissing me all around my throat. I can only explain it that way.

"Then there are the clothes. The feel of everything: the smooth, slick, cool feeling of the dress against my skin; my breasts, my nipples pushing against the bodice waiting to be set free; the shimmering lamé on my back and the sheer stockings on the legs, from my thighs right down to my toes. It tickles me all over. I love it. It's like electricity. Lord knows how much I love feeling this way."

At that moment, she had made certain that Guilermo was hers to have.

During the orchestra's fifteen minute interlude, they finished their drinks, smoked and exchanged murmured suggestions, emotive glances and allowed soft touches to do most of the talking. They had set their course and were forging ahead at full speed when the lighting dimmed and a stagnant cigarette fog shrouded the ballroom. The breath of human chatter subsided, and was replaced by the dull drone of whispered anticipation. It was a signal that the music was about to resume.

Neither partner needed more of an invitation to return to the parquet for the second set. Phryné and Guilermo were on the floor in seconds and opened the tanda^{**} center stage.

Biagi's guest songstress, torch singer Lamarque, opened with *Tango Negro*. Her sultry vocals and Biagi's emotive violin electrified Phryné's spirit. It was a dance-floor casting call.

Guilermo began to feel Phryné's animated enthusiasm and brought a new-found zeal to the dance. They kept perfect cadence, performed parallel and cross walks, multiple pasadas[*], step-overs and suggestive leg hooks. The dance was theirs until the mishap.

He had sandwiched her left foot with his and pushed her into a deep, waist-high leg wrap. Her dress restricted her movement and forced her to stop in her tracks, break her partner's embrace, stand on her right foot and quickly recover equilibrium without an embarrassing fall. In a split second, Phryné reached down to her hemline and tore the tightest, inner semi-sheer tulle fabric upwards, halfway up her hip to the garter and stocking top.

It seemed choreographed. The finesse that followed seemed rehearsed. Despite exposing her garter, stocking and thigh during the rip, Phryné managed to maintain a modest decorum.

She spoke into his ear, "Lead me in a walk. There's more."

Guilermo stepped to the music and began to lead his partner with a short, four-step, defined salida[*].

Phryné repeated the performance of her impromptu, untried, dress-tearing tango step with a full turn and an overhead, high-handed flourish two more times; once for each additional layer of soft purple silk tulle. Biagi's violin and Lamarque's vocals paired perfectly with each tear of fabric. Biagi's orchestra ended *Tango Negro* with a strong set of bandoneón and concertina riffs, a rolling drum flourish and a vocalized, impassioned grunt from the band leader.

Phryné and Guilermo had made an unforgettable impression on the sedate audience as well as the dancers on the floor. Her actions also garnered a boisterous fan base throughout the ballroom and there was applause, not overwhelming, but applause nonetheless, accompanied by a few isolated boorish whistles and cheers.

Guilermo was surprised and bemused. He asked, "I am sorry for my error. You are all right?"

"Of course! I'm fine. I had to finish that dance!"

They passionately finished two tandas of three tangos before returning to the calm sanctity of their table, seeking rest and refreshment.

La valse de l'amour (The Waltz of Love)

*"Corte de pierna abierto"*** (Open leg finish)*

He put a match to a Marlboro, handed it to Phryné and said, "I must apologize again for my amateurish mistake on the dance floor. But as a dancer, you didn't miss a step. It was very brave of you to tear your dress so you could finish the tango."

"In a way ... it was brave, but not unusual. The tango is a bold dance and can change with every step. Bold dances require bold decisions and I consider myself to be a bold woman, and I've had to be bold throughout my life. But don't you dare blame yourself for that little misstep. There was no harm done, and at the very least, the tango is a complicated dance. And we had fun didn't we?!"

She took a small puff of the cigarette, exhaled from the corner of her mouth and continued with a devilish Mae West smile, like the Cheshire Cat of *Alice In Wonderland,* "I took a big chance ripping my dress. From my flashy white pearls to my ivory-white Cuban heels, the only thing between me and the rest of the world was the silk of my dress and my periwinkle stockings. I loved it!"

Guilermo guessed at what Phryné meant, and knowing that she had her own way with words, he teased, "What are you trying to say?"

She playfully blew a little cloud of smoke his way. "Exactly what I said: I loved it!

"I'll never forget Miriam Lowenstein, my very first Hollywood dance coach. She told me: *'Phryne,'* she said, *'if you dare to dance barefoot you can feel the Earth move, but don't let him step on your toes.'*

"And if you think about it, what she said makes perfect sense. Sometimes we need to take chances to get on with our lives."

Guilermo admitted, "I imagine that's true."

Phryné continued with a slightly oblique grin, "What Miriam told me goes hand-in-hand with another saying that every hotshot cowboy actor always throws around at Hollywood parties. They say that *'you have to ride bareback if you really want to feel the horse.'*"

"There you go again, telling me those silly American proverbs ... and expecting me to understand them."

"There is nothing really to understand. Proverbs tell of wisdom learned."

He sent her a wry smile and asked, "You ride horses, too?"

"I have never been upon a horse."

They shared a salty laugh just as a waiter appeared tableside, ready to take their order.

Guilermo asked for another packet of Marlboro cigarettes, ordered a pousse-café*** for Phryné and a neat double brandy for himself.

She asked, "What's that drink you ordered for me?"

"First, it's a test for the barman because it requires a bit of skill to build one ... and ..."

Phryné interrupted him mid-sentence, "The name makes it sound terribly erotic, it does."

"It does sound erotic, and it's supposed to be ... and something more ... it's a *night-cap* like I have heard you Americans say. It is meant to be a drink to end the evening."

"I'm ready."

15 Hours After Departure from New York City

Tuesday, October 14, 1 AM Eastern Standard Time

Phryné practiced self restraint and relied on her patience. She successfully fought the urge to wrap her legs around his thighs and writhe beneath his weight like captured prey. Instead, she stealthily took command of the situation and rolled on top of him. She sat up, her hands upon his toned midriff, straddling his hips and holding his thighs firmly between her calves. Between their soul-deep kisses she ran her hands and fingers over his chest and stomach.

Phryné knew from past experience that the ultimate climax and sensual rapture does not always compare to the combined *joie de vivre** enjoyed during extended foreplay. Over the years, she discovered that if the coupling is carried out with care and self-control, slowly peeling back the wrapping paper can be far more exhilarating than simply ripping open the box to find out what's inside.

This time it was no different. After their first pairing ended in a flash of rocket fire, the second pounded her with a tidal wave of rapture. Her intimate capstone rocked the boat.

They basked in amour's afterglow. He held her close, her head on his upper arm and her right leg over his.

Half an hour after the roaring tsunami, Guilermo had drifted off, giving Phryné a convenient opportunity to secure the evening's events forever into memory and consider her exit strategy. He was on his back, snoring softly. Even in sleep, he looked confident; in control of his destiny.

Two hours had passed since he turned the key to Stateroom 235, *"B Deck"*, and invited Phryné to come within. Since she took those first steps inside her newfound lover's cabin, she was silently considering her options. A sleepy Guilermo presented the perfect opportunity for an easy exit without any awkward goodbyes before returning to Hugo and Suite 162. For the first time in her thirty years, she would be the one leaving a lover's bed. Her silent departure would mean gathering her belongings and walking out the door alone.

She slid out from between the crisp sheets, picked up her battle-scarred dress from the floor, stepped into it and zipped it up to her shoulders. Walking to the powder room, she discovered her evening wrap atop a chair in the sitting area and her shoes on the floor a few feet away. She found her pocketbook on the vanity, checked her reflection in the large oval mirror, ran her lacquered nails through her curls and touched up her lipstick. The mirror gave evidence that one of her pearl teardrop earrings was missing.

A cursory walk through the cabin did not reveal the wayward bauble, but brought the realization that her pair of lace garters and stockings were also among the missing and nowhere in sight. She could only assume that the AWOL[*] items were likely hiding somewhere under the sheets with her Spanish lover.

There was nothing to fret about. The missing items were only an inconvenience and not of any great value, either monetary or sentimental. Rather, Phryné saw opportunity in her loss.

It was an excuse to knock on Guilermo's door the next day with the pretense of a search. She was selfishly wondering when their next rendezvous would be and what pleasurable excitement it would bring.

She took one last look across the bedroom at sleeping Guilermo, lustfully hoping to see him once again within hours. She walked quietly across the carpet to the anteroom, exited without fanfare and shut the door to Stateroom 235 behind her.

Sometime earlier, the lighting had been turned down in the Grand Salon, Main Corridor, vestibule and deck gangways to reflect the time of day and signal that the evening's entertainment had ended, the night's parties were over and it was time to refresh and replenish for the coming day. There were still dozens of passengers walking about; some decent and presentable, others disheveled and soiled, and some in questionable states of sobriety or awareness. A few were alone, some in small groups of three, four or five and some in pairs. For a passing moment, Phryné wondered how many other lovers aboard ship were left behind and alone in beds. She knew of at least two.

Head over Heels in Love

17½ hours after departure from New York City
Tuesday, October 14

Unsure of what she would find on the other side of the door, Phryné cautiously slid the key into the slot and opened Suite 162. The room was dark, with only dull swords of incandescent light slicing under and around the dressing room door. Hugo wasn't in the sitting room, leaving Phryné to believe he was asleep in bed.

Through the patio doors she could see that the sleepy light of morning was just beginning to cut through the black of night and brighten the North Atlantic. She slipped out of her Cuban-heeled dancing shoes and crept quietly toward the bedroom.

Hugo was in his black silk pajamas and sprawled across the larger bed. He was atop the sheets and blankets, with an arm around a pillow, holding it in a gentle embrace. His doting, sleepy hugs endeared him to her.

An empty brandy snifter and a half bottle of Evian water were on the bedside table along with the envelope of his prescription barbiturate sleeping tablets. He didn't move a muscle or display the slightest flinch to indicate that he was awake.

Phryné silently took eleven steps across the Persian carpet to the dressing room and stealthily closed the louvered door behind her. She gingerly set her torn, tattered lilac evening gown onto the dressing bench and ran the water in the sink until the pink marble basin was full. She indulged in a slow, warming cat bath and dried with one of the large, supple Egyptian cotton towels.

She crept back to bedroom and discovered that Hugo had not moved. She stood stoically still for the better part of a minute and detected no movement. She untied her bathrobe and let it fall silently to the floor before she slid her naked form between the sheets of the smaller of the two beds[**].

She looked to Hugo in the next bed before she closed her eyes hoping that a warm, restful blanket of sleep would soon cover her.

But Rudolfo Biagi's eight-piece Argentine orchestra selfishly performed *Tango Negro* endlessly in the ballroom of her brain until the sandman could work his magic: silence the band and grant Phryné the quiet and rest she needed.

Tuesday, October 14, 1 PM, Western Greenland Time

Five hours later she awoke and opened her eyes to find that Hugo was not in the neighboring bed where she last knew him to be. She called out, "Hugo! I'm awake!" She stood, and wrapped herself in her robe.

The empty silence prompted her to look to the bedside table for her watch. The hands pointed to ten o'clock: exactly 24 hours since the Normandie sailed from Pier 88, New York Harbor.

She was still tired, anxious and now slightly curious about Hugo's whereabouts. Since they began their trip in Hollywood, Hugo had never struck out on his own.

111

In fact, since they met in March, Hugo had nearly always been at her side. She could only assume that he must have become overly bored sitting alone in the spacious stateroom and ventured out for a meal. And lately, because of his recall to Paris, he had seemed unable to shake his blue mood.

Phryné needed to start the day anew, but *Tango Negro* began coursing through her head once again, setting up musical road blocks that stymied her thoughts and stopped them dead in their tracks. Her mood gradually turned unexpectedly dark. Dreamy romantic interludes with Guilermo fizzled out like stale seltzer water spilt onto a dirt floor. Her hopes for a meaningful conversation with Hugo were thrown against a brick wall and fell to the ground like twisted, rusty film canisters.

She knew fully well that her fling with Guilermo could only be categorized as a flash-in-the-pan affair. Although it was as refreshing as a spring breeze, it was destined to end as quickly as it started. Her future, uncertain as it may be, was currently tenuously tied to Hugo and would not begin to reveal itself until she set her feet upon French soil.

Still, unanswerable questions with unforeseen solutions and an unscripted, insecure future plagued her morning. She saw her only escape from nagging reality and recourse to be a shower, a fresh change of clothes, hot coffee and something to eat.

Perhaps then she could start her day.

2 PM, Western Greenland Time

Phryné exited the dressing room squeaky clean, wearing a fresh outfit and feeling refreshed and invigorated. Hugo had returned. She believed that she was ready to answer any questions about her night of dancing and diddling that he could ask. Still, she knew that she needed to tread softly.

Although she and Hugo had been lovers for nearly four months, and there weren't any relationship commitments either verbal or implied, she would conveniently keep her romp with Guilermo a secret. The guilt she carried wasn't heavy enough to weigh her conscience down.

Hugo was stretched across the settee, paging through his stale Friday copy of the Paris newspaper *Je suis partout.* He looked up from the page and said, "Bonjour, ma chérie ... good morning, my dear."

Phryné breathed a discreet sigh of relief. She rationalized that she had no need to be nervous about her indiscretion, given that yesterday he had drugged himself into a stupor after dinner and was certainly in no condition to party, dance the tango or even listen to Gypsy Jazz. He chose to pass out rather than celebrate with her. Furthermore, she didn't actually sleep in another man's bed.

When he laid eyes on her, Hugo had smiled and seemed in good humor. Those two elements by themselves were a marked improvement over the last few days.

"Good morning, Hugo, darling ... or maybe I should say good afternoon! Who knows what time it is?!"

"Did you have a good time last night, ma chérie? How was the music ... and the musicians? I hope you danced. I know how you love it and I apologize for not feeling well. Maybe I had a touch of the sea-sickness."

His response settled her nerves; his tone seemed cheerful enough; pleasant and amiable.

Phryné began her response by encouraging him, "I am so happy that you are feeling better. Perhaps all you needed was a good night's sleep so we can enjoy the remainder of the crossing together. This is such a beautiful ship with so many things to do."

She continued, "I had a wonderful time last evening, listening to Gypsy Jazz by a Paris night club band and then enjoying an Argentine tango orchestra. What a treat that was! And you'll never guess who I bumped into completely by accident ..."

"Tell me." His tone and demeanor telegraphed both interest and curiosity.

She stepped to the settee, squeezed in next to him and began, "The very same gentleman we spotted on the platform at the train station in Los Angeles and once more in the dining car on the train to Chicago. He was well-dressed and I know you must remember that dashing couple on the train platform. He was with a bottle blonde, a platinum blonde woman. And later that night, they sat at the table next to ours in the dining car. I know I pointed them out to you."

Hugo dived into his memory, formed a few creases on his brow and said, "Maybe. Maybe I remember them. But I don't remember thinking that they were anything special. To me ... if it's who I think they are ... to me, they seemed to be nothing but typical Hollywood Americans pretending to look important and trying to be fashionable. So, you say that you spent most of the evening with them?"

"Just him. He's traveling alone. She's a Broadway actress and didn't make the trip to France. And he's a Spaniard, a wine maker, and his name is Guilermo and he's returning to Spain. And he's not the least bit precocious or blue-nosed*."

"Well, if I know you like I think I do, you must have danced. Certainly you danced with this Spaniard. Did you have fun?"

"We danced, maybe ten, twelve times. Maybe some more. I got back in the wee hours, maybe two-thirty, three, and when I got in you were asleep so I washed up and went to bed. I didn't think to wake you just because I was back."

Hugo's answer put her nervous wondering to bed, "No, no, ma chérie. It is fine. There was no need to wake me."

He hesitated in thought for a split second, and continued, "But you must be hungry, yes? You had such a late night and it is still some hours before dinner, but we can go to the Café Grill for coffee and a profiterole[*] or if you would like something more, perhaps we could find something off the menu for *le brunch*[*]."

Phryné leaned in and kissed him on the cheek. She didn't expect him to be angry with her, but it was comforting to know that there was no ill will. She purred, "That's perfect, thank you. It will be nice to enjoy something to eat and drink and relax and talk now that you're feeling better."

J'ai deux amours (My Two Loves)

Halfway through brunch, Phryné had a sense that Hugo was being overly cautious with his conversation and that he was actually wrapping his words in cotton to avoid a squabble over what may or may not have happened overnight. She believed he had no reason or foundation whatsoever to be jealous and considered his caution to be misdirected. Phryné knew him to be generally polite and considerate, but never before had he walked on eggshells. She laid the blame on his employer, Pathé and his occasional overuse of his prescription sleeping salts. Silently, secretly, she longed for the Hugo of Hollywood.

Since he first learned of his recall to Paris, their intimacy had waned to only a scattered few, brief, awkward sessions; not the least of which was aboard the Los Angeles Limited bouncing on a two-inch-thick, forty-inch-wide cotton tick mattress.

After their lunch in the Café, and a four-ounce snifter of Benedictine and Brandy[***] they returned to their stateroom. Once inside, Hugo stepped close, leaned in and pressed a passionate kiss onto Phryné's lips. Feeling the weight of guilt-driven intimidation upon her shoulders, she believed that her only recourse was to surrender and accept his advances.

The ensuing love-making was lack-luster. Hugo's passion burned hot and fast, quickly running out of fuse and exploding prematurely. Phryné's libido never left the warming plate.

He began snoring within moments, and with worldly knowledge of past his performances, although not typical, it was not surprising behavior. Phryné also considered that he was still recuperating from drink and drug.

She saw an opportunity in her lover's state of snooze as an unexpected chance to visit her Spaniard on B Deck with the pretense of retrieving her errant earring, stockings and garters. There were still four hours before dinner so the possibility of a gratifying late afternoon liaison was not out of the question.

Phryné slid stealthily out of bed and stepped to the dressing room where she quickly and quietly showered, powdered and perfumed her form. She selected a fitted, bias cut, below the knee, pink rayon dress with a tiny blue forget-me-not print, and a pair of peep toe white pumps.

She left a one-line note on the settee, "I am above decks, strolling through the shops." On her way out the door, she wrapped a white silk scarf twice around her neck and set a wide-brimmed, soft blue hat atop her curls. It was certainly unintentional, but she heard Hugo send a little good-bye snore her way out the door and into the hall.

Stepping quickly through and around the moving mass of passengers, she made her way to the Grand Salon and the staircase down one level to Guilermo's "B Deck". As an attempt to implement a measure of convenient avoidance, she angled her big hat to the left; just enough to cover one eye, but it wasn't enough of a disguise to fool the Gold Diggers. She purposely kept up her brisk pace and was able to dismiss

Joan Blondell and her friend Ginger with only a wave and a smile as she approached the stairway and kept walking.

It was that afternoon that Phryné came to realize that the halls, dining rooms, stairways, vestibules and walkways of the Normandie were unavoidably full of recognizable faces. She may as well have tried to remain anonymous inside the Trocadero on a Saturday night.

Up-and-coming, sequined French actress Simone Simon, bejeweled Academy Award winner Janet Gaynor and director Irving Cummings were standing center stage, at the foot of the "B Deck" down staircase. Cummings was waving a publicity poster for *Girls Dormitory*** and the women were chatting with Marvin 'Squeaky' Nesbitt, a journalist with the *Hollywood Reporter*. The Normandie was packed with blue-nosed members of New York society as well as Hollywood types marketing their way across the Atlantic.

She stepped around the human roadblock and sensed her heart beating just a bit faster as her feet touched the carpeting of "B Deck". Thirty yards and fifty faces down the hall she stopped at Stateroom 235, tucked her pocketbook under her arm, and knocked.

She didn't know what to expect if and when her knock was answered and her lover stood in the doorway. She imagined the look on his face and all sorts of scenarios from an impassioned embrace to an off-putting, emotionless "oh, hello, it's you'. She stared at the door a few more seconds before she ended her pointless speculation and moved her gaze innocently to the activity around her in the hall.

Courtesy forced her to greet a few overtly curious passers-by with a smile as she waited for an answer to her first knock. An awkward thirty seconds ticked by before an unanswered second attempt, followed by a final, softer rap with her knuckles. Yet another punishing thirty seconds passed before she turned and started back down the hall to the staircase. An eternity of romantic fantasies vanished in a little more than a minute outside Stateroom 235. Last night, in the wee hours of the morning, when she and Guilermo entered the room, she didn't remember so many people milling about. Her thoughts had been elsewhere.

At the stairway leading up to the Main Deck, the *Girls Dormitory* entourage was still there, still in the way and still schmoozing*. Phryné was greeted with a blinding flash from a young photographer in a suit, tie and newsboy cap wielding a sparkling new, jet-black Leica camera. This time she couldn't pass without the stubborn reporter, Squeaky Nesbitt, stepping in front of her and blocking her path.

His offensive breath betrayed a lunch of liver pâté*, duck mousse, gin, and cigarettes. The odor soured his question beyond palatability, "My darling Phryné, tell me do, are you making this passage to France for pleasure or the arts?"

Phryné stepped back, held her breath against the stench and spoke rapidly, "Why, you know me and you certainly must know the answer to that question, Squeaky! It's always about the arts!"

Squeaky had earned his nickname honestly. He had the voice of a pubescent thirteen-year-old.

Phryné wasted no time and continued with her answer, not allowing the photographer or reporter any room for an interjection or retort, "I'm off to Paris for a time and who knows what trouble I can stir up! Toodles*!"

She executed a perfect relevé*, spun around, and spoke to the others, "It was certainly nice seeing you, Simone, Janet and of course ... Director Cummings ... perhaps we'll meet again during this trip and we can chat longer!"

As her last words left her lips, Phryné briskly stepped away from stinky Squeaky and the camera boy, and started on her way above decks, back to Suite 162. She kept an eye peeled the rest of the way through the Entry Hall and Grand Salon, still holding onto foolish hope for a glimpse of her Spaniard. She stopped outside the Café Grill and quickly surveyed the crowd inside for Guilermo's face or form without a satisfactory result.

She could only imagine what would have happened had she met up with him. She eerily felt she was walking on eggshells and fought the urge to constantly look over her shoulder, fearing that Hugo was lurking somewhere in the shadows and ready to throw sand on her fire. In the deepest, secret compartments of her thoughts, Phryné nervously suspected that her whirlwind romance was a one-off affair, but continued to stubbornly hold out hope that her Spaniard was her man of destiny. She thought, *"Ships that pass in the night"* but hoped it wasn't so.

Forty-five minutes after she began her pursuit, her search was over. Disappointed, dejected and minus her missing earring, stockings and garters, Phryné's quest for her dark, mysterious lover ended as a fruitless, frustrating endeavor. She grudgingly decided to nix any further Guilermo expeditions, but doggedly refused to dismiss the possibility of a chance encounter.

She stopped at Suite 162, brought the key from her pocketbook and went inside, hung her hat and scarf on the valet stand and picked up her unread note from the settee. Quietly, she stepped to the bed and her still-napping Hugo and kissed him softly on the cheek, whispering, "It will soon be time for dinner, my darling. I just got back from a stroll on the upper deck and checking the shops in the Entry Hall. Did you have a good little sleep? I think I walked up an appetite."

He opened his eyes, smiled at her, rolled onto his back, stretched his form and reached out for her hand, "Good evening, ma chérie."

The light of day had disappeared hours ago from the blue-black sky. It was still an hour before dinner, late evening, and the SS Normandie was steaming east northeast at 30 knots, 500 nautical miles southwest of Godthåb[**], Greenland and more than 800 miles from New York City. Their destination, Le Havre, France, remained about 2400 nautical miles beyond the eastern horizon.

Phryné sat on the bed, "Let's have a nice quiet dinner together, Hugo, like we did last night. We should relax and enjoy the crossing, there's so much to do and see. And after dinner, if you like, we can share a drink in the Café Grill. I really think that you would enjoy the jazz band from Paris playing at the Grill. I know you would. I just know it."

Hugo sat up, set his feet on the floor, put an arm around her waist, kissed her cheek and spoke softly into her curls, "That sounds wonderful, ma chérie. The evening will belong to us alone."

His words were a refreshing breath of fresh air. The Hugo of spring and summer had returned. It was a welcome change for Phryné.

How Deep Is the Ocean?

Dinner was served at their assigned table punctually at eight o'clock. And as the night before, the food and service were first class; just what the French Line promised its passengers. Afterwards, they drank, danced and were entertained by The Hot Five in the Café Grill. The second day of their four-day transatlantic crossing went exactly as Phryné had hoped, and even more so.

Before returning to their stateroom, she and Hugo meandered hand-in-hand along the Observation Deck, below the Wheelhouse and through the glass-enclosed walls and ceiling of the Winter Garden. It was a starlit, fairytale walk through an oceangoing, tropical Garden of Paradise.

That evening, she briefly allowed Guilermo's image to recklessly trespass and tread through her field of thoughts. But passing memories of her Spanish fling didn't plow under the fertile furrows of Hugo's reseeded, amorous advances.

That night, the Hugo that Phryné had known in Hollywood reignited her flame and warmed her soul. She slept soundly.

10 AM, Central Atlantic Time

Next morning, they were awakened by a brisk, purposeful knock at the door. Sleepy-eyed and annoyed, they looked at one another in bewilderment.

A second later, there was another, more affirmative, resounding knock that further exasperated their shared state of confusion. Hugo became increasingly aggravated and Phryné's irritation grew. About forty winks earlier, she had anticipated an intimate cuddle with Hugo and a leisurely, romantic brunch in the Café.

Hugo shouted, startling his bedmate, "Un moment!"

He slid out from under the sheet, stepped into his pajama bottoms and stepped into his slippers.

Again, a knock.

Phryné quickly crossed to the dressing room, donned her soft pink robe, returned to the bedroom and stood next to the bed, discombobulated, barefoot and disheveled. At the fourth noisy clash of knuckles on mahogany, Hugo was in the foyer and opened the door. Two men wearing stern faces and stiff uniforms pushed past Hugo, not stopping until they were well into the bedroom. They hadn't offered an introduction or granted any semblance of decorum.

The tallest was definitely a ship officer and presented a confident, authoritative, refined demeanor. He appeared to be about fifty, dressed in a dark blue military-style uniform embellished with gold trim and carrying an air of aristocratic, inherent pomposity. He came to a stop, stood squarely five feet in front of Phryné, removed his service cap and stuck it under his arm.

The other man appeared ten years younger and was dressed in black with a high, stiff-collared jacket and jodhpurs with red piping. He was clearly spit-and-polish with police-issue knee-high boots, gleaming brass buttons and a shiny patent leather kepi atop his head. The entire uniform was typical of French police. Hugo followed him inside and stood beside Phryné. He held her by the hand.

The ship's officer spoke in a steady monotone as if he was reading from prepared text, "Good morning. It is unfortunate that we have awakened and disturbed you, but it is most necessary. I shall speak in my best English if that is acceptable?"

He didn't wait for a response. He trod upon and spoke over Phryné and Hugo's unsteady, nervous replies of 'yes'.

"I am Georges de Villenueve, the Second Captain of SS Normandie and this is Ship's Security Officer, Inspector Claude Bohec. I have examined the passenger manifest and assume who we have here are Monsieur Hugo Grétillat and Mademoiselle Phryné Truffaut. I am correct?"

Again, he didn't give them a chance to answer and continued, "Inspector Bohec and myself apologize for this inconvenient intrusion, but some extremely troubling safety and security concerns have arisen. An unfortunate incident has occurred aboard ship and during the first stages of the inquiry that is now taking place, it is suspected that Mademoiselle Phryné and Monsieur Hugo may be of importance to our investigation."

Villenueve cleared his throat and went on, "And further, Monsieur Hugo may prove to be of significant assistance not only because of his relationship with the Mademoiselle, but also his knowledge, and the personal nearness, you could say."

Hugo appeared puzzled and glanced sideways at Phryné.

"The incident that I mention demands immediate attention and a resolution must be achieved at the earliest possible time to ensure the continued safety of all passengers aboard the Normandie. I am here to escort you to the Command Deck and the Captain's Conference Room to help make clear some questions that have come to light. You may, of course, get dressed, but then we must proceed with no delay. As I mention, there are safety and security concerns of the highest priority that must be settled.

"Again, I apologize on behalf of Compagnie Générale Transatlantique for the inconvenience. But please, do not misunderstand or ignore the gravity of the situation. These matters are most important and need to be addressed. The faster we can proceed and finish, the sooner we shall bring this matter to its end."

Phryné's scalp tingled. Her thoughts were twirling wildly, as if in a centrifuge. She was searching frantically for a reason behind her and Hugo's rude awakening, and like all nervous worry, it was fruitless.

Her frustration and aggravation were voiced as an attempt at sarcastic humor, "This is absurd. It feels like I'm reading for a part in the next Charlie Chan[**] movie: *Charlie Chan Sails to France.*"

Her statement fell on deaf ears, and nobody was smiling.

Hugo was flushed and clearly embarrassed by the intrusion. He asked in futile protest, "What is this about? What could we have possibly done to become a part of this vaudeville act?"

Like Phryné's verbal protest, his also was ignored.

Rather, Second Captain de Villenueve affirmed his authority and replied sharply, "The sooner we begin, the sooner we all can be educated by the facts I will reveal, the questions I will ask and the answers I will get. You must now quickly find what to wear today and we will proceed above deck. Inspector Bohec and I will wait here in the sitting area for you to dress and prepare yourselves. But I must advise you: do not waste my time."

Hugo asked for and was granted fifteen minutes of personal time for himself and Phryné. They spent it between the dressing room, wardrobe, shower and wit's end.

Neither could guess, let alone share, what they considered this mystery investigation could mean or how it may affect their situation. Whispered questions and suppositions bounced back and forth, up, down and sideways between the walls, ceiling and floor. There were no answers to be heard. Captain de Villenueve had them all and wasn't about to show his hand until he was ready.

Although Hugo had showered, shaved and dressed well ahead of Phryné, she asked him to remain in the dressing room until her preparations were complete.

"Stay by me, Hugo. Please. We must not be led like sheep."

He agreed, and sat patiently on the dressing bench.

She was determined to make a silent protest and demonstrate her point by using at least the full fifteen minutes to step in and out of the shower, apply her morning Pond's cold cream and complete her makeup regimen. Wide-bottom grey slacks, a white blouse, black beret and a soft yellow jacket would be her uniform of the day.

She purposely dillydallied seven minutes over the initial quarter-hour time allotment, prompting Villenueve to shout through the door, "You must finish now. Now! Or we will drag you out by the ears."

Hugo stood abruptly, and answered, "We are coming now."

Phryné capped her lipstick and smiled into the mirror, "I'm ready, my darling."

The Upper Echelon and the Upper Deck

2 days, 2 hours after departure from Pier 88, New York

Rather than using the stairway and passing through the Grand Salon, Second Captain de Villenueve led Phryné and Hugo along the Main Deck hallway from their stateroom to an unmarked, key-operated elevator, which was effectively disguised as a frescoed door. Inspector Bohec stayed a few steps behind. Not a word passed between anyone along the way.

The Command Deck was two decks above, the topmost of the ship, excepting the Wheelhouse. The Captain's Conference Room was, in fact, a glass-ceiling, mahogany-panel atrium with two doors on each of three walls (port, starboard and aft) leading to separate office suites and meeting rooms. The morning sun angled into the atrium from the chilly Atlantic skies above, drowning one side of the room in light while starving the other.

Villenueve stopped outside a sunlit door adorned with a gilded letter "F", opened it, and allowed his guests and Bohec to enter ahead of him. Inside, the room was minus the glaring sunlight, much more subdued, and like the Dining Salon, illuminated solely by incandescent lights behind floor-to-ceiling columns of Lalique glass. There was one highly polished, eight-foot table, with two chairs on one side and four opposite, four large crystal ashtrays, four composition booklets, several pencils and a black and chrome telephone in the middle. The Second Captain motioned to the two chairs, "Please sit and we can begin."

The Inspector and Captain did not sit, but stood beside two of the four chairs on the near side of the table.

Without the slightest inkling of what to expect, Phryné wriggled a bit in her chair and looked around the spacious room in nervous anticipation. For the second time that morning, she felt her scalp tingle.

She asked with a hint of defiance, "What's going on here? Are you putting us on trial?"

Hugo snickered, "It looks like a meeting of the Pathé Frères Production Board at 30 Avenue Corentin in Paris!"

Villenueve seemed preoccupied. He wasn't amused and went directly to point, "One, perhaps two, of our passengers are missing and it is suspected that they were on the wrong side of the deck railing."

He picked up the trumpet of the pedestal telephone and clicked the receiver hook multiple times before speaking into the mouthpiece, "We are ready here, sir."

Hugo and Phryné shared nervous glances.

Phryné said, "I don't understand. Did somebody go overboard? What does that have to do with me? Or Hugo?"

Hugo interjected, "Or me? Either of us?"

Second Captain Villenueve suddenly realized that he had likely let the cat out of the bag when he mentioned that someone may have gone overboard. He could only hope that he didn't ruin the investigation and decided that it was best not to mention it to the Ship's Captain.

Villenueve did not utter one word in reply, grant either Phryné or Hugo the courtesy of eye contact, or give them a passing sideways glance. He remained standing as Bohec sat at the chair furthest to the right.

Moments later, three men came through the entry door.

Villenueve began with the introductions as the newcomers took the three remaining seats at the table. One of the men set a small paper box on the table.

"This is Ship's Captain Paul Baudelande, Chief Inspector Amié Veblynde, and Lieutenant Inspector Erec Lamonte."

More ornate and frivolous than either Bohec or Villenueve, the newcomers were dressed in uniforms that showcased their official capacities.

Already seated, Captain Baudelande snapped a token salute and spoke, "Merci, deuxième capitaine de Villenueve. You may assume command of the wheelhouse. Thank you."

Phryné and Hugo were sitting across from a highly decorated veteran man of the sea. Captain Baudelande's official portrait and biography were highlighted on page one of the SS Normandie Welcome Packet as a twenty-plus year veteran of the French Line.

The triumvirate of policemen at the table sat without human expression, hands folded next to their patent leather kepi hats to the left and pad and pencil to the right.

Phryné feared that the coming ordeal could last for hours and ruin her plans for another romantic evening. Hugo wished that he could return to the stateroom and consume a measure of brandy and sleeping salts. He didn't have the slightest inkling of what was about to occur but feared the worst.

Ship's Captain Baudelande reintroduced himself and the three Inspectors before he began, "Mademoiselle Truffaut and Monsieur Grétillat ... first, let me say we will conduct this inquiry in English if possible, and if needed, I will translate the word or phase that we stumble over.

"Inspector Bohec and Second Captain de Villeneuve have been working on this investigation for more than eight hours and have conducted several interviews overnight and this morning. We are getting close to the end and it seems that a conclusion is near and we shall try to finish this inquiry as soon as possible. As Ship's Captain, I am here as a moderator and fact-finder in this matter, not as a judge or jury, but as Ombudsman. My responsibility is to enforce the Maritime Laws of France. The only enforcement power here stands with the Ship's Security, and they alone determine the status of the investigation and if it merits legal and judicial action ashore.

"So, understand that what we have here is an initial primary investigation and not a Maritime Ship's Court."

Phryné looked to Hugo for answers he couldn't know and comfort he couldn't provide.

He asked the Captain, "Do we need a lawyer? Has there been a crime?"

Captain Baudelande didn't reply. Instead, he nodded to the three police seated to his right and said, "You may begin, Chief Inspector."

Chief Inspector Amié Veblynde was about to give an overview of the ongoing investigation and the incident that prompted it. His voice was deep and rough, like a dull saw butchering through oak timber.

He began, "Nearly nine and one-half hours ago, the Office of Ship's Security was notified of a disturbance on the portside of "B Deck". A passenger in Tourist Class had reported a loud noise outside his cabin that sounded like something struck or fell onto the port gangway. Ship's Security Inspectors Bohec and Lamonte investigated and found evidence of violence. There was a small amount of blood smear along the ship's hull below Stateroom 235, limited splatter on a lifeboat tarpaulin and on the gangway railing. Directly above was "B Deck", and Stateroom 235."

Veblynde paused, lit a cigarette and watched for a reaction from across the table.

Phryné and Hugo sat silent and attentive. Phryné's gaze was intense. Hugo's eyes were inquisitive.

The Chief Inspector continued, "After entering Stateroom 235, Inspectors Bohec and Lamonte had discovered that the Suite was unoccupied, several lights were left burning, the patio door was unlocked and open, and the bed appeared to have been slept in. Articles of men's clothing were scattered in the sitting area and around the bed. Some ladies' intimates were on the floor next to the bed and a piece of jewelry was found lying on the dressing room floor. A chair had been knocked over and an ashtray was shattered on the marble floor of the washroom.

"On the patio deck, Inspector Bohec noted a blood pool on the teak deck, a smear on the railing and one patio lounge that was tipped on its side. These discoveries had pressed Inspector Bohec to notify Second Captain de Villeneuve of the probability of foul play or a physical altercation that resulted in bodily injury and the possibility of a passenger gone overboard."

Inspector Veblynde paused his story.

He looked Phryné directly in the eye, "Mademoiselle Truffaut, this morning, Inspector Bohec interviewed one female witness who knows you from Hollywood. That witness placed you in the Café Grill with an unknown companion. And yet another witness claims to have seen you in the Lounge with a passenger who may or may not have been Monsieur Grétillat. Can you explain?"

Phryné gave a slightly delayed reply, "Yes ... I was. My darling Hugo, Monsieur Grétillat, wasn't feeling well and I met someone in the Café and we listened to music and danced. I have nothing to hide. I told my Hugo everything very early this morning."

Veblynde prodded further, "Was this man the Spanish national named Guilermo Gaeta?"

Phryné flushed and answered, "Yes."

"Did you go to his stateroom?"

"Yes, we had a nightcap."

"How long did you stay?"

"I'm not certain, but perhaps an hour. Guilermo was sleeping when I left. It was perhaps two o'clock. I still have New York time on my watch."

Inspector Veblynde reached for the paper box, removed the lid and dumped the contents onto the table: a pair of lilac stockings, white lace garters and one pearl teardrop earring.

His next question was emphatically expressed as a demand rather than an inquiry, "Are these your items, Miss Truffaut?"

Without a second's hesitation, Phryné replied, "Yes. They look like mine. I think they are mine. My dress was torn during a tango, and my stockings had runs, so I took them off. I must have dropped the earring when I left to return to my stateroom."

Veblynde cleared his throat and directed his next question to Hugo, "Where were you during this time, Monsieur Grétillat?"

"I was asleep. I had a few glasses of brandy and sleeping salts. It was a very tiring trip from Los Angeles to New York and I was still struggling with sea-sickness."

During Chief Inspector Veblynde's questioning, Inspectors Bohec and Lamonte were busy with pencil on paper. Occasionally, Ship's Captain Baudelande also took pencil to paper and made notes of his own. Of the four men sitting opposite Phryné and Hugo, Baudelande was the most attentive, and would squint an eye or wrinkle his brow now and again.

Chief Inspector Amié Veblynde folded his hands and sat up straight. "I have one last puzzling question for both of you."

He looked around the table. There was an uncomfortable, lengthy pause that allowed everyone to understand the possible gravity of what he was about to ask.

"Where is the passenger traveling with the Spaniard, Monsieur Guilermo Gaeta? Her name is Nancy Kenyon. She is Mademoiselle Nancy Kenyon from Ohio, United States."

Velblynde twisted in his chair, grunted, pushed his shoulders back and wrenched his back. He then found it necessary to clear his throat again. It echoed between the paneled walls as a slushy gurgle.

Phryné grimaced. Baudelande noticed. Bohec smirked.

Inspector Veblynde glared at Phryné and Hugo and said, "No answer? No one knows? Then I must tell you. Passenger Mademoiselle Nancy Kenyon is missing along with passenger Monsieur Guilermo Gaeta. They have likely met the same fate together and are swimming with the little fishes at the bottom of the ocean."

Velblynde went on, "I am finished, Captain Baudelande, sir."

Phryné and Hugo exchanged glances, each hoping beyond hope that they were also finished and their ordeal was over.

Phryné shuddered. Tremors coursed through her body. She suddenly found herself burdened with new worry: *Where is Guilermo and was he telling the truth about the mystery blonde he was with in Los Angeles and New York? Did she really return to Hollywood? Is it possible that Guilermo and platinum blonde Nancy Kenyon met an unscrupulous demise together in Stateroom 235? Did someone push them overboard or was it a murder and suicide or just a lovers' suicide?*

Captain Paul Baudelande measured his words, and spoke clearly, "As Ship's Captain, my primary responsibilities are the safety of the passengers and crew. Secondary is the Normandie and the interests of the French Line. Suspect individuals and detainees stand in third place. Because there are individuals of foreign nationality involved, I was obligated to send the details of this incident by radio telegraph to the National Police, in Paris.

"These are the factors that dictate my actions, Mademoiselle Truffaut and Monsieur Grétillat. This unfortunate incident and this investigation has not only cast grave doubt on your innocence but also revealed cause for concern for your safety as well as that of all Normandie passengers.

"Under the laws of the French Republic, and considering the circumstances, it is my duty to remand each of you to separate cells below decks in the ship's brig* for the duration of the crossing. There will be no contact or communication allowed between you. You may dress in your own comfortable clothing, but only essential items. You will be served three meals daily while you are in custody, and offered medical attention should the need arise. After Normandie docks in Le Havre, we shall transfer your custody to the civil authorities of Department Seine-Inférieure, Normandy Province.

"You are not the first passengers to be placed into custody aboard the Normandie, nor will you be the last. We have done this before and we do it well.

"Inspectors Bohec and Lamonte will now escort you back to your stateroom. You will be advised what clothing you may wear during your two-day confinement. The clothing that you will be wearing today will be what you wear until tomorrow. Your baggage and personal items recovered from your stateroom will be stored for you at the French Line

Cargo and Baggage Offices at the Port of Le Havre for a period of up to six months. Your travel papers and negotiable assets will be documented, verified and secured for you at the French Line Purser's Office in Le Havre for a period of up to five years.

"Remember, you are permitted to pack only one day of fresh clothing, what you will wear, nothing frivolous and only the simple articles that you need. No belts, no scarves, no stockings, no sashes, no knives, no scissors, no razors of any kind. Inspectors Bohec and Lamonte will closely observe and assist you when you have questions. It is necessary to heed the direction they give. I am allowing this as a courtesy, so do not test my patience or humanity. I could demand that you wear service dungarees and nothing more.

"I do not see the need for wrist or leg irons, so again, do not test my patience or humanity. Go with the inspectors to your stateroom and do as you are instructed. Show respect to the authority of the French Line and you will be treated with due dignity in return. There are all forms of printed material for you to read and entertain yourselves during your internment. In the coming days, you will come to appreciate your treatment aboard Normandie."

Somehow, Phryné controlled her nerves and managed to speak through the lump in her throat to plead their case, "We are innocent, Captain. We do not know Nancy Kenyon. Guilermo Gaeta was asleep when I left him. Hugo and I have hurt no one."

She was flushed with nerves. Her stomach churned. She was incredulous, embarrassed. She feared for her immediate future and well-being, but fought the tears. She likened her situation to a nightmare.

Hugo piped in, "We are guilty of nothing ... nothing."

He was insulted, apprehensive and nervous. Beads of sweat stuck to his forehead. He felt threatened. This was far beyond what Pathé had done to him.

Captain Baudelande tried to reassure them, "The Normandie Security Officers will continue their inquiries in this matter. And I repeat: I sent a Radiogram to Paris because I am under obligation to share information about foreign citizens with the proper French authority, the National Police, the *Sûreté Nationale*. And of course, in addition, this case will be examined by the civil authorities in Le Havre and you will be granted the opportunity to obtain gratis legal counsel if they should charge you with a crime.

"Mademoiselle Phryné, I suggest that you ask after the Consulate of the United States as soon as you are in custody of the Department of Justice in Le Havre. And Monsieur Hugo, as a citizen of the French Republic you should certainly ask after a legal advocate.

"You will go now, and I must wish you luck with the civil investigation in Le Havre.

"There is nothing more that I can do for you. I wish you good fortune."

The second half of their transatlantic trip was to be spent in the brig.

The Brig and Bilge Water

Life below decks stood in stark contrast to that they had experienced in Première Classe. In fact, it was in stark contrast to anything they had known since the day they were born.

The detention cells aboard the Normandie were ten-foot square cubicles with riveted steel sheets on all four walls and ceiling. Ventilation was limited to six, three-by-twenty-inch, ceiling-height vents on three walls. The solid metal door had an eight-inch square, steel-barred window at eye level and an eighteen-by-six-inch slot for the transfer of food trays and other items. Each opening had a sliding steel door on the outside. A single incandescent bulb cast dreary yellow light from a steel mesh-covered ceiling recess. Amenities were few: a bar of brown soap, a twelve-inch square linen cloth, and five sheets of tissue paper.

The sanitary fixtures were a stainless steel commode and a twelve-inch round stainless wash basin tucked in the right entry-side corner.

On the left side of the cell was an eighteen-inch-high, six-by-three-foot, steel-clad rectangular box attached to, and built as a permanent fixture, against the wall and floor. A two-inch mattress, wool blanket and twelve-inch pillow were the only items of comfort. Once inside, they were allowed only the clothing on their backs. If anything could be positive, it was that the accommodations were clean.

Although they were held in separate cells, their experience was the same. They shared feelings of degradation, isolation and desperation.

At the end of day one, Phryné believed that she'd cried her last tear. She hadn't.

She remembered the flash from a Leica camera and newspaperman Squeaky Nesbitt. Any day now, she could be on the front page of the Hollywood Reporter.

Hugo's anger-driven anxiety and depression wanted for the barbiturates and brandy that he couldn't have.

He had constant worry about the security of his position at Pathé and what consequences he could suffer if his current predicament became the fly in the ointment.

During their second and final day of internment, they each asked several times for updates on their situation. They were assured by Inspector Bohec that the investigation was ongoing and if there were new developments, they would be informed.

Bohec's positive attitude did nothing to soothe their nerves, nor did it soften the reality of their impending confinement. Neither Hugo nor Phryné had any amount of restful sleep during their period of captivity deep in the bowels of the SS Normandie.

Phryné spent much of her time second-guessing the choices she had made in the Café Grill, Lounge and behind the door of Stateroom 235.

Hugo wondered how long it would be before his life in Paris returned to what he had known before his tumultuous Hollywood assignment.

5. Bienvenue en France
(Welcome to France)
~ 1935 ~

Was That the Human Thing to Do?
Police Central Command, 36 Rue Michelet,
Le Havre, district Danton, Normandy

The SS Normandie docked at Pier Meunier, Le Havre at 7:35 PM, Friday, October 18; four days, three and a half hours after steaming away from Pier 88 in New York City.

Phryné and Hugo had arrived in France. Although they dreaded the day ahead, when the ocean liner's five-foot tall, three-trumpet brass air horn announced its arrival in Le Havre, they could not imagine that another, much more harrowing ordeal was about to begin. Their transatlantic crossing had ended with an isolated confinement below decks that left them questioning not only their individual futures, but their commitment to one another.

Before leaving the brig to go ashore, Ship's Security Inspectors Veblynde and Bohec afforded woolen blankets around Phryné and Hugo's shoulders to fend off October's chill and the evening dampness of the harbor. They were subsequently handcuffed and led along the crew and supplies gangway well ahead of the disembarking passengers.

They came ashore and stepped around piles of rolled hawser[*] and mooring posts as large as an elephant's thigh, and were shuffled along toward the Arrivals Building. Mere minutes after the Normandie was moored, two Ship's Security officer's and their two prisoners were inside the Welcome Center and Customs Hall. Veblynde and Bohec solemnly transferred custody of Phryné and Hugo to the Le Havre

Police without a single word passing between them or their detainees during the hand-over. The senior of six French policemen examined the paperwork and finalized the transfer with his signature and initials on the form where Velblynde had pointed his long, bony finger.

With only a nod and a half-hearted smile, Velblynde and Bohec expressed an unspoken farewell to Phryné and Hugo and silently watched as the gaggle of a half dozen French Police frog-marched them through the Welcome Center, past the Customs and Duty desk to the docks outside.

Floodlights eerily illuminated the dock and the starboard side of the Normandie with a dusky glow as if it were twilight. Wispy fingers of fog drifted off the harbor waters attempting to reclaim the pier into the murky darkness. It seemed that the ocean liner was the backdrop for Scene One of a Hollywood murder mystery. As if it was scripted, a clanging ship's bell indicated that the curtain was about to go up.

Outside on the shadowy dock, the unexpected sighting of black-uniformed French police escorting blanket-clad prisoners off the French Lines' premier ocean liner prompted an explosion of flash bulbs among a growing swarm of reporters pushing their way toward the activity. A swarm of newspapermen had populated the dock much earlier, anticipating the arrival of the Liner of Legend. Since its first Atlantic crossing in May, the docking of the Normandie spurred hopes and presented the opportunity for an exclusive interview from an arriving Hollywood figure or returning European luminary. The surprise of fresh police activity presented an unexpected chance at a fiery hot, scandalous headline. Photographic flashes lit the dock like tiny bits of ball lightning[**].

Unfortunately for the photographers and press, the entourage of French police threw water on the flames. They responded quickly to the minor melee and shouldered through the press, surrounded Phryné and Hugo like a flock of penguins and pressed them into a waiting, windowless police van.

The short-lived ruckus on the dock was witnessed by a mixed crowd of about fifty individuals awaiting the arrival of relatives and friends. Further along the boardwalk and pier, the docks were alive with longshoremen pushing carts, wagons and wheelbarrows. A handful of newspaper and magazine vendors called out headlines and offered souvenir trinkets. Notwithstanding the police activity, it was a normalized scene of organized chaos.

Once off the dock and inside the prisoner transport van, Phryné and Hugo were given a short, bumpy, seven-block ride along cobblestone streets to the Rue Michelet police station. Inside, they were doggedly processed into a legal system that was shackled by nineteenth century traditions preserved and practiced within eighteenth century stone walls. But, despite the obsolete and rickety equipment, mug shots and fingerprints were taken.

One younger policeman spoke in labored English and informed them that they would be taken across the street to temporary detention dormitories pending their first court appearance.

Hugo pressed him, "Pouvez-vous nous dire quand nous pouvons nous attendre à ce que notre affaire soit entendue par le tribunal, mon ami?"

With apologetic eyes and a long face, the officer replied, "I cannot say."

Hugo's use of French frustrated Phryné. She never felt so threatened, fearful, helpless and alone.

They were summarily shuffled to a dimly lit room to fill out forms requiring input of name, place and date of birth, citizenship, address, occupation, income, employment status and passport numbers.

To finalize the process of conformity and degradation, their blankets were confiscated and they were issued a pair of grey, shapeless, linen trousers and a tunic top. A pair of hand-sewn slip-on, cotton duck canvas shoes with thin leather soles made the prison uniform complete. Every stitch in each piece of their new wardrobe was made by the convicts and prisoners in Le Havre Prison across the street.

Insecure about their immediate future and beaten about by the inefficiency of embedded bureaucracy, a darker sheet of new worry was unfolded and covered them. Circumstances deteriorated further after Phryné believed it was time to heed Captain Baudelande's advice and asked that the American Consulate be contacted. Her request was poorly timed. The single French officer who was able to understand and communicate with Phryné in English had left the room. It appeared that words had left her lips and fell to the stone floor with as much weight as a speck of dust. No one noticed. Not one of the other policemen attempted to acknowledge her existence or recognize her request.

A few painful, silent seconds later, Hugo spoke in his native tongue and asked that he be granted access to an attorney.

An older, thin, slack-jawed officer evidently felt that he was obliged to answer a fellow countryman, and remarked, "C'est fin de la semaine. Peut-être le lundi."

Phryné piped in, "What have you been asking him? And what did he answer? Did you ask about the American Consul?"

Hugo sighed, "I asked for a lawyer and he told me that it's the weekend. He said perhaps something will get done on Monday."

Hugo's tone telegraphed defeat.

Phryné sensed her world spinning round and round; sucking her life down the drain. Her heart had dropped into a bottomless pit with an ache she had never known.

Le Havre Prison, 25 Rue Lesueur

It was just past midnight when they were placed in leg irons and three officers escorted them down six stone steps of the police station, and four yards across, and five yards down a cobblestone street to the Rue Michelet entrance of Le Havre Prison[**]. The prison grounds occupied an entire city block bordered by Lesueur, Duroc, Michelet and Messéna Streets, and were surrounded by a thick, twenty-foot high, haunting, ominous, grey stone wall.

They stopped when confronted by a ten-foot wide black iron gate as perilously foreboding as the entrance to Hell. A few seconds after they arrived, a gate keeper appeared from the shadows, bouncing toward them with three or four long, rattling, heavy keys attached to a large black ring. He acknowledged the policemen with a genial "Hallo[*]! Allô[*]!". Without blinking an eye at Phryné or Hugo, he inserted one of his oversized keys into a smaller man-door on the right side of the massive gate. It unlocked with a weighty click and opened with a screech and groan. To Phryné's ears, it also seemed that the gate keeper had allowed a two-syllable giggle to escape. For the first time in her life, she genuinely feared for her future, and looked to Hugo only to discover that she wasn't alone with her feelings of dread. Missing her blanket, the cold and damp violated her essence.

A hand on her upper back purposely pushed her forward through the noisy, rusty door and onto the prison grounds. A shiver crossed her shoulders. Behind her, she heard Hugo's leather-soled slippers shuffle and slide. She turned and realized that he had likely received a stronger shove upon his back and had been stumbling to catch his balance.

Inside the stone walls were six large, time-beaten, brick and stone, three-story dormitories, with scattered narrow, barred windows on the first floor and very few on the top two. Gaslights flickered at the corners of the buildings, casting more gloomy shadows than yellow light. Within moments, they were pushed inside the second closest building and into a small room where they found themselves facing four sturdy prison guards in steel-grey uniforms embellished with yellow insignia and pewter buttons. The policemen from the station across the street removed Phryné and Hugo's handcuffs and leg irons, and exited without a word.

The four guards that remained stood emotionless and staring into the eyes of the new prisoners. At first glance, the four appeared to be two men and two women. They each kept one hand upon the hilt of a holstered truncheon, using it and their hardened gaze as weapons of control.

Without a word, two of the prison guards swarmed upon Hugo like turkey vultures on carrion, before mumbling a few unintelligible words in muddled French, and jackbooted him out through the door. Overwrought, Phryné sensed her heart leap from her breast toward her lover and became overcome by a growing, stronger apprehension. She was left helplessly alone to ponder her immediate fate, but fearfully acknowledged that it wouldn't be a long time coming.

The two guards who remained appeared to be female Matrons, prejudiced not by body shape or demeanor, but rather facial features and hair length. One of them pulled her black baton from its holster, stepped beside Phryné, placed it firmly onto her lower back and applied a steady pressure. The other took Phryné by the shoulder and led the way through the door to the courtyard and across the pea-gravel paddock to the adjacent three-story jailhouse. The faded, painted words *aux femmes** were barely visible above the wooden plank door.

One Prison Matron spoke a few words that drew a response from the other, who removed her hand from Phryné's shoulder and beat a beefy fist upon the door, and announced the new prisoner, "Nouveau prisonnier!" Six or seven apologetic words came from within just before the door creaked open and revealed another female guard, the resident dormitory Overseer.

A few more words passed among the three Prison Matrons before Phryné was once again pushed into a place where she would rather not be. She was forced a few feet into a dark, yawning room and forced down onto a creaky, rickety metal bed topped by a hard, lumpy straw mattress that had been made by inmate labor. Sharp spikes of straw pushed through the linen cover of the mattress and nipped at her backside. She slid, twitched, shifted and fidgeted her buttocks to no avail. Surrender to discomfort was inevitable. She gave up, abandoned her pride and slowly laid her body down upon the prickly mattress.

Phryné had no idea what time it was and could only assume that she was in the company of other female inmates. She did know that she was in an antiquated prison that reeked of body odor, urine, smoke, coal soot and wet straw.

Her eyes gradually acclimated to the dim light and her new surroundings. She discovered that the room was as dark and foreboding as it was cavernous; fifteen yards long and five yards wide with a ceiling that reached perhaps six feet from the floor. Dozens of beds were lined perpendicular to the walls on both sides and all but a few were occupied. Four dirty, naked light bulbs that glowed with the candlepower of a single match, hung from the ceiling on skinny, cloth-wrapped power cords.

There wasn't a spoken word to be heard, and Phryné assumed that talking was not allowed. There were, however, guttural sounds. A groan, a cough, a rhythmic snore and an errant sneeze polluted the forced silence within the dingy dark.

Halfway down the dormitory, built into each of the long walls was a brick and mortar, open-pit coal fireplace, casting a steady red glow, throwing an occasional spark and providing inconsistent radiant heat to the huge hall.

In the bed to her right was a skinny form covered by a badly tattered wool blanket. The occupant's long black hair was spread across what likely was once a pillow and looked like a gigantic hair ball. There was much less hair on the person lying in the bed to her left and a bit more of meat under another beaten blanket.

Phryné sensed countless eyes studying her through the creepy darkness. Her eyes burned with the salt of countless tears, and at that moment, she genuinely didn't care about anyone else's eyes.

She thought first of Hugo, then faulted her infidelity and selfish actions for his perilous position. She wondered how he was being treated on the other side of the prison yard and privately vowed that she wouldn't stray again.

She couldn't help that her thoughts then drifted to Guilermo. She found herself pondering his fate and that of the missing mystery blonde. She worried for his safety and somewhat for that of his Ohio companion, but reassured herself that any misfortune of theirs couldn't be directly faulted upon her.

Phryné may not have been the only soul in the dormitory, but her thoughts were her only confederates. Peace of mind became a forgotten, foreign concept and her only resource to whittle away the time was woeful worry.

She had lain awake for most of the night, drifting back and forth between foggy cognizance and dreadful, nightmarish visions. Phryné's senses were battered by conscience thought, sensory triggers both real and imagined, bodily sounds, repulsive odors, frightening uncertainty and the unrelenting, dark, ominous unknown. Occasionally, sleep stole away a few moments of reality that were able to grant her precious seconds of unconscious peace.

An eternity passed before Saturday morning pushed a few slivers of grimy light through the filthy, decades-old, skinny window glass of the dormitory. Glazing had been added to the prison windows in 1889, and protected from breakage by wire mesh on the inside. After nearly fifty years, a thick grey-green film had covered the glass and cob webs dangled from the mesh, greatly limiting the amount of light allowed inside the building. The four light bulbs precariously hanging from the ceiling struggled to remain the main source of lighting in the dormitory. The half-light of day only worsened Phryné's first impressions.

The building's single door was the one through which Phryné had been shoved the night before. A brick and stone trough along the opposite end of the dormitory served as drainage for two metal wash basins and an open, four-seat wooden latrine. Gravity drew the waste water from the second and third floors sloshing along angled, half-round terracotta gutter tiles in each of the furthest corners and out to a wooden-plank covered cesspit in the center of the prison yard. Sawdust from the men's carpentry hall had been scattered on the stone floor to absorb spills, accidents and seeping odors.

Water was drawn from a hand-dug well inside the prison walls at the corner of Duroc and Michelet streets.

The Le Havre penitentiary's *aux femmes* building could not be described as a dungeon. It was above-ground.

Accentuate the Positive

Rise and shine.

145

The high-pitched screech of a brass police whistle signaled to the dormitory population that it was morning. Whether prisoner or convict, all detainees jumped from their beds en masse. Dozens of bare feet smacked the stone floor in near perfect unison. A few women got out of bed wearing their smocks, but most of them were a naked match to their bare feet. Startled by the whistle and ensuing commotion, Phryné followed seconds later and stood wearing the slept-in uniform she was issued hours earlier. She could only watch as the rest of the population immediately dressed, put on their shoes and stood squarely, military style, at the foot of their beds and facing the opposite wall.

Three Prison Matrons in their standard grey gabardine uniforms with yellow trim, pewter buttons and black, holstered nightsticks, stood hands-on-hip, motionless at the entrance door and scowling at the population. The dormitory Overseer was standing near the doorway to her room with the brass whistle dangling between a pair of pinkish-red pursed lips. Phryné expected that her late performance and lack of conformity would prompt a necessary show of authority. She was correct.

The Overseer took a dozen steps toward the new inmate, stood nose-to-nose with Phryné, screamed and spit a mouthful of indiscernible French words.

Carelessly foolish and inexplicably bold, Phryné found the courage to speak, "Excuse me ... I am an American."

Two, perhaps three, snickers came from within the dormitory. The Overseer growled something more in French, landed an open-palm slap on Phryné's right cheek, growled again in French, turned and returned to position at her door.

Everyone, excepting Phryné, understood what she had said, "I will teach you French! Welcome to France, Hollywood whore!"

With that retort, the entire population had a chuckle and wore a smirk. Phryné didn't flinch, suffering no pain except for indignant humiliation. She understood four words: 'French', 'France', 'Hollywood' and 'whore'.

Phryné garnered all the pride she could and stood tall.

Soupspoons and Salvation

Another emphatic blast from the brass whistle brought the dormitory back to attention. The piercing noise had thrust a dagger through Phryné's skull. Her thoughts already numbed by lack of sleep, she stood at her bed with a ringing in her ears.

Without a verbal command, the inmates on the opposite side of the barracks made a quarter-turn to their right and marched out the door with one Matron in front and another following at the rear.

When the first column had finished filing out of the building, the Overseer blew on the whistle once again.

The night before Phryné had been shoved onto the bed nearest the Overseer's room. She unwittingly found herself in the uncomfortable position of being first in line.

Without recourse, she bravely made a quarter turn to the left. When she heard the leather-soled shoes of the remaining women do the same, a great sense of relief settled upon her shoulders. And after her first two steps toward the door, the sound of feet behind her confirmed her choice of action. It seemed her fortune had changed and she had twice made the right choice. The remaining Matron stepped in front of Phryné and assumed her position of authority at the head of the line, pressing the Overseer to the rear.

Quietly, solemnly, the column of women braved the cold, grey October overcast and stepped in time across the prison yard to the dining hall; a building identical in size and architecture to the *aux femmes* dormitory, excepting that it was limited to one floor, and included a door on each end. Inside, nine eight-foot wooden tables and sixteen benches were placed end-to-end, running the length of the hall.

Once the column was fully inside the mess hall, the Matrons and Overseer broke ranks and stood at evenly placed positions at every other table. The cooks, kitchen help, servers, orderlies and dishwashers were male prisoners assigned to dining hall duty. The work was considered to be an assignment of privilege and was earned through bribery, patronage, favoritism or good behavior.

Each female prisoner in the serving line plodded along without emotion, picked up a wooden spoon and watched a ladleful of gooey oatmeal and barley porridge plop into a shallow, hammered pewter bowl alongside a spoonful of soft white fromage* and a melted gob of rendered pork fat. A tin cup of water was handed out at the last station on line.

Phryné found herself in a quandary. In one hand she held a wooden spoon and a bowlful of questionable French cuisine that she wouldn't consider giving to any dog; pedigreed or cur. In the other, she had her fingers around a beaten metal cup filled with water from sources unknown.

A potentially life-altering decision was sprawled out in front of her. She needed to decide which role she wanted.

She could play the wild-west wife of tough western rancher Randolph Scott, bite the bullet, eat the food and drink the water. If she played this leading lady, she could achieve a higher spot in the prison pecking order and make her incarceration easier.

The alternative was safer but less likely for successful survival within prison society.

Her other option was to act it up as a goody-two-shoes Shirley Temple type, and turn up her pert little nose at the dog-food mush, sing a happy song, do a lively tap dance, and dump the polluted drink.

Each role would come with a clear, concise consequence and a co-star; survival by selection or elimination by default.

Phryné made her choice and had the spoon to her lips when she heard an authoritative voice shout *"Mademoiselle Phryné Truffaut"* from the entranceway. She looked to the door and set the spoon down into her bowl of wretched muck. She wasn't alone in her reaction.

All eyes traveled to the voice; a tall, thin man wearing a triple-breasted grey topcoat, brown over black wingtips and a dark grey fedora with a white silk band. Standing at his side was a woman wearing wire-rimmed eyeglasses and carrying a black valise. She appeared to be a professional, with strong cheek bones, overdone red lipstick and curled black hair to her shoulders. She too, wore a topcoat, camel in color, a tan beret tipped to the left side and brown pumps. The pair stood in the company of three stern-faced, French National Police. All stood at attention and peered into the mess hall with a steely gaze. The senior Prison Matron removed her nightstick from its holster, smacked it into the open palm of her left hand and repeated "Mademoiselle Phryné Truffaut" with firm emphasis on the last name. The Matron, unlike the two well-dressed visitors and policemen, knew exactly who the name belonged to and directed a glaring stare at the name's owner.

Phryné stood and felt the weight of more than a hundred eyeballs fall on her. The Matron used her baton and hands like a New York City traffic cop, and motioned Phryné to come forward.

Her spirits soared. Somehow, she had escaped a repulsive meal and was about to meet some people who may or may not help her out of prison. Perhaps the visitors were from the American Consulate or attorneys that Hugo or Pathé were able to hire. She held out hope that her fortunes were about to change.

The woman with the briefcase smiled and said, "Please come with us to the Administration Offices, Mademoiselle Truffaut. We have what may be considered good news about the charges that you were facing."

The Revelation

$\mathbb{F}$our men and two women left the dining hall and proceeded across the prison yard. It was obvious to Phryné that something out of the ordinary was afoot; she wasn't in leg irons or handcuffs and a Matron wasn't pressing a night stick into her lower back. The only sounds were the crunch and rustle of pea gravel beneath their feet and a wayward moan from an upper floor of *Men's Number Three* dormitory.

Daylight did nothing to improve Phryné's impression of Le Havre Prison. Like the overcast sky above, everything appeared grey and dreary, but she held out dubious hope that her first day in Purgatory was about to get brighter.

The Administration building was the time-worn showpiece of architecture inside the prison walls. Unlike the other brick and stone structures, it was constructed of white marble blocks with large, multi-light windows on each of two floors under a terracotta tile roof. The marble exterior was streaked with black mildew stains and the tile roof was spotted grey-green with lichen. An oversized, French tri-color flag was draped over the double entry doors and decorative, hammered brass fleur-de-lis[*] were above each first-floor window.

Up five marble steps, through a set of double doors, across a terrazzo floor and inside a paneled meeting room, Hugo was sitting at a polished table next to yet another officer of the French National Police. He sprang to his feet when Phryné and her official French entourage entered the room.

The woman spoke to Phryné, "You may sit together, and we can get started. The sooner we finish, the sooner you may leave this place and resume your lives."

Hugo and Phryné held one another like lovers separated for years, but maintained their embrace only briefly. The woman's words *'the sooner we finish'* had made a strong first impression.

Everyone settled in at the table. The gentleman and his female associate removed their coats, sat directly across from Hugo and Phryné, and introduced themselves as Lieutenant Aimé Onboyne and Colonel Jules Chayriguès of Renseignements Généraux[**], the RG, or the National Police Intelligence Bureau.

Phryné and Hugo exchanged glances and silently reacted to the introductions, each experiencing a renewed fear for their freedom and worrying that their first impression could be wrong.

Phryné felt her heart in her throat. Her stomach churned.

Hugo sensed his palms sweating. His temples prickled.

The colonel took a pack of Gitanes from his breast pocket and encouraged Hugo to take one for himself and one for Phryné.

The policeman seated next to Hugo lit the French cigarettes for the nicotine-starved prisoners.

Lieutenant Onboyne began, "Colonel Chayriguès and I have been working on the disappearance of Spanish national Guilermo Gaeta and American citizen Nancy Kenyon since we first received the radiogram from Captain Baudelande two days before the Normandie docked in Le Havre."

Chayriguès continued, "Because of valuable information our Spanish friends in Madrid have shared with us and what we have learned from our own ongoing investigation into this Spanish national, we have determined that socialist activist

Señor Gaeta was very strongly involved with the revolutionary Popular Front of Catalonia[**].

"It is known that Señor Gaeta was in California to gather financial and material support for continued civil unrest and armed conflict against the legitimate Spanish government. Madrid has protested his actions in California to the United States Ambassador. The Spanish authorities estimate that Gaeta was returning to Catalonia with about five-hundred-thousand United States Dollars in bank notes and cash."

Phryné and Hugo exchanged looks of surprise.

Lieutenant Aimé Onboyne explained further, "At first, it was assumed that robbery was the motive. But the bank notes were found in his luggage and there was a large amount of cash discovered in a shipping crate full of wine grape vine cuttings"

The Colonel lit a cigarette for himself and went on, "Initially, we believed that your suspected involvement was baseless, and now, after our investigation, we have completely exonerated each of you in the incident. Madrid agrees with our finding and together we have concluded that he was the unfortunate victim of partisan violence. Although the American, Nancy Kenyon, was listed as a passenger aboard the Normandie, at this time we cannot find verification that she boarded the ship in New York City.

"Your statements to the Normandie Security Officers are in agreement with what our investigation has uncovered. Witnesses have stated that the Mademoiselle Truffaut was seen intentionally tearing her dress while dancing the tango and that she left the Café Lounge in the early morning hours of Tuesday in the company of Señor Gaeta. Additional eye witness accounts place you, Mademoiselle, knocking at Señor Gaeta's door about one hour after he was discovered missing, and you, Monsieur Grétillat, were not seen outside your stateroom after dinner on Monday evening, 15 October until mid-morning on Tuesday.

"A witness statement from British citizen Nelson McIver details that the Mademoiselle was in the Café Grill looking after Señor Gaeta on Tuesday, and a French national, cinema star Simone Simon, also places the Mademoiselle near Señor Gaeta's suite on Tuesday. It is a simple deduction that a murderess does not return to the crime scene to visit her dead victim.

"And, I do not intend to insult your physical ability, Mademoiselle Truffaut, but it would be impossible for a woman to throw Señor Gaeta's body overboard, because the deck railing of Stateroom 235 is nearly four feet high."

Phryné reached out and held onto Hugo's hand. They breathed silent sighs of relief.

Lieutenant Aimé Onboyne was sitting across from Phryné with the same sterile look of satisfaction that her Paramount Pictures talent agent had when she signed her first movie contract for *Murder at the Vanities* in 1933 Hollywood.

Colonel Jules Chayriguès asked, "Do you have questions?"

Hugo answered, "How soon can we leave this torture chamber and how soon can we claim our baggage and possessions and how soon can we find a hotel?"

Phryné stated the obvious, "First we need to get out of these jail clothes."

But It Didn't Mean a Thing

Their transport from Le Havre Prison to the French Line offices on Rue de la Vallée, Port of Le Havre, was provided by a forest-green Citroën Traction Avant** sedan rather than a pitch-black paddy wagon.

Together, they appeared as sleep-starved vagrants. They were released from custody at Le Havre Prison wearing the wrinkled, soiled clothing they were inducted with: the slacks, shirts, socks and underwear that they were wearing on their last night in the brig aboard the Normandie. Hugo had a three-day growth of whiskers and neither he nor Phryné had been near a wash basin in the past thirty hours. Their fingers were their sole grooming tools. Hugo was uncomfortable, but Phryné could feel her skin crawl. They sat close on the back seat; each detecting an odor from the other but necessarily ignored it.

Phryné held on to Hugo's arm, squeezed and said, "Good God, I'm glad this ordeal is over."

Hugo suggested to front-seat passenger Colonel Chayriguès and driver Lieutenant Onboyne that if a Frenchman kept a flock of sheep housed in conditions like those at Le Havre Prison, he would be charged with animal cruelty and face death by guillotine.

Without turning around, Chayriguès nodded. Onboyne was too busy driving the large car to have a reaction, and didn't express as much as a flinch.

Regardless, after spending two harsh nights below decks in the Normandie brig and one inside a beaten, run-down nineteenth century prison in Le Havre, the weight of the world had been removed from Phryné and Hugo's shoulders. Burning fear was replaced by smoldering frustration over circumstances that they each believed were no fault of their own, but imposed upon them by the luck of the draw.

Phryné lamented to Hugo, "This experience proves one thing: that it's impossible to know everything about anyone you know. And it is possible to know nothing about someone that you think you know very well."

Hugo looked puzzled and blamed his confusion on his imperfect mastery of the English language and his lover's use of confusing American idioms.

Although her statement seemed to make sense while she formed the words, she did not intend for it to sound like a prophetic epiphany. She knew that she was exhausted; physically strained and mentally stressed.

She decided to clarify and restate her case, "I'm sorry, my darling ... so sorry. I should have explained it better. This whole affair was my fault. I apologize sincerely. I have nobody to blame but myself. All I can say in my own defense, that although I didn't think so at the time, when it comes down to brass tacks, it didn't mean a thing. The whole affair; it didn't mean a thing. I'm truly sorry if I hurt you."

Hugo took her by the hand to console her, "You caused me no trouble or worry, ma chérie. I did not believe that you did anything wrong and now it has been proven. We were simply the target of unfortunate circumstance and no one is to blame except those revolutionaries that profit from political unrest."

As Normandie Ship Captain Baudelande had promised, their baggage and documents were secured and available at the French Line Cargo Offices.

The clerk at the baggage office was more than sympathetic to their situation and helped them get first-class lodging at Hotel La Perouse.

Phryné and Hugo discovered a privilege that is easily overlooked and far too often taken for granted: freedom.

They pampered themselves and tightened the bond between them for two days and two nights at La Perouse. On Monday afternoon, October 21, 1935, Hugo bought one-way tickets on the Le Havre-Rouen narrow gauge rail line for the four-hour trip to their new life in Paris.

6. Boulogne~Billancourt, Paris ~ 1936 ~

J'suis Mordue (I'm Hooked)
96a Rue du Château, Paris
10 AM, Tuesday, May 12

Hugo's second floor walk-up was in a row house fronted with century-old brick on a quiet cobbled street on the west side of Paris. The accommodations had been refashioned from two smaller flats according to Hugo's personal direction. His undefined floor plan included a pantry married to a compact kitchen that opened to a dining and sitting area that completed the street side of the apartment. The furnishings, although used, were tasteful and functional. Three pairs of double, swing-open windows allowed for ample morning and midday light to enter the welcoming, renovated living space. A small iron-rail balcony that overlooked Rue du Château was assessable from the sitting room. The only doors in the flat opened to a dressing room and bath, and an ample adjoining bedroom that occupied the other exterior wall. Those rooms faced the west with a view of Pierre-Adrien Park and overlooked a narrow alleyway, ruelle Vernes, which connected two shop-lined streets to the north and south.

It didn't happen often, but Rue du Château below was so narrow that when opposing vehicles met, both would slow to a crawl or one would cautiously place two wheels up and onto the sidewalk. Bicycles traveled in a separate dimension, yet comingled with the motor vehicles while ignoring their precarious proximity. On the opposite side, the ruelle Vernes alley saw plenty of foot traffic.

Paris wasn't Hollywood, but it wasn't far from what Phryné had imagined. On more than one occasion, she believed that she was playing the lead role and shooting a scene in a modern Parisian romance. It wasn't immediate, but she accepted the changes she faced. Experiences and expectations were altered by pace and attitude. Life experiences moved at the speed of Paris and daily expectations were tempered by romantic patience.

Settling into a new lifestyle can be as irritating as a wool overcoat in July, refreshing as the first breath of spring, miserable as a cold, driving rain or as foreboding as black storm clouds on the horizon. Adding a foreign country, language and culture into the mix creates a churning potpourri of surprises, not all of them pleasant. Phryné made every effort to make life comfortable for her and her Hugo, but it wasn't always easy to cope with everything foreign.

Everyday life was filled with small adventures such as those encountered at the baker, butcher, or grocer. Whether Phryné was acquiring the essentials or the frivolous, shopping in the 14th arrondissement of Paris was a three-step process that involved first pointing to her selection, followed by mumbling French words and fumbling with paper script and coin. Her daily immersion into Parisian life not only prevented cyclic boredom, but provided education in language and culture.

Phryné's first attempts at securing employment in Paris were exercises in futility. Following country-wide general strikes during the winter of 1935-36, the newly organized French Academy of Cinema Artists began flexing its muscles. The brotherhood strongly asserted that the film studios hire French union labor exclusively. Despite Hugo's affiliation with Pathé and Phryné's membership in the Associated Actors and Artistes of America**, Pathé Frères would not commit to an interview or schedule an audition. The movie makers were shackled by powerful new union restrictions and threats of wildcat strikes. Additionally, the administrative offices of the Gaumont and Méliès film studios would not open their doors for the American chorus girl.

Phryné compared her plight to that of an infant swaddled and sent adrift on an uncharted river. Restricted in movement and with limited freedom, she began to look outside the world of cinema for work. Because so many doors had been closed to her, she needed a starting point, and elected to rely on the skills and professional experience she garnered as a teenager.

Her employment history began in 1924, immediately after high school. She was earning while learning alongside her mother, Selene and owner Rita Palladio at Ritzy Rita's Beauty Salon at the corner of Main and Genesee Streets in Buffalo, New York. For a bit longer than three years she cut, colored, clipped, manicured, set and styled patrons from Buffalo and Niagara Falls. In fact, it was at Rita's salon where she got her feet wet in the entertainment world and began to lust after a career in Hollywood. Much of Ritzy Rita's clientele was part and parcel of the *'Little Broadway'* vaudeville and theater circuit that filled venues such as Shea's Hippodrome, the Gayety, Savoy, Palace and Olympic theaters. In 1928, her experience at Ritzy Rita's provided Phryné the stepping stone that she needed to walk into a job at the Cosmetic Studios of Paramount Pictures in Los Angeles, California.

Nine years later and nearly half a world away, and with a little help from Hugo's friend Alfonse, Phryné found an outlet for her pent-up energy and emigrational blues at a beauty shop named *Le salon d'Brigitte* on Rue Froidevaux, three blocks northeast of their apartment.

In mid-December, she began working Wednesday through Saturday at Brigitte's salon. In short order, she acquired a dependable base of regular customers. Her job immersed her so deep into Parisian life and French culture, that within a few months, her working knowledge of spoken French was on par with much of the general public. Her work at the salon had also helped her cope with the grey mood of a Paris winter and fend off that blue feeling when Hugo was out of town and filming on location.

Six months after Phryné's arrival in France, the overcast, dreary skies of winter gave way to warm sunshine. Her heart began to beat in time with the harmonious rhythm of Paris. Songbirds returned from northern Africa, daffodils and cherry trees began blooming along the Avenue des Champs Elysées, and the streets became alive with humanity.

After she weathered the first storms of culture shock, Phryné gradually adjusted to life in her new environment. From day one, she was fully aware that the pace of living slowed.

Phryné not only enjoyed her work at the salon, she formed congenial relationships with co-workers and clients, including one particularly close bond with Pigalle** cabaret performer and former danseur*, Gael Vennard.

Phryné may have been black-balled from French film, but the unions couldn't keep her away from the colorful and dramatic Paris theatre district.

On any Friday or Saturday night, Gael, Phryné, and co-workers Marielle and Nicole could be found in one of the many dance clubs or cabarets on Rue Lepec or Rue de Douai in the Montmarte district of Paris.

The nights out were good fun and in good conscience when Hugo was working away from the city. Phryné didn't ask, but because Gael never joined in bawdy talk or laughed at off-color stories, she assumed that he was either gender neutral or had a feminine penchant for rouge and soft pink lipstick.

Without doubt, however, Gael was a dancer beyond reproach, an impeccable dresser and knew that a pousse-café was an after-dinner cocktail. And he would unapologetically give an unsolicited opinion on fashion, cosmetics and social etiquette.

Phryné discovered that Gael was not only a provocative conversationalist; she also found it very easy to open the pages of her life to him. Perhaps it was their shared background in dance that drew them together and made their back-and-forth discussions as upbeat and lively as a vaudeville tap-dance performance. While Marielle and Nicole were socializing at the bar or high-stepping out on the hardwood floor, Phryné and Gael could be found at a table, sitting close and holding onto one another's undivided attention.

Gael was a few inches shorter than Phryné, perhaps five-foot-six, reddish-blonde, good-looking and toned. He never revealed his age to anyone, but some of his life stories hinted that he was at least in his early to mid-forties. He had a voracious appetite for everything theater, film, photography, Hollywood and America. He confessed that his dream was to dance with Hollywood neophyte Fred Astaire[**]. He was fascinated with Phryné and her story, wanted to know more, but had never prodded or pried beyond the polite.

It was early into one of their nights at the *Cabaret à Cheval*, when she postulated to Gael, "The biggest difference between Hollywood's Sunset Boulevard and Paris' Boulevard de Clichy is that Hollywood isn't a community like Paris. It's an entertainment colony, a gypsy camp full of transients from all over the globe chasing a celluloid[**] dream. Certainly, there are a few true artists, but they are the minority. Most of the Hollywood population is made up of dreamers chasing a pot of gold at the end of a paper-mâché[*] rainbow that's been painted and glued onto a cheap back drop on some back lot studio. And that same rainbow has been painted over and over so much that the colors are all smeared and running together like cheap eye shadow and tear-stained mascara. It's sad."

Phryné put a match to a Gitanes[**], paused a moment, inhaled and continued, "American movies are made in Hollywood with make-believe settings and painted backgrounds. French movies are made in France with real settings and backdrops. I've only been in France about seven months, but so far I haven't seen anyplace over here that you could compare to Hollywood."

She took another puff, and added, "Well ... maybe the dressing room of the Moulin Rouge."

Gael twittered like a fledgling tit.

Phryné giggled too, then paused, and went on, "But over there ... in Hollywood ... the movie stars, writers, directors, producers, dancers ... they're all huddled together in some make-believe, sequined world all their own. From what I've seen, Paris is full of artists and lovers. And cafés."

Gael laughed lightly, "Don't forget the cabarets!"

"Right. We're in a cabaret now, aren't we?"

Gael's eyes laughed along with Phryné and said, "Some people say that all the true stars are in the heavens, and they only descend onto the movie screen to produce real art."

Phryné sipped at her glass of champagne, feigned insult and put the Gitanes cigarette to her lips. She teased, "I suppose that leaves me stranded out somewhere in the Milky Way!"

Once again, they laughed together, and showed how much their personalities meshed. Phryné found Gael to be the easiest person she could to talk to in years, perhaps decades.

Gael reached across the small, round table, put his hand on hers for a moment, and pled, "I meant it only in good fun!"

Gael had a flash of thought, and saw an opportunity to find out more about the American transplant. He asked, "Is it too bold for me to ask ... can you tell me your American adventure and how you arrived in Hollywood?"

Phryné took a final puff, blinked the sting of smoke from her eyes and crushed the Gitanes into the ashtray. She looked to Gael and asked, "Are you sure? My story could frighten you away."

Once again, he reached across the table to her hand and held it. His words asked, but his eyes begged, "Please, Phryné. I want to know all about you."

She sat back into her woven wicker chair. It creaked. She studied the Frenchman who had asked her to open the window to her soul. Although they had kept casual company for perhaps five months, it seemed as though she had known Gael all her life. She answered, "Fine. But my story will cost you another glass of champagne."

Gael smiled in agreement, sat straight and settled in for the long and short of it.

Phryné began, "Early on, when I was young, they called it the Roaring Twenties, and I had no direction ... I couldn't avoid temptation and believed that life would forever be a party. My fiancé and I had a dustup with the police and we ran. We left Buffalo, New York ... that's a city near Niagara Falls ... we got married in Chicago and came to Los Angeles ... to Hollywood ... California. That was in 1927. I was a naïve new bride and we had dreams of making a life for ourselves in California.

"But the marriage ended up in the toilet. Ten days after we arrived he was gone and I had the marriage was annulled. I was alone in a lousy one-room apartment in a strange city with maybe fifty dollars to my name. I had to do something. So I bought a dress, some shoes and stockings and hopped a street car to Paramount Famous Players studios. I wiggled and charmed my way into a job in the makeup department fixing the hair and painting the nails of young starlets.

162

"In a few weeks, I found out I was pregnant by my no-account, no-good first husband Leopold, and then Abner ... Abner Mandelbaum, a Paramount producer who was fifteen years older than me, rescued me and married me. The birth didn't go well. It weakened me, stole my fertility and hurt the baby. My daughter died a week after birth.

"It took a few months, and a lot of encouragement from Abner, but I got up and dusted myself off and went to the Paramount dance studios and in a year or two I was in my first picture as a walk-on, stand-in, real live dancing chorus girl. Over the next six years I had song and dance parts in a dozen or more musical comedies, mysteries, romances, and even a couple westerns.

"But it wasn't long before old Abner found greener pastures and I gave him the boot and he gave me a divorce. That was last year. And then I met my Hugo, we fell for each other and we came to Paris. That's my story.

"It's been difficult at times, and only God knows how many tears I've cried over some of the men I've known. Now, today, I can safely say that I've never really been in love. I don't mean hot-blooded, impetuous, toe-curling love. I mean the real, heart-warming kind. Once I foolishly shared my bed just to forget my loneliness, but that was a decade ago. Certainly ... I carry some regret for some of the things I've done and I'm the first to admit that I've made mistakes and made some of them willingly. But I promised myself that I would never, ever forget their names."

She sat back into her chair and took a breath. It wasn't a sigh of relief, but a signal of finality. She considered it strange that, of all the people she knew through the years, no one had shown such an interest in her as Gael did. It gave her pause to think that Abner likely knew the most about her life and Hugo the least. Now, Gael was somewhere in between.

Phryné and Gael lit cigarettes and sipped at fresh glasses of champagne. She wore a demure smile and his was softly endearing.

He dared to break the silence, "You are a brave woman, Phryné. Nobody can dare cast you into the role of an unsuspecting ingénue. It's not you. Far from it. You know which side of your bread gets the butter. Someday you will be happy. I know it. You will make sure of it."

Le jour où je te vis (The Day I Saw You)

Boulangerie et café de Bonney
32 Rue de Sablon, Versailles
11:30 AM, Tuesday, September 15, 1936

Café Bonney was Hugo's preferred spot for a relaxing lunch in Versailles, so much so, that when he extolled its merits to Phryné, he said that he considered the quaint bakery to be his only respite from the drudgery of editing.

Depending on an infinite number of variables, there was usually a daunting amount of film to be cut and altered after returning from a remote filming location. He oftentimes lamented his displeasure to Phryné when he was required to work at the Versailles offices of Pathé Frères. He explained that the cozy café allowed him the feeling of being close to home, if not back in Paris. He told Phryné of his affinity for the boiled egg and Roquefort baguette served with a half-bottle of Bordeaux Sauternes. Hugo explained that on particularly lazy days, he and his production assistant Alfonse could spend the entire afternoon at a sidewalk table rather than return to the editing room work benches.

For the previous two weeks, Hugo had been using the Gothic and Medieval backdrops of Le Mans for a period drama set in the late sixteenth century during the reign of King Henry IV. On Monday he was to return to Versailles Pathé Frères for the first edits, and was expected to make the trip home to Paris sometime on Wednesday afternoon.

On Monday, Phryné acted on impulse and decided to leave Paris and meet him at his favorite café in Versailles on Tuesday. She felt like a conniving schoolgirl, and believed that she had concocted the perfect mischief.

Her plan was to surprise him at Café Bonney on Tuesday for lunch, share a bottle of wine, have dinner, another bottle of wine, spend a romantic night together at a hotel in Versailles and return to Paris together on Wednesday.

Under a warm, bright September sun, the Montparnasse bus from Paris delivered her at the corner, and left only a dozen or so steps to the café. She had purposely dressed inconspicuously for a day of shopping; not wanting to unduly endanger the surprise she had planned. She sported a below-the-knee, rayon crepe, town-tailored dress in emerald green with puff sleeves, belted waist with large yolk and collar. A beige waist coat and wide-brimmed, straw sun hat finished her disguise. Inside, she claimed a table tucked into a corner and nestled adjacent to the waitress station. From her vantage point, she had full view of the street and the customer traffic entering the café. She ordered only coffee, assuming that she and Hugo would each have one of his cherished egg and cheese baguettes.

The noon hour was approaching and the little café was beginning to feel the midday crush. Tables were filling up and customers were at the counter claiming take-out orders. The murmur of humanity mingled with the cling of dinnerware and the tinkle of glasses. The smell of butter, hot coffee and warm baked bread teased every working nose.

For the next fifteen minutes, customers came and went, traipsing in hungry and walking out of the door with full bellies or wrapped sandwiches. The clientele was largely professionals out for lunch, with a good number of shoppers and a few pensioners. Phryné was sure she couldn't be seen sitting in interior shadows from the bright, sunlit outside, but took no chances and pulled the brim of her hat down to her eyebrows. She nervously wondered if her Hugo would appear, or if he had indeed, left Le Mans on Monday as scheduled.

It was nearly half past twelve when Hugo came into her line of sight. She spotted him crossing the street, stepping quickly and brusquely walking toward Café Bonney. He was alone, without Alfonse. The storyline was developing as written.

Suddenly, everything went off-script. The scene changed.

Hugo walked past the café entrance, and stopped at an occupied table; third past the door. Phryné's heart jumped. She strained her eyes.

At the table sat an attractive young woman with shoulder-length, curled black hair, pulled back and restrained by a wide, red ribbon. Her red dress revealed a youthful form and a trim waist peeped through the open-back chair. Hugo took a seat at the third chair, leaned over and placed a lingering kiss on her lips. A young boy, who Phryné guessed to be three or four, occupied the second chair. Hugo kissed him on the forehead and playfully mussed the boy's full head of curly black hair. The young fellow had one arm wrapped around a small stuffed bear. It wasn't a certainty, but from where Phryné sat, it appeared that Hugo could claim paternity.

The high-wheeled, wicker perambulator sitting at the woman's side was definitely not the boy's mode of transport, but from her vantage point, Phryné could only see blankets under the buggy's sun bonnet. An infant was certainly aboard.

The mischief that she had envisaged collapsed. What she got instead was a heart-piercing arrow of painful surprise and a mind-numbing load of new worry.

166

Phryné painfully watched as Hugo, the woman and young boy talked and traded smiles. She felt the ache move from her heart deep into her gut, and waited forty minutes for tears that never fell. However, her heart jumped at half past one, when Hugo and his guests stood to leave. Phryné watched him pull a blanket back in the baby carriage, smile proudly and peer lovingly at its occupant. The infant was undoubtedly asleep, prompting Hugo to replace the blanket and engage in an endearing embrace with the mother. He kissed the woman one more time; passionately.

They left together, crossing the street with all the appearances of a family unit. Hugo was pushing the carriage with the young boy and his mother walking close at his side.

The scene she had witnessed brought back the burning pain of losing her infant daughter nearly a decade earlier and the painful realization that she could no longer bring forth a child into the world. That pain, when coupled with her realization of Hugo's betrayal, became all but unbearable.

For the next two hours, Phryné sat alone at her table, ordered a half bottle of Hugo's favorite sauternes and smoked four Gitanes. She was aware that what she had witnessed and her initial pain could have shattered her emotions. Instead, she became numb.

At five o'clock, the Montparnasse bus stopped at the corner. Phryné dropped a franc** into the driver's palm for the one-hour ride back to Paris.

Don't Do Something to Someone

Le restaurant Maxim
3 rue Royale
7:45 PM, Wednesday, September 16, 1936

Gael was sitting on a gold and burgundy flocked settee in the foyer, a few feet away from the maître d'hôtel* and his busy desk. Gael had cashed in a favor from his friend Jean Sablon[**] and was able to finagle reservations for two at eight o'clock.

Phryné had telephoned him that morning, before she was to leave for work, and asked if it were possible to meet him that evening. Her voice had telegraphed the serious nature of her request, and it was apparent that she had something to discuss. Gael agreed of course, but persuaded her to come to dinner with him, and said that he would telephone her at Brigitte's salon with the details. Because Phryné had taken the early morning initiative and reached out to him, he knew something was amiss. Gael was concerned, but not worried. It wasn't his nature to worry and he had faith in Phryné.

He stood and started walking toward Phryné as soon as he spotted her stepping through the glass and brass doors of the restaurant. Their eyes locked, they briefly embraced and stepped to the head waiter's station.

Gael announced, "Sablon-Vennard table for two."

A hostess led them into the restaurant, stopped at their table and helped with their chairs. It was business as usual at Maxim's[**]; the place was packed.

The décor was nineteenth century opulence blended with twentieth century art nouveau. Sateen, sheer balloon curtains covered the windows, red velvet draperies, golden ropes and tiebacks; brightly patterned carpets on the floor, recessed tray ceilings supported by carved Grecian pillars, Louis XIV furniture, massive carved mirrors, large glass-door armoires, Queen Anne chairs and linen-draped tables occupied the interior. Customers and restaurant staff were relegated to what space remained.

During dinner, Gael and Phryné verbally sashayed around one another like paired figure skaters. She never mentioned Hugo or what she had witnessed in Versailles. Phryné had tip-toed over the rink like Tinker Bell**, barely scratched the surface, and didn't crack the ice or kick up any sharp shards.

However, after the Grand Marnier soufflé dessert course, Phryné skated directly to center rink and confessed, "I need your help, Gael. I witnessed something that I cannot run away from. I've got my back up against a stone-cold wall that's chilling me to the bone. I'm facing a double-barrel problem with no simple solution. It's a Man problem and a French problem. That's it ... I'm looking at a Frenchman problem. My friends at the salon told me that I'm taking this too seriously, and that it's really nothing to fuss over."

Phryné leaned back, waiting for a reply, a signal of some kind, something, a willingness to help. Gael lit a Gitanes, handed it across the table and another for himself. He sipped at his glass of brandy, and said, "Well, tell me what it is, Phryné. Tell me this Frenchman problem."

She explained the events in Versailles and Gael listened.

In conclusion she said, "I'm hurt, Gael, but not destroyed. Hugo and I never swore out a till-death-do-us-part allegiance or made a blood-pact or anything ... it's just that he kept this secret from me. I've got secrets, we all do, but this one never should have been a secret; not between lovers anyway. What do you think?"

"Did you ask him about the woman and children?"

"No, but I will when I see him. Sometime tonight or tomorrow; it depends when he's finished in Versailles."

"Well, it's one of two things. First, she could be his sister, which is unlikely because of the kiss and bits of endearment that you saw. Second, and most likely, it's that she's either his wife or his mistress**. Either way, that means you are at least Mistress Number One or maybe Number Two or Three or more."

Phryné puffed on her cigarette and exhaled a grey cloud from the side of her mouth with the words, "That's the conclusion I came to. But I really can't stick what just happened to me in a jar and hide it away on some dark shelf in a closet. It's all lopsided and crooked and it just wouldn't sit right. This whole situation just wobbles and wiggles too much. I need to nail it down or something. It sounds like I'm talking gibberish, I know. I've been wounded but I'm not dying. I need to let Hugo know how I feel about this. I deserve the truth.

"I think what I'm trying to say is this: knowing everything that's happened in my life, and where I am today, the only things that are important are those children and my pride. I'm going to tell Hugo that his secret hurt me, but I've got to remember that I've kept a secret affair from him, too ... a lover who he doesn't know about."

Gael picked up his drink and took a sip before he began, "As a default Frenchman by birth, this is what I think you should do. Tell Hugo what you just told me, and ask him to explain his feelings. You are correct: this is a *Frenchman* problem that I know Americans don't understand. This is a cinq-à-sept[*], and acceptable. Hugo has a wife and a mistress. That's all, nothing more. It has gone on since the beginning of time and French culture has embraced it. It is commonplace here in France for those who are fortunate enough to afford it. For the man, it is a status symbol. And it may be shocking to hear, and it's nothing to be ashamed of, but in France, being chosen as a mistress brings pride to many women. Not everyone is asked. Only the pretty ones."

Phryné took a final draw on her cigarette, and then ceremoniously crushed it out in the ashtray, pushing the ashes into one little pile.

"Thank you, Gael. You've helped, and you've helped me understand some things. But, maybe it's because I'm not

French ... that I don't think I can take pride in being a mistress. But, I think a woman can certainly be happy about someone loving her. I think I can do that. Sometimes it's enough to know that somebody loves and cares about you."

Boum! (Boom)

96a Rue du Château, Paris
7 PM, Friday, September 18, 1936

The street-level entry door was certainly as aged as the building and made from heavy wooden planks painted bright geranium red with three white ceramic tiles at eye-level that displayed the number: 96a. Black, wrought iron strap hinges squeaked mercilessly and noisily telegraphed Hugo's arrival to the occupant in the upstairs apartment.

Hugo had returned from Versailles as he did so many other times over the past ten months. Phryné heard his steady stride conquering the thirteen steps up to the landing and still had plenty of time to meet him at the door.

He stepped inside, lowered his leather suitcase and valise to the floor and greeted her, "Hallo, hallo, ma chérie."

They shared a brief embrace and quick peck on the lips. Phryné asked, "Have you eaten?"

"Yes, in Versailles, before the return bus."

"Very good, my darling. Then it should be enough with a bite of bread and brie with our glass of chardonnay this evening."

From the time she left her bed that morning, Phryné had nothing on her mind but the new set of circumstances that she found herself in. She was uneasy and frustrated over her inability to pin down her feelings about her discovery in Versailles. She expected to be upset and certainly was, but found herself holding the short end of the stick when it came to anger. There wasn't any.

Phryné began to doubt the sincerity of her feelings about Hugo. She was left questioning her moral standing and commitment to their eighteen-month long affair.

Her conversation the previous day with Gael combined with bits of well-intentioned advice from co-workers Marielle and Nicole, left her with a stark realization. She was stuck behind the eight ball in a foreign land in an awkward situation that she should have anticipated.

Phryné had been dealt an emotional blow that may not have knocked her out, but had certainly left her staggering. She still felt surprised by the numbness that she felt when she'd expected acute heartache and pain.

That evening she and Hugo sat on the divan, sipped wine, nibbled bread, shared small talk and listened to Paris Radio Cité**. There were forty-five minutes of crooner Charles Trenet followed by a quarter-hour of national and international headlines. It was a repeat of old, distressing news: French labor unions continued to threaten countrywide strikes and Adolf Hitler and his Third Reich forged ahead with their saber-rattling in central Europe.

In Phryné and Hugo's second-floor apartment there were no harsh words or emotional outbursts. Earlier that afternoon, Phryné had decided not to discuss what she'd witnessed in Versailles until Saturday. She couldn't remember when, but sometime, somewhere she'd heard that it's never a good idea to go to sleep angry with your bed partner. She also recalled words that her mother had once driven home: *you make the bed you sleep in.*

My Last Affair

Café Desprez
22 Rue Vercingétorix, Paris
9 AM, Saturday, September 19, 1936

Phryné didn't want an upsetting confrontation. She awoke that morning from an unsettled sleep and decided that she was as far downhill as she wanted to go.

She suggested breakfast at the little café around the block and down Bretagne alleyway. Hugo agreed.

His coat and tie and her woolen wrap weren't enough to hold back a brisk Autumn chill and permit them to take a seat at one of the sidewalk tables. Instead, they stepped inside the café, sat at a window table and ordered blueberry crepes and creamed espresso.

Phryné summarily set the scene and broke the ice, "I intended to meet you for lunch on Tuesday and I went to Café Bonney in Versailles."

Instantly, Hugo knew Phryné had discovered his secret. After a split second of shocked silence, Hugo said, "You did?"

"Yes, I did. I want you to know that I'm no longer angry, but my heart is wounded ... because you kept this secret so long. I need to know ... is she your wife? And are the children yours? Who am I? What is my role in this production?"

He nodded. His thoughts were racing too fast to form words. His emotions ran from embarrassment to angry arrogance. He was speechless.

"You need to talk to me, Hugo. The silent treatment won't work. This is a conversation that we must have. You need to know that I am firm in the position that I have taken and that I will not walk away from this wobbling and out of balance like a little bird with clipped wings."

Hugo remained silent, pulled his pack of Gaulois Bleu from his coat pocket and lit one. A puff and a sip of coffee only fed the needling silence. He searched for words.

Phryné held her ground, "You need to talk to me, Hugo. We have to discuss this today. Now."

Another puff and another sip preceded his nervous, careful reply, "I love you deeply, Phryné, and you know how much I love you, believe in you and trust you. Now I know that I must show you the respect that I have for you."

"Don't you think you're a little bit late with that respect? I mean, I've supported you and your work and I came with you all the way from Los Angeles and you wait until now to respect me? That's generous of you, Hugo. Real generous.

"Who am I, who is she and who are the children?"

A two-day growth of whiskers roughened his appearance, but his eyes telegraphed the insecurity of a lost puppy. His voice was uncharacteristically meek, "The woman you saw is my wife of five years, Natalle and my three-year-old son Henri and the infant you saw in the carriage is my precious little girl, nine-month-old Aimee. You must understand how much I missed them while I was with you in Hollywood. In America."

"And me, I'm your mistress? Your lover, that's all? And you probably never miss me, do you?

"And if you missed your wife and children so much, why did you never mention them?"

Hugo inhaled deeply and allowed the smoke to settle into his lungs before he expelled a grey, foul smelling cloud. He pled his case, "I love you. I have loved you from the day we met. I love your spirit, and your love of life and what drives you to perfect your art. I respect your strength and your ability to hold on. I love to be with you and I love being seen with you. You breathe life into my soul and refresh me when I'm feeling poorly. I cannot imagine being without you. So many times you lifted my spirit when I thought the world was crumbling around me. And you helped me escape from my depressed state when Pathé forced me back to Paris. I will never forget that and I owe you my future for it."

Hugo sat quietly and granted her eyes admission into his blurry, secretive soul.

Phryné studied him inside and out, and then asked, "Does she know about me?"

His reply was immediate, "Of course, she knows. I told her as soon as I returned to her from America."

"No! I don't believe you."

"It is true, I tell you. I told her that you are my artistic inspiration and I need you for my creativity. As my wife, she understands the stress of my work and accepted my truthful explanation."

Phryné stubbornly kept her eyes holding onto his, and was not about to let him go until she was finished. For a day and a half she had been thinking of what action she could take to lift herself out of her current quagmire and get back on a smoother track to her future.

She needed to play her hand. She started, "You have pushed my back to the wall. I can't back up. I must break free and you must help me stand alone. You must. From this day forward, you must be honest. I do not own you body and soul. I never did, nor do I want to claim you as mine exclusively. However, I have always expected honesty and respect in all of my relationships.

"I'm not going to curl, cut or color hair for the rest of my life, Hugo. I want to be involved with film. Movies have been my world for years and I won't sit by and watch my shadow walk away and fade to black. I expect you to do everything you can to help me.

"I don't give a damn what the unions want or what the French Actors' Guild says I can or cannot do. I need to be in film and entertainment. Tell them that I'm French or whatever else you need to do. You owe me that. I won't settle for being a footrest anymore. You must help me with my future career if you want to keep me."

Phryné had unwittingly thrown Hugo a lifeline.

He didn't see it coming until it splashed down in front of him. He quickly thought of a resolution that may appease his American mistress.

He wasted no time, and reached for it while stretching the truth.

"I have been working on an outlet for your talents for some time, ma chérie, and I think you will be happy with what I think I can arrange. I am so happy now that I can help you satisfy your desires. I know you will like it."

She warned him, "Don't think you can sell me cheap Belgian bubbly wine and call it champagne. I am serious about this, Hugo ... dead serious."

Hugo felt the need to warm the air and clear the fog. He reached across the table for her hand. Phryné instinctively flinched, and then reluctantly surrendered to his touch, hoping for a resolution to her predicament.

Still hoping to calm and convince his lover, Hugo believed that his proposition could be accepted. He attempted to sell his idea, "The unions can burn in Hades. You can manage a cinema ... a movie house ... a motion picture theater. It would be your duty to plan and select and schedule the secondary presentations. The Property Division of Pathé has always been very receptive of American films, but of course, the primary content source would be Pathé Frères Productions and other sources with Pathé's exclusive approval and consent for distribution. Remember, it was Pathé that sent me to Hollywood and now they have secured two-way market sharing agreements with your Paramount, RKO Pictures and Columbia."

Phryné did not expect such a seemingly simple, rapid fix to her problem and was intuitively skeptical.

"A movie theater? I could manage a cinema and choose some content? Approved American content? Where?" she asked.

Hugo smiled with self-gratifying satisfaction, "Anywhere in France. Pathé owns hundreds of theaters, many hundreds, all across France. But of course, I hope that you will choose to manage one in Paris. I want very much that you remain close to me and my work, ma chérie. You are my lover, my muse. Your inspiration breathes life into my soul and my work comes alive."

Phryné envisioned a fulfilling future and became cautiously optimistic. It seemed possible that what first appeared to be a hopeless, loveless and emotional disaster was salvageable. The day started to show promise. Warming rays of sunshine began pouring through the window, spilling over the table.

New Position, New Apartment, New Direction
85 Rue Beaugendre, Chatou
Noon, Monday, November 2, 1936

Eleven months after she first arrived in France, Phryné found herself facing new challenges and more change. She granted a good deal of thought to her situation and decided that she needed room to grow if she was to establish roots in France. She concluded that it would be best if she loosened some of the knotted ties that bound her so closely to dallying Hugo.

Once she discovered his marriage, it became apparent that the apartment at 96a Rue du Château had been Hugo's Paris love-nest of convenience long before they met. She came to the realization that she was likely not the first lover to warm his bed at the Boulogne-Billancourt address.

Phryné didn't jump at the first opening or opportunity, but took some time, considered her options and selected a newly-renovated, once-popular movie house in the northeast suburbs of Paris. Pathé had recently acquired the Poissy Theatre and Cinema and completed a full restoration in the Art Deco style. She believed that a shiny glass, chrome and brass theater lobby was the perfect backdrop and an apropos setting for her renovated life.

With Hugo's familiarity and experience with Pathé, Phryné entered into an employment contract and signed a five-year lease agreement with the French cinematic giant for the Poissy Cinema and Theater at 6 Rue Saint-Sébastien, Poissy.

However, the commute from Phryné and Hugo's apartment in Boulogne-Billancourt to Poissy would require a fifty-minute, one-way bus ride. The inconvenience, distance and time involved in such a commute afforded Phryné a pragmatic reason to leave Hugo's Paris love-nest and strike out on her own in Poissy.

While it was apparent that her situation had been that of a mistress, Phryné did not have the mindset or reservations of a kept woman. Now more than ever, she was determined to be independent. Her new situation afforded her the chance to broaden her horizon beyond the city of Paris and get out from under Hugo's thumb.

In less than a month after she and Hugo had come to a mutual understanding, Phryné was able to secure an apartment in the Île-de-France region at 85 Rue Beaugendre in Chatou. Her new nest was a second-floor walkup in an older, well-kept, French provincial home directly across the street from the Reformed Church of Saint-Esprit. It was an efficient, one-bedroom space with a sitting room, kitchen and adjoining bath. Two large windows opened out to the narrow cobbled street, barely a block away from the city bus route. She was still close, but comfortably away from the bustle of mid-city Paris. The Poissy movie house was ten minutes away.

Phryné gradually settled into her new surroundings and soon realized her freedom to select secondary film features from the cinema giant's vast international library. Within her first six months as Theater Manager in Poissy, the newly renovated Art Deco Pathé Theater at 6 Rue Saint-Sébastien had garnered an enthusiastic, dedicated clientele from Versailles to Saint-Denis. The Poissy box-office receipts subsequently skyrocketed to the highest in France, prompting Pathé Frères to invest in a new, wide-screen 35 mm Paillard-Bolex projector for the movie house. Phryné hired an accounts assistant, custodian, electrician and a second projectionist to staff the busiest Pathé franchise. The movie house at 6 Rue Saint-Sébastien, Poissy was no longer simply an address where films were shown on a silver screen inside a darkened auditorium. It became a cultural attraction and the destination for international cinematic entertainment in northern France. For the next three and a half years, Phryné presented an international library of film to the Poissy Cinema.

Hugo's visits to Poissy became markedly infrequent and predictably sporadic. Phryné discovered life without the weight of a man standing over her and restricting her life decisions. She learned to enjoy the freedom to move within a circle of trusted friends who shared her laissez-faire, live-and-let-live lifestyle.

Gradually, subtly, life in Poissy began to change. Many citizens didn't notice and others simply ignored the approaching storm. Dark, ominous clouds had formed in the East and began threatening the status quo. On May 10, 1940, the German Blitzkrieg[*] cut through The Netherlands, Belgium, and Luxembourg like a hot knife through butter. Six weeks later, France whimpered and surrendered.

Yet again, Europe was on fire and in the midst of its second world war inside of thirty years.

7. POISSY, ÎLE~DE~FRANCE
~ 1940 ~1942 ~

Ich nenne alle Frauen Baby (I Call All Women Baby)

Cinéma et théâtre de Poissy
6 Rue Saint-Sébastien
2 PM, Friday, June 14, 1940, (Bastille Day)

☞ *Troops of the German Third Reich marched into Paris and its suburbs without resistance on June 14, 1940. Four days earlier, on June 10, officials of the French government deserted the city and escaped the inevitable German occupation and rule**. On June 22, the Second Armistice at Compiègne was signed by France and Germany, which resulted in the division of France. Nazi Germany occupied the northern three-fifths of France along the Atlantic coast. The remaining area to the south was centralized in the city of Vichy and ruled by a "neutral" French puppet regime. The French State (Vichy France) was headed by Marshal Philippe Pétain, who pledged loyalty to Germany and the Third Reich.*

Hugo opened the door and walked into the street-level office of the Poissy Cinema without knocking. A startled Phryné stood, the back of her legs pushing her chair away from her desk. Hugo had two thirty-centimeter, ninety-minute film canisters under his arm and two uniformed German soldiers and a woman following at his heels.

Hugo's unusual and unannounced visit had shocked Phryné and set her heart racing. She was not alone; all of Paris and her suburbs were on pins and needles. All of France was fearful and shuddering.

Hugo set the films down onto Phryné's desk with a metallic plunk, and announced, "These are the films for this week.

From this day forward, the Reich and only the Reich, will provide films for this theater, and you must show them on the days listed inside the cans. There will be no foreign films. There will be no exception."

"Of course." She had no idea what to expect; tried to regain some composure and feared that her nerves could betray her stoic façade.

Hugo took two steps to the right, stood alongside Phryné and introduced the Germans, "This is Luftwaffe[*] Hauptmann[*] Dieter Dientz, Unteroffizier[*] Erik Pfaltz and Agent Erica Zoller of the Filmausbildung, the Reich Chamber of Film[**]."

The German flyers were in blue-grey dress uniform, complete with braided aluminum epaulets, service medals, gravity daggers and holstered Lugers. Dientz carried a riding crop in his left hand, and had an oval, four-inch burn scar on his right cheek alongside a deformed, burned ear. Pfaltz was a bow-legged, short, stocky fellow. The appearance of Agent Erica Zoller brought back chilling memories of the prison matrons in Le Havre. She certainly wasn't a film agent, but rather an enforcer.

Hugo was obliged to introduce Phryné, and did so with a tone of possessive smugness, "This is the Pathé Frères cinema manager who we were talking about, Mademoiselle Phryné Truffaut."

Captain Dientz interjected, "That's French! You told me she was American. She cannot be American! American women are plain and plump. This one is very, very attractive."

The Nazi studied Phryné from head to toe with luring, piercing grey eyes. He snapped his riding crop into place under his left armpit.

Hugo answered with arrogant self-importance, "Phryné isn't French. The name is Greek ... she is an American. Her parents were French ... French Protestant Huguenots[*] to be exact. She has assured me of her firm desire to fully cooperate with the Chamber of Film and assist Der Fuehrer in all ways possible, all of the time."

Dientz abruptly extended his right hand to the American.

Phryné reached across her desk and took the Luftwaffe captain's outstretched, gloved hand. The glove was fashioned of soft, black leather without fingers. She was unsettled by the disguised deformity, but managed a meek smile. It seemed that the German had purposely forced his hand to her, and without a saying a word, had ordered her to accept it.

Hauptmann Dientz spoke with a heavy Schwäbisch[*] accent, "Happy to meet you, Mademoiselle Phryné. I look forward to working with you. I will be traveling today to the West, to Évreux for more inspections, but I will be back tomorrow evening at your Rue Beaugendre apartment in Chatou to complete my interview. Make certain that you are there when I arrive. After my interview, if I am satisfied with your answers, I will submit my report to the Reichsfilmkammer and authorize a residency and work permit for you."

A shudder crisscrossed her shoulders, causing worry that it may have been detected. She felt her heart thumping heavily and pounding out a warning within her breast. The German knew where she lived. Of course, he did. She knew what it meant.

Dientz kept his hand outstretched, silently demanding that she continue to hold the aberration until he had finished speaking. He coarsely whispered a brusque affirmation into her ear of his intention to visit her the following day, snapped his heels, turned, nodded to Hugo and left the room with Corporal Pfaltz and Agent Zoller walking in step directly behind him.

Phryné was left alone in her office with her estranged lover and two feature films of unknown subject matter and the unsettling dust of a forced visit. She refused to expose her discomfort and worry to Hugo.

Hugo sat in an arm chair across from Phryné's desk, lit a cigarette and spoke calmly, "Pour some brandy, ma chérie. For both of us."

Phryné deftly brought a bottle and two glasses from the file cabinet and carefully poured the drinks. The visit had triggered her nerves. She noticed a tone of aloof confidence in Hugo's words and believed that he had detected her anxiety. He was talking down to her.

She felt betrayed, short-changed and foolishly gullible. She needed to ask, "What happens tomorrow? That one-handed boche* Dientz said he'll be back to interview me and give me a resident and work permit. What did he mean?"

"You know what he meant. You should be thankful. I used my influence and membership in the Reich Film Ministry and I submitted your name as a collaborationist. I convinced the Pathé puppets that it is in their best interest to confirm your dedication and loyalty. It was either that or allow you to face arrest as an unregistered foreign national and beg for your life. Not everybody gets a choice, ma chérie. You should know that, so consider yourself one of the lucky ones. You are not in prison and you are not on a train to a labor camp. Tomorrow, you will tell Hauptmann Dientz exactly what he needs to hear. You will do what you need to do and you will be allowed to stay. The Reich recognizes that the cinema is a very important information tool. You are part of that tool."

Phryné's voice quivered, "I'm a collaborationist tool? Like you?"

Hugo became agitated and loudly defensive, "I am loyal to the Reich and you need to be as well. You must realize that you don't have a choice. Once Der Führer* secures the defeat of the Socialists and Communists, things will be better. This

183

war won't last long. The French have surrendered, the British are cowering sheep and had their royal asses handed to them at Dunkirk. And the Americans ... they are neutral, selfish, gutless pacifists and an ocean away."

Phryné swallowed what was left of her brandy and poured another for Hugo and herself. She didn't want to talk but she had questions. "What does Pathé want with you now?"

"The Waffen SS[**] has shut down the Paris offices of Pathé Frères. Only Versailles remains and it is controlled by the Reichsfilmkammer. Now Pathé can only say that they have released all employee contract obligations. That's a lie. Pathé no longer has administrative or production employees. We work for the Reich. I work for the Reich. The Chamber of Film has acknowledged my talents and ordered me to Berlin where I will become part of the production team for Ufa[**]. I'm taking the train to Berlin, either Tuesday or Wednesday, depending on availability and the needs of the Reich."

"What about Henri, Aimee and your wife Natalle?"

"For now, they will remain in Versailles but it has been approved that they will come after. I will settle in Berlin and they will follow. France has fallen. Paris has fallen. Pathé has fallen. The Reich will survive a thousand years."

Hugo stormed out of the office. He purposely slammed the box office door behind him. The ticket window glass rattled.

Phryné felt abandoned, yet freed. It wasn't the first time that a man turned his back to her and walked out the door, but Hugo's departure was a confirmation of the end of their affair. It fell upon her as a heartless desertion. Although there was finality, emotional relief and an ending of sorts, it was also a time of confusion and trepidation.

Before the abdication and exile of the French government and the resulting collapse of the French army, Phryné and thousands of others were encouraged by daily positive news reports and upbeat government broadcasts urging calm and assuring peace. Things changed when German troops marched down the Champs-Elysées.

Following the surrender, there were days of depression when Phryné blamed the French government and herself for missing the warning signs of the impending German onslaught, lack of foresight, and ignoring the advice of so many other Parisians who had escaped ahead of the invasion. However, it wasn't long before she came to realize that the thousands who had fled their homes in the city were only able to go so far before the invading German troops had caught up with them and made them homeless refugees in their own country.

The German invasion and forced occupation of Paris was met with minimal resistance and effected without significant casualties. Paris fell without so much as a whimper, but Phryné felt the booming aftershock. Without warning, her life was turned inside out. For the first time in her life, she feared for her safety.

The Spoils of War
6 PM, Saturday, June 15, 1940

Phryné answered the knock upon her door and discovered Luftwaffe Captain Dieter Dientz standing on her landing. He was smiling with the confidence of a high school quarterback. Under his left arm was a small, black leather valise and in his good, gloveless hand was a bottle of wine.

They exchanged pleasantries and Phryné invited him into her small sitting room.

Since yesterday, when the German announced that he would be returning, Phryné knew that this scenario would unfold. It read like the script of a low-budget RKO picture. Five minutes into the film, the entire audience knew how it would end. It was no comfort to her, but she saw it coming. She knew that Hauptmann Dientz had arrived to demand a Hollywood-style casting couch audition.

Last night before she fell asleep, she uselessly weighed her options and ultimately realized that there was no workable alternative to what was about to happen. She was in the comfort of her bed, looking up at the grey ceiling, and thought of the French Foreign Legion's motto, *"marche ou crève" (March or Die)*. Phryné did not want to die and believed that she was about to march onto stage in the role of her lifetime. Quite possibly, her life could depend on her performance.

She succumbed to the inevitable and surrendered to the unpreventable.

That first night they shared a glass of wine before Hauptmann Dientz suggested dinner at a corner restaurant a half block down the street. They walked to the corner *Restaurant L'Esturgeon* on Rue Beaugendre and Allée de Pissises and enjoyed beef Burgundy served in a terra cotta cassolette, chanterelles mushroom risotto and steamed asparagus. There was more wine with dinner, coffee and cognac afterwards.

Dientz reached into his breast pocket and presented Phryné with her Reichsfilmkammer Identification, Residence and Work Permit. As Phryné expected, there was no need for an interview. Back at her apartment, the captain took advantage of Phryné's supposed appreciation and forced himself on her. An hour later, he kissed her softly on the lips, gently on the forehead and left.

Phryné recognized the parting insult for what it was. She slowly, reluctantly accepted her fate and the uncertain, precarious future that lie ahead. She stood in the narrow shower stall under the hottest water she could bear and wept. Eventually her tears dried. She wasn't comfortable, it took hours, but she was able to fall asleep that night.

Pillaged and Plundered
6 Rue Saint-Sébastien
Poissy, Île-de-France
Monday, June 24, 1940

On an otherwise quiet Monday morning late in June, one week and two days after Captain Dieter Dientz despoiled Phryné of her pride and three weeks after the fall of Paris, a squad of German Wehrmacht barbarously announced their presence at Phryné's door. Soldiers of the Reich stormed into her compact apartment at 85 Rue Beaugendre in Chatou, presented her with a printed order in German and informed her that the entire property was being seized to house Hitler's occupation forces. She sat in her small kitchen, cowering in fear on a wooden chair as close as she could possibly get to the wall. All she could do was watch as they rummaged through her belongings, wardrobe and pantry. Most of her wardrobe and all of her foodstuffs were looted, commandeered and seized. Everything from her black, Russian sable shoulder wrap to her prized silk stockings and delicates were manhandled, tossed aside or confiscated. More than half of her wardrobe was plundered.

Half an hour after the plundering began, Phryné was left standing on the street with what remained of her belongings stuffed into a paperboard box, a railroad bag and a canvas rucksack. The skies were grey and a light rain began to fall.

She had only one place to go for a roof over her head: the theater. With a cardboard box under her arm and a bag in each hand, she walked the length of Rue Beaugendre to the bus stop and waited for the noon bus to Poissy.

Noon came and went without a bus. It began to rain steadily. Phryné and a half dozen other potential passengers inside the bus shelter began to wonder if the bus would appear at all. No one talked. The air was too heavy. There wasn't room for conversation.

A burning anger flared up inside her. She wondered if Dientz knew of the impending trespass and plunder of her small apartment when he shared her bed two Saturdays earlier. She made herself a promise that she would confront him with that question at her first opportunity.

However, when the opportunity arose weeks later, she voided her promise and decided not to kick a sleeping dog. Her question was better left unanswered.

The noon bus from Chatou to Poissy arrived at one forty-five. Phryné and seven others clambered onto the Renault Parisien, 40-seat bus and somehow found standing room among the other human sardines aboard. There were one or two empty, forced smiles but still no words were shared.

The ride to the Poissy movie house at 6 Rue Saint-Sébastien was torturously quiet and tense.

Nestled next to the balcony-level projection room of the Poissy Cinema, an austere, ten-by-twelve foot storage room became home for Phryné. Martin, the Poissy cinema's fifty-eight-year-old projectionist helped Phryné settle in and move some old furnishings from the storage shed that were removed three years earlier for the theater renovations. A tattered old sofa, two wobbly floor lamps, a dented and dinged card table, and a three-drawer cabinet helped fill Phryné's makeshift living quarters. Her lavatory facilities were downstairs, off the lobby.

The certainty that tomorrow would bring another day had vanished. French radio stations had gone silent and only German-filtered news came across the airwaves. Reports from the German War Information Office stated that Luftwaffe bombers were exacting heavy losses on strategic British targets in the Battle of Britain. The BBC broadcasts from London were jammed with static pops and whistles. An occasional friendly smile could be seen on the streets of Ile de France, but they were few and far between. Most pedestrians kept their eyes focused on the sidewalk or street ten feet ahead of them.

The German Chamber of Film mandated that fifty percent of the box office receipts be forwarded to Berlin, twenty-five percent to the French provisional government in Vichy, and the remainder was earmarked for the Poissy Cinema. Because Phryné lost access to Pathé's library of American content and there was little interest in watching nothing but two alternating titles of German propaganda for an entire month, attendance at the movie house collapsed to less than a fourth of what it was prior to the invasion. Phryné was left with twenty-five percent of nearly zero ticket revenue and made the painful decision to cut the theater's hours and showings. The Poissy Cinema opened its doors only Wednesday through Saturday for shows at six o'clock in the evening and for noon matinees on Saturday.

Hugo had promised that he would provide a living allowance, but so far his cash stipends from Berlin amounted to sporadic and infrequent pittances. Hauptmann Dientz however, made regular visits with his canisters of Nazi film. Every three to four weeks the Luftwaffe officer took full advantage of Phryné's predicament but did, however provide for her. The townsfolk took notice and soon turned their heads and looked away whenever the American ventured out in public.

Phryné lived an unsettled life in Poissy, jumping around like a piece of bacon on a hot skillet. There was no place to turn without getting burned. Life was harsh. Although Abner's monthly alimony payments were being deposited to her existing account, the funds were inaccessible outside of Switzerland during wartime. Her pre-war, one-thousand-dollar Paramount stock debenture was worthless both back in Hollywood and Europe. Everywhere Phryné went, either inside her cubbyhole apartment or on the streets of Poissy, she found her back against a wall of war.

Hugo's Departure

Poissy, Ile de France
Six months after the fall of France,
January 1941

𝕻hryné answered a knock on the lobby box-office door one cold, grey afternoon in late January and was surprised to find Hugo standing on the other side. She hadn't seen him in at least six months.

His words, "Hallo, ma chérie" were followed by a brotherly kiss on the lips before he sidestepped, shut the door and walked inside. Heel plates on his oxfords clicked across the wooden floor. He was well dressed in a somewhat oversized, wide-shoulder, black overcoat and a triple-breasted, dark blue pin-stripe suit. Topping off his curly locks was a black fedora.

On his right arm was a wide red felt band with a white circle and a central black swastika. Hugo had become a card-carrying Nazi; a member of the National Socialist German Workers' Party.

Phryné sensed her skin crawling. She became a collaborator for survival. Dientz was a Baden-Württemberg German and a Nazi by default. Hugo was a member of the Nazi party by choice.

"Here, this is for you," and handed her an envelope.

Phryné peeked inside, fingered the contents and found ten, one-hundred-Reichmark[*] notes.

Hugo continued, "I haven't been able to keep up with all my contributions and I apologize, but it may not get better for some time. I'm leaving Berlin and travelling to Rome for a few months with the great Roberto Rossellini ... to create a documentary film for *Il Duce*[*], the Prime Minister of Italy and a strong ally of the Reich, Benito Mussolini."

Hugo walked to her desk, stared out the narrow office window through the lobby, to the street and lit a cigarette. He started talking low and softly, through the glass to the world outside, "I don't know when I will see you again, ma chérie."

Phryné ignored his melancholy. She disguised her contempt, "I've heard about the Italian dictator. He's as ruthless as they come. It should be an interesting film for you. But tell me ... how have you been?"

Phryné hadn't seen him in more than six months and yet it seemed like yesterday. He hadn't changed a hair on his head or the intonation of his meaningless prater, but she had never before felt so uncomfortable in his presence. The crimson red of his armband burned her eyes. She worried that he may want and expect her favor despite his darkened demeanor.

Hugo mused, "I'm doing fine. Things are going well enough with me."

She took two steps to her desk, set the envelope of money down and asked, "I have no food to offer, but can put this morning's coffee back on the warm if you would like a cup."

Hugo's mood abruptly changed. He spoke hurriedly and almost tripped over his tongue, "No, no thank you. I really must leave. My train is scheduled to leave in about an hour and I can't miss it. I just wanted to stop by and give you the money. I really have to leave."

She felt relief, and decided to stroke his ego and prod him for information. She began, "Well, it must certainly be and unfortunate coincidence that you are leaving Berlin so soon. But, thank you for coming by, Hugo. It was nice to see that you're still doing well and your career is advancing. It must be truly exciting to film such a good ally of the Führer as Il Duce is."

Phryné then feigned concern, "But, tell me, please. I worry about your family. Are Henri, Aimee and Natalle doing fine in Berlin? Aren't the English bombs dropping there?"

Hugo became markedly agitated and nervous. He spoke coarsely, "My family is safe. Who told you that the British are bombing Berlin?"

His voice cracked and he continued hurriedly, "Where did you hear that information? You could be shot for treason. Or worse. You could be on a train to Poland tonight."

Phryné had heard the stories about bombing raids, but had doubted that they held water. However, Hugo's jittery reaction seemed to verify the validity of the rumors.

She explained her worry for the children, "I heard some gossip on the street but of course, I didn't believe any of it was true. I'm happy it's false and that your children are safe."

Hugo didn't likely intend it so, but he appeared shaken and in a hurry to leave. His eyes briefly pierced hers with a frightening glare.

"Be careful of who you listen to and what you say, my dear Phryné. Words can kill almost as quickly as bullets and ..."

She sensed an opening in his arrogant façade and boldly interrupted him. Hugo had let his guard down. She saw a chance to discover the truth. She prodded him, "Tell me, Hugo. Something has been troubling me. Did you kill Guilermo? Was it you? You weren't in the stateroom when I woke up that morning."

He crushed his cigarette underfoot, ground it into the wooden floorboards and immediately put a match to another. He filled his lungs, wrinkled his brow and looked at her over the bridge of his nose.

"Yes, I did. I killed him. And I tossed that revolutionary dago[*] bastard overboard to the fishes ... but don't flatter yourself. I didn't kill him because you shared his bed. I killed him because I was following orders from Versailles. I like to think that I helped win the Spanish Civil War for the right side. History will prove that fascism is the right side."

For the previous four years, Phryné held suspicions that Hugo had killed Guilermo. She spent some troubled, sleepless hours wondering how her Spanish lover met his demise. Now she knew for certain.

"You do not need to return to Poissy, Hugo. I cannot be with you anymore."

She walked to the door and held it open.

Hugo scowled, pushed past her, started toward the doors to the street, turned momentarily and suggested, "You better learn German, ma chérie. Heil Hitler!"

As Long as You Live (You'll Be Dead if You Die)

Poissy, Ile de France
8 PM, March 3, 1942

Phryné was inside the Poissy Cinema and Theater, upstairs in her one-room apartment when the bombs started to fall and the tin, plaster and lath ceiling collapsed around her. A few minutes earlier, when the sirens first sounded, she feared another sleepless night. The previous night she could hear the bombs exploding miles away. Now they were not only closer, but she could hear them screaming through the air as they hurtled down toward the earth. Air raid sirens wailed. Like a toddler, she scurried under her bed to escape the bogeyman. There just wasn't enough time to run or walk to the shelters located in the bus depot basement.

She not only heard the explosions, but felt each detonation to the tips of her toes. The air smelled of ammonia and burned eggs. Hell was attacking her soul. She heard the Devil's footsteps coming nearer with each conflagration. She sensed his breath stealing the warmth from her body core. Her ears ached with the piercing pain of his trident. Flashes of light from the swords of demons attacked the darkness of night. Satan threw piercing pillars of flame from every point of the compass. A demonic blacksmith's red-hot poker struck her. She felt the fire cleave through her flesh and deep to the bone. Blood was running across her forehead, over her brow and down her cheek. She put her hand to the wound and felt her pulse. Smoke scorched her eyes. Her ears rang in pain.

Clouds of black soot as thick as tar could be seen hanging in the air, threatening to smother all breathing life below. Relentless, fiery explosions fell mercilessly from the skies above. Flaming fingers of fire reached out from the broken windows of burning homes. There were explosions in the street that tore up a century's cobblestones and threw them into a whirling maelstrom of brick, glass and mortar. Aircraft engines groaned like dying dinosaurs. The trembling of the floor beneath her was unrelenting. Pounds of plaster fell from the walls and ceiling. Anti-aircraft shells exploded in the boiling skies above. An errant scream was heard through the thunderous noise outside. The night sky blackened as the darkest cave to be lit up again with a flash of lightning-white fire. Hundreds upon hundreds of explosions shook the night.

The Earth trembled. The air split. The fists of war had pounded on every door in Paris. Death and destruction were on the steps, waiting impatiently to be invited inside.

Eventually, dead silence descended from above and passed through the city. The bombing[**] ended an hour and fifty minutes after it began.

We Three (My Echo, My Shadow and Me)
Poissy, France
7 AM, Wednesday, March 4, 1942

She remained under her rickety bed for an unknown length of time, fearful, trying to regain her composure, waiting for the dust to settle. She was on her belly, stretched out and holding a piece of her torn dress to the painful wound over her left eye. She didn't trust the silence and worried the bombs could return.

Her trembling body eventually calmed, and like the earth beneath her, she regained self-control and breathed a sigh of relief. She slowly, gingerly slid out from under her bed, reaching and feeling across the floor for a familiar piece of furniture, fixture or wall. She discovered her nightstand, lying on its side. The drawer where she kept her flashlight was opened and without its contents. Phryné went to her hands and knees searching for the battery-powered source of light. The fingers of her left hand discovered the prize as her forehead started once again to drip blood down along her eyebrow, around her eye and onto her cheek. She switched on the torchlight, set it on the floor, ripped off the bottom three inches of her dress and made a headband bandage. The memory of a brazen tango performance flashed through her mind.

When she dared to venture out from the supposed safety of her apartment, she peered through the clouds of plaster dust and noticed a ten-foot hole in the roof over a gaping crater where the orchestra pit and the first two rows of seats once were. The movie screen was sprawled across the stage like a backstreet drunk, but torn and scorched beyond repair.

The balcony stairway leading down from her apartment and the projection room to the lobby was littered with bits of wall, ceiling and exterior brick. The precious, 35 mm Paillard-Bolex film projector was smashed to pieces and scattered along the stairway.

Downstairs, through the once-opulent foyer, she discovered that the Poissy Cinema's entrance doors were broken, bent, cracked and barely hanging on strained hinges. Every street-side window was shattered. Glass shards covered the carpeting.

Daylight struggled to brighten the devastated city. Bricks, boards and broken shutters littered the cobblestones and sidewalks outside. A course, filthy white dust permeated the air. The world smelled of pyrite and charred wood. It was a war zone.

Cries of pain, suffering, misery, loss and pity coursed through every street and alley, violating and insulting every soul alive. Babies wailed. Adults wept. People rummaged through the rubble. Dogs wandered the streets without direction. Down the block, a forlorn rooster dared to declare that life goes on.

Fire, first aid, search, rescue and recovery personnel had been on the streets as soon as *all clear* was sounded at three in the morning. They worked in teams, in pairs, in squads or individually throughout the blackness of night and into the breaking daylight. Sirens, fire bells, police whistles and vehicle horns belched their coarse noise over the city. Persistent fires continued to blaze despite the best efforts of man. Human anguish was compounded with grief. An occasional, isolated gunshot could be heard in the distance.

Squads of German occupation troops scoured the streets looking for looters or saboteurs. They offered what little help they could within the bounds of wartime protocol, such as direction, blankets or emergency medical triage.

Phryné's world had crumbled and fallen down upon her. In a stupor of shock and disbelief, she walked away from the theater and down Saint-Sébastien Street without direction. Ruin and rubble were everywhere. Nothing was recognizable. All known landmarks were gone. Someone told her that hot coffee, sliced baguettes and the comfort of human company were available at the bus depot shelter at the corner of Rue Pouchete. She didn't know where to turn.

She recognized a handful of neighbors and cinema patrons seated on make-shift benches of salvaged boards set across piles of brick and ruin. Others were standing and remained huddled in clusters of two or three. Phryné stood alone. Someone handed her a tin cup of lukewarm, weak black coffee and a three-inch piece of bread ripped from a long loaf.

An older, round woman, without the courtesy or courage to stop, slowed her pace, waddled past and gruffly mumbled, "Your man, your janitor, your projectionist, Martin died last night, but I see you're still alive."

The pang in her stomach was aggravated by the nonchalant comment which, she believed, put the blame for Martin's death on her shoulders. She was left standing alone and distressed when a young woman in a clean but drab, blue-grey dress approached carrying a bulging, black leather bag.

The woman pointed to a dirty, ragged sofa cushion atop a pile of smoldering rubble and said, "Sit there, and allow me look at your forehead."

Phryné had forgotten about her injury and gingerly sat down on the beaten cushion. She noticed that the woman was wearing a small, Red Cross lapel pin.

The young woman went to a knee and introduced herself, "I'm Renée-Ffion Delacroix ... I'm a service corps volunteer for the District Charmille, Poissy."

"I'm Phryné. Phryné Truffaut. I manage ... I managed the cinema back there."

Renée opened the bag and brought out a small bottle of alcohol and an eye-dropper bottle of mercurochrome[*]. She placed a warm, reassuring hand on Phryné's thigh and said, "I know who you are ... now ... let's have a look at your hurt."

Renée unwrapped the wound, daubed it with alcohol and asked, "Do you remember how this happened?"

"I'm not sure, but I think it was a piece of the tin ceiling."

The aid worker reassured Phryné, "It's going to need a stitch or three or four. But it's a clean cut and should heal well."

"You can do that here?"

"Now and then, this job requires a good deal of improvised field work and a bit of bold initiative. But you'll be fine. I'll be finished in a blink of your eye."

Phryné asked, "I'm indebted to you. How can I repay your kindness?"

Renée threaded the suture needle and teased, "Perhaps one day I'll ask a favor of you."

Duty Calls
Monday, March 9, 1942

After the bombing, Phryné and Renée gave three full days to volunteer efforts in and around Poissy, wherever and whenever, and performing whatever tasks were organized. They found themselves on fire brigades battling stubborn flare-ups, clearing rubble from the streets or carrying buckets of water from the city cistern back to the shelter. They spent the first four nights after the bombing sleeping in a coat closet in the bombed-out lobby of Poissy Cinema. On the fifth day, the police and fire marshal declared the theater to be unsound, unsafe and uninhabitable. The women were ordered out of the theater and into the bus depot and shelter. Phryné's heart sank further when she learned that her old neighborhood in Boulogne-Billancourt was flattened and reduced to unsalvageable rubble.

The only pleasant development to evolve over those disastrous days was the relationship that Renée-Ffion and Phryné forged from the unrelenting human tragedies that surrounded them. Renée-Ffion Delacroix had an extraordinary ability to talk to and comfort the needy souls around her who were in distress. Phryné admired Renée as she went from person to person, from one sorrowful individual to another with words of kindness and encouragement. Like a butterfly on the wing, the French volunteer became especially beautiful when she stopped to spread life's sweet nectar of hope and caring.

Whether she was comforting a grieving spouse, setting a broken bone or mending the torn arm of a baby doll, Renée rendered selfless help. She had a voice that soothed and a touch that healed. She listened without prejudice and spoke with compassion.

Phryné could not help but wonder how such a young woman had acquired such a varied skill set and the ability to use it.

An unlikely visitor arrived at the shelter on Monday, March 9. Luftwaffe Captain Dieter Dientz descended upon Pouchete Street at midday, lunch time, sitting in the back seat of an open-body Horch [**] staff car. He swaggered into the bombed-out bus depot shelter with his left hand resting atop his pistol holster. He looked around, spotted Phryné and Renée handing out pieces of buttered bread and walked toward them. Every eye in the shelter saw the attention that the German afforded the women, but not a single eyeball dared to stare. Phryné introduced her new friend Renée to Dieter and placed glowing praise on the French volunteer's stamina and humanity.

Although the introductions and pleasantries were nearly over as soon as they began, they were fully wiped out when Dientz motioned Phryné and Renée to step out of line. He handed Phryné an envelope.

He needed to ask, "Your head, the injury, it's not too bad, is it?"

Phryné explained, "No, no. It's fine. It's only a scratch, I'm fine."

The captain took her at her word and pointed at the envelope in her hand, "Those are your travel papers and the authorization for the position of manager at Cinema Boos, about one hundred kilometers to the northwest. The old manager needed to be replaced and has volunteered for service elsewhere."

Renée turned and took a step away before Dientz said, "Stop. You do not need to leave. You may remain until I am finished here. There is no secret or I would not have said a single word in your presence."

The young French volunteer did not dare refuse but did not lay her gaze upon the German.

Hauptmann Dientz's arrival, visit, apparent assignment and travel orders put Phryné on edge. She could feel the glare of dozens of eyes burning on her body. She asked, "You knew of the destruction of the Poissy Cinema?"

The German affirmed, "Of course," and returned his focus to the business at hand, "You must be in Boos tomorrow evening. It will be safe for you there. I have arranged for your travel tomorrow at one o'clock in the afternoon with a Wehrmacht escort. I have also arranged your living quarters. There is a comfortable cottage for you some meters from the Cinema Boos-Manoir."

Phryné pressed him, "You knew I survived the bombs and I was alive? How?"

The captain stiffened his posture and replied, "Of course, I knew. It's my job. And I care about you, but I must leave."

He added, "I must now visit the targeted western areas and the Renault factory damaged by the English bombs. I expect to be in Boos with new films for the theater by the end of next week. Travel well and Heil Hitler, Fraulein Phryné."

His stiff-arm salute was perfunctory, his tone non-committal. He was outside of the shelter's broken walls, back inside the staff car and gone before the dust from his jackboots settled.

The shelter had been as quiet as an open-air picnic of cloistered monks. However, the volume was turned up to a low, steady clamor after the German left. Renée and Phryné became the topic of whispered conversation.

"I've got three cigarettes left, Renée. I need one, how about you?"

The women started for the open door and immediately felt the harsh stares branding them. Renée and Phryné moved quickly out of the shelter and onto the sidewalk. Together, they sized their cigarette ration.

Renée offered her pack and said, "I've got a half dozen. Take one of mine."

One match, two lit cigarettes and two puffs later, Renée asked, "That Nazi clearly cares about you. What does he do? Don't you think he does more than deliver film to cinemas?"

They leaned with their backs to the station's battered wall, smoking their cigarettes.

Phryné exhaled slowly, "He cares for me. I don't care for him. I believe he has a district that he oversees. I think he spies on people, to tell the truth. He told me to tell him if I hear about anyone who is plotting sabotage."

Renée pressed her, "Would you? Would you tell him about any sabotage or underground activity, I mean? You wouldn't, would you?"

"No. I would not get involved. I'm not a soldier and it's not my job. I would not rat on anyone and I will not kill for anyone."

"Well, I think you'll like it in Boos. It's all farms and no factories, so you shouldn't need to worry about British bombs falling on your head anymore. But you cannot avoid the obvious. I do think that Nazi has thoughts about you and wants to keep you safe. And he wants to keep you for himself."

Phryné sighed, "For the last two years he's had me to himself. I tell myself over and over that he might want me, he might be with me, and he may take me, but he doesn't own me."

She took another puff, and spoke of the destruction around them, "Look at this ruin. What a waste. Now the cinema is gone and I need to leave here to keep my job. The only friends I had in Paris lived in Boulogne-Billancourt. Who knows where they are now ... or even if they're still alive? You and I just met and I like you and was just getting used to being around you and now it's over. Everything is kaput. I will miss you, Renée."

Renée inhaled, let the smoke penetrate her lungs, exhaled and said, "You won't be alone up there in the Boos farm country. It is a very close community with many farms and it is not at all like Poissy or Paris. Everyone is friendly and they will make you feel right at home. And there are people in Boos who I visit occasionally. I know some very good people there. I think I'll see you again before too very long. And if we get the chance, perhaps we will work together again. Perhaps we could help one another."

8. Boos, Rouen, Normandy (One Year Later) ~ 1943 ~

American Patrol
5 Rue de Andelys
Boos, Normandy
6 PM, Friday, June 18, 1943

To see the timber and stucco cottage at 5 Rue de Andelys, an observer would find it difficult to believe that the property was in the middle of a war zone at the center of the largest, costliest, and most deadly war the world had seen. The closest cross street was a half kilometer down the road, a narrow, unpaved country lane with access to fields of wheat, oats and barley. Its name was puzzling: Rue de l'Avenir, which translates from the French as "street of the future".

For the past fourteen months, Phryné had been enjoying a peaceful, pastoral life in rural Boos. The population hadn't fluctuated much over the past half century and had remained at about two hundred since the end of the First World War.

The four-room cottage she called home was snuggled under the shade of an aged, spreading linden. A flagstone walkway led from the roadside garden gate to a bright blue, round-top wooden door. Blooming pink hollyhocks embraced the doorway on both sides and a single pot of red geraniums sat atop the stone steps.

The business section along Boos' main street, Rue de Andelys, consisted of a co-op grocery and general store across the street from the post office, and a black smith, petrol-station combination set cross-street to the cinema.

The movie house was tiny, and perhaps microscopic when compared to the once-opulent Cinéma et théâtre de Poissy. The Boos theater had a packed-house seating capacity of forty.

Dieter Dientz visited Boos twice a month, bringing two or three, sixty or ninety minute canisters packed with Nazi propaganda film for the Boos movie screen.

Early on, Phryné wound discover a few Reichmarks in the cans, tucked underneath the film but never removed them. She relied on her suspicions and assumed that they were a test.

Over the course of the past year, the German gradually revealed his humanity. It could well have been a combination of factors, such as Phryné's emotional influence, the softening of his Nazi persona or the weariness of war.

Phryné slowly, reluctantly accepted her fate and the uncertain, precarious future that lie ahead. She wasn't comfortable, but she could sleep at night. Dieter Dientz was fastidious to a fault, and his one redeeming quality could have been his cleanliness. She slowly warmed to him, and attempted to convince herself that he was genuinely sorry for the initial circumstance that led to her rape at their first meeting in Poissy after the fall of Paris. Try as she might to rationalize a personal relationship with him, she still struggled not to flinch at his initial touch and always suspected that he noticed.

She could never relax in his company and continued to see him as a temporary yet necessary evil required for her long-term survival.

However, Dientz persisted with his tokens of supposed appreciation. It wasn't long before he began bringing along black-market gifts of food, wine, banned soaps, perfumes, stockings and intimates.

It didn't carry much water with her, but during an emotional, wine-infused confession of his trespasses, he eventually apologized for, as he put it; his "inconsiderate" behavior following the German occupation. He was Phryné's junior by at least five years and blamed his erratic behavior on his youthful insecurity, poor judgment and the pressures of war.

Another interesting revelation came six months following the Poissy bombing. After sharing a bottle of wine, Hauptmann Dientz suggested that all wars could be ended permanently if the belligerent parties were placed in an open field and commanded to fire at will until every last soldier and politician was dead.

Phryné learned that a battle injury Dientz sustained during the Spanish Civil War in Guernica, Spain in April of 1937 had ended his career as a pilot. His scared cheek, deformed ear and hand were the result of the fiery crash of his Junkers Ju-87 Stuka** dive bomber. An inexperienced Spanish field surgeon had dressed his wounds, removed part of his ear and wrapped his burned hand. During the healing process, the tight wraps on his right hand caused three of four fingers to weld together.

Hauptmann Dientz became fascinated with Phryné's stories of her life in Hollywood and rubbing elbows with the glittering stars of the silver screen. He was befuddled by her decision to leave Los Angeles for Paris and when he discovered that Phryné had attended private parties with Marlene Dietrich, Clark Gable and a slew of others, his reaction was over the moon. Dieter held Phryné as his ticket to the stars and could listen to her tales of Hollywood for hours.

Without method or predictability, a pre-war Porky Pig or Bosko *Looney Tunes*** animated short by Harman Productions would sometimes appear in the mix. In December 1942, Dientz delivered what was likely intended as a surprise birthday gift for Phryné: a spliced and partially burnt copy of

Shirley Temple's *Bright Eyes*[**]. The 1934 Fox Film was placed in a film can that was intentionally mislabeled, *Robert and Bertram*, a pre-war German musical comedy.

On June 18, 1943, the Boos box office sold a total of seven tickets for that particular evening's showing. Two were purchased by a local, love-struck young couple who vanished from their back row seats within the first ten minutes. Pierre Dugay, the town's walking-talking gossip columnist, purchased a ticket for himself and one for his wife Claire. Two transient farm workers from the Saar Valley bought the fifth and sixth. The last ticket was bought and paid for by Luftwaffe Captain Dieter Dientz.

The propaganda film showing that evening at the Cinema Boos-Manoir was already a year old, *Vienna 1910,* a dramatized 1942 biography of an Austrian mayor who had banished all Jews from the city.

Phryné wasn't in the audience, but she couldn't avoid viewing the film. She was the projectionist.

The heavens above Boos were usually quiet during the week, but on odd days, the heavy, growling drone of hundreds of American Boeing[**] B-17s could be heard racing toward Germany at an altitude of 8,000 feet.

A year earlier, the skies over Boos weren't so crowded. As the war progressed, the Americans launched more and more, day and night, bombing sorties over Normandy en route to targets deeper and deeper into Germany. To counter the increased air traffic, the German Luftwaffe installed 88 mm anti-aircraft batteries in Normandy along the flight paths of Allied bombers.

On the night of June 18, an airborne swarm of giant aluminum bumble bees passed over Boos that could not be ignored. Each B-17 Flying Fortress had four engines. That night, there were at least a thousand Wright 1200 horsepower engines screaming above the clouds. Six pair of ears inside the movie house heard the thunderous noise. The evening's Nazi-sanctioned entertainment ended for Hauptmann Dientz, Phryné Truffaut and four civilian patrons.

Dientz stood, turned, looked up toward Phryné in the projection booth, signaled to her and exited the theater. The film stopped.

German antiaircraft guns positioned between Rouen[**] and Boos, began to throw so much flak skyward that Boos was subjected to a barrage of deafening explosions that lasted nearly half an hour. Cinema Boos-Manoir was emptied in moments.

Because of the large number of aircraft that were obviously involved in the American raid, it was likely that Dientz was automatically detailed other duties and wouldn't be spending the night. He had arrived in Boos about five o'clock that afternoon with the film and his usual packet of goodies for Phryné. They shared a half bottle of wine over an otherwise boring, bland dinner of potato soup and buttered bread at her cottage next door. Although the captain had planned a late evening rendezvous, Phryné did not expect to see him until his next visit.

Two Days Later; 10 AM, Sunday Morning, June 20

5 Rue de Andelys
Boos, Normandy

Church necessarily became a part of Phryné's routine in Boos. Her choice was to attend church or be damned by the locals. Weather permitting, she attended church.

On Sunday, June 20, she had unexpected but not unfamiliar company. A forest-green 1938 Renault Ville bus stopped outside the Boos Cinema and delivered one female passenger.

Renée-Ffion Delacroix arrived at the cottage just before Phryné was about to bicycle to the Evangelical services at Temple Saint Éloi in Rouen. Over the last fourteen months, Renée hadn't been a total stranger. Twice she made the two-hour bus trip from Paris to Boos and visited Phryné: once in August and once again over the Christmas holiday. However, Renée had always either written or telephoned the theater to advise Phryné of her arrival. Renée would overnight and Phryné would share her oversized straw mattress.

That Sunday morning, Phryné was sleep-deprived from the noisy American fly-over, the German antiaircraft and the compounded nervousness of Friday and Saturday nights; so much so that she had been looking for an excuse not to attend church that morning. But Renée encouraged her to take the one-mile bicycle ride north of town and dutifully say her prayers if only for the sake of appearance.

Renée pled her case and explained that it could be important to show her face in church after Friday night's air-raid and antiaircraft barrage. Throughout France, the local citizenry were becoming more and more war weary and less tolerant of Nazi collaborators. She urged Phryné, "Carry on with business as usual. I've got a favor to ask, so I'll put together a little lunch for us and explain it all after you get back."

12 PM, Sunday Afternoon

Renée had the table set, the bread sliced, the cheese shaved and a pot of tea under the cozy. She had brought a tin of liver pâté as not only a treat, but as an icebreaker and deal maker. She was about to ask a favor of someone whom she didn't know all that well.

Outside the cottage, Phryné dismounted, gathered her skirt and propped her bicycle against the weathered white fence in front of her home. She removed her straw hat, loosened and removed her scarf and stepped inside.

"Church was not pleasant, Renée. I don't enjoy blazing stares or the buzz of whispered innuendo."

"Sit and have some lunch. Get your thoughts away from the petty peeves of ignorance. Someday this war and its rumors will end."

"It's not easy, Renée. I tried to keep it secret, but somehow they all know that I'm an American and my work papers have me listed as a trusted member of the *Greater Reich* whatever the hell that is. And this stubborn boche Dientz keeps coming around. I'm sick of it. I don't care who the hell wins this war. I just want it over with."

"I know you don't mean that. I know you don't."

"I want a cigarette. Did you bring any from Paris?"

"Yes, I did. And they're American!" Renée took a packet of twenty Lucky Strike** cigarettes from her bag.

Phryné was mildly excited, "Wow. This is like Christmas."

She carefully opened the pack, tearing the foil only one-third across the top edge, pulling it up and off, neatly exposing the tops of six cigarettes.

Renée watched closely and remarked, "Aaahaa! Oui, oui! That's how it's done!"

"Where did you get these?"

"I got them about a month ago, south of Brussels, in the Ardennes, from a downed American flyer. They were intended as a thank-you gift to me. My Free French friends and I were about to get him and a few others out and back to England."

Phryné was wide-eyed but not shocked. She tapped two cigarettes out of the pack, put them between her lips, lit them both, handed one to Renée, and said, "Keep going, tell me more."

"I'm not a service corps volunteer. I'm a trained Free French operant. We use our combined skills to plot, plan and assist in the war to defeat Nazi Germany any way we can. Any way ... always."

"I had that figured out months ago. You must be here to ask for that favor you mentioned after the Poissy bombing."

Renée nodded, "Yes. You are in the perfect place at the perfect time under the perfect circumstance. Your Nazi will never suspect you."

The Root Cellar

The favor Renée sought was to conceal and care for a wounded English pilot whose plane had been downed by German flak on Friday night. The flyer was part of the British fighter escort for American B-17s targeting a ball bearing factory in Schweinfurt, Germany, on a flight path that brought the Americans directly over Rouen and Boos.

Renée devised the plan: An American would keep an English flyer in a French root cellar directly beneath a German's nose. The Free French would attempt to spirit the pilot out of France and back to England as soon as practical.

Luftwaffe Hauptmann Dieter Dientz had known Phryné for nearly three years and maintained a convenient intimacy as well as a professional, working relationship with her. Additionally, Phryné had established a presence in a quiet, isolated agrarian community and lived in a cottage with a concealed root cellar barely large enough to harbor a foreign fighter.

Renée knew Phryné. She also knew the place: the root cellar at ⁿ5 Rue de Andelys: a hand-dug ten-foot-square underground hideout with an old, tumble-down, timber ladder that ended at a dirt wall.

Tears in My Heart

5 Rue de Andelys
Boos, Normandy
10 PM, Monday night, June 21, 1943

A powerful Ardennais draft horse snorted in defiant compliance to the guttural grunt and sharp pull of the old driver seated at the reins. The sun was setting and twilight was knocking on the horizon.

Seconds later, Phryné opened the door and witnessed a full wagonload of freshly cut forage hay come to a stop in front of her cottage. Seated on the time-worn bench next to the aged driver was another older man in faded, worn, jade-green coveralls and knee-high boots. The third person on the wagon appeared to be a pipe-smoking younger fellow wearing work trousers, an oversized, long-sleeved, cotton duck shirt and a black beret.

A pubescent voice cracked and broke while asking for water for everyone and the horse. Fifty meters down the dirt and gravel road a group of a half dozen boys was playing soccer with a ball fashioned from empty burlap sacks and barnyard twine.

Phryné stepped back into the house and came out with three mismatched cups and a bucket.

It was the summer solstice, the longest day of the year along with the most hours of daylight available for harvesting. There were festivals, bazaars and harvest celebrations to commemorate the extended daylight. In years past, a traditional bonfire was lit to symbolically lengthen the day, but the war put a stop to that ritual, leaving the over consumption of wine as the evening's main event.

The young farmhand half-stepped and half-jumped off the wagon and hurried toward Phryné at the water well and hand pump.

It was Renée-Ffion under the beret.

She spoke with urgency, "We cannot stay long, only to water and oat the horse. Our flyer is in the back, under the wagon in a cargo box. He's on morphine, but it's due to wear off. Gitan and Jules will bring him in on a stretcher. Those two are a good deal stronger than they look. Is everything ready here?"

"Yes."

The men still on the wagon didn't have Renée's youthful exuberance. They carefully stepped off the bench seat, and methodically toe-and-heeled their way down off the wagon, and onto the ground.

Renée thumped out the spent tobacco on the heel of her boot, stuck the pipe in her pant pocket and walked to the horse. She grabbed his bridle and angled the big beast to partially block the view of any passersby. The boys had kicked their way further down the street. Gitan and Jules dropped open the side of the cargo box and pulled both stretcher and flyer out into the fresh air. They started toward the cottage.

Phryné stayed at the well, pumping water into the rusty tin bucket. As Gitan and Jules came closer and walked inside, all Phryné could only see were blankets and bandages. She followed them to the doorway and peered inside to watch their progress.

Gitan was the younger, biggest and burliest of the men. He set his end of the stretcher on the kitchen table and lifted the trap door to the cellar. Together, he and Jules wrangled the bundle of bandages and blankets down the ladder, into the hand-dug cellar and out of sight.

Renée took the bridle again and persuaded the horse to take a few awkward steps backwards. Luckily, the burlap soccer boys were the only townspeople in sight and still kicking up dust in the road. Gitan and Jules took the ladder up and out of the cellar and closed the cottage door behind them. Up from the cellar, outdoors and free of their human cargo, the men leaned against the wagon and rolled cigarettes.

Renée watered the horse and strapped on his feed bag of oats. Gitan walked to the outhouse and Jules went to the other side of the wagon and peed on a wheel.

Renée thanked Phryné for her help and encouraged, "There's morphine tablets for the collarbone, two a day if he needs them and sulfa powder to sprinkle if you see infection on the arm break. The bleeding has stopped, he's alert when he's not on the dope and he seems able to withstand what pain he has. He's had one pill today. He knows he needs to be silent. I brought one book in English, I'll bring more. It's Scott Fitzgerald, *The Gatsby* or something. There's a flashlight and batteries and candles but keep them out of sight. You know what to do. I'll get word to you this week. Be careful."

She stepped close and gave her friend a hug.

Phryné asked, "What's his name?"

"Morris. Lieutenant Morris Sutcliffe."

"Explain his injury."

"A compounded fracture of the upper arm, and a cracked collar bone, and a sprained ankle that looks like a sack of potatoes. And I think that may have a case of battle nerves. But he's proved to be a tough one. Physically, anyway."

Don't Hit Your Head
Tuesday morning, June 22

Phryné spent the night in the cellar and although she didn't sleep, she was able to capture forty winks from time to time.

The English flyer didn't appear to move a muscle, nor did he make a sound. Initially, it made her nervous enough to hold her hand to his face and detect his breath.

That first night it was Phryné and not the Englishman who was uncomfortable. The basement brought back haunting memories of what she considered to be the dungeons of Le Havre.

In the morning, she was sitting cross-legged and close at his left side. From what she could see with the flickering yellow light from a paraffin candle, she estimated the lieutenant to be a few years younger than she and guessed his height to be a match. He had sandy, red hair and four or five days of brownish whiskers.

He stirred and came to life while she studied him. She was startled and felt slightly ashamed.

She leaned away and apologized, "I'm sorry if I got too close. Good morning. You're safe. The Resistance brought you last night. I'm sure you know that. I'm Phryné, an American, I live here and I'll be taking care of you."

He only nodded and remained motionless with the exception of two eyelids moistening his powder blue eyes.

"Are you hungry?"

He moved his head back and forth sideways, ever so slowly and ever so little.

She asked, "Do you need anything? Your pain medicine, water, anything?"

His lips formed the word: *water*. His left shoulder was wrapped and bound against his chest. His bandaged left arm was in a sling and rested on his abdomen.

"Let me help you." She came to her knees, put a hand behind his neck, and assisted him, and raised his head enough to sip from a beaker of water.

She aided him, guided and lowered his head slowly onto a ragged, skinny pillow.

It was then that she realized she had work to do. She stood, felt a thump and painfully, abruptly remembered that there wasn't enough head room to fully stand.

Embarrassed, she joked, "If you want to stand up and stretch, watch your head. I'll be back soon. I'll bring some bread and hot tea. Is it all right if I call you Morris?"

She didn't get a reaction.

Let Your Eyes Get Used to the Dark
Tuesday evening, June 22

A twenty-foot length of sound wire from the cinema, a chamber pot, a chicken-feather pillow from her bed, *The Great Gatsby* from Renée, a winter-weight comforter, her wool overcoat and two blankets went into the root cellar that afternoon.

With encouragement and perseverance, together Phryné and Morris struggled and were able to pile and form the comforter, coat and blankets into a narrow make-shift mattress atop the dirt floor. With a kitchen knife and bandages, Phryné used some sound system cord to fashion a power source for a naked light bulb. The flyer was set for the long haul.

Morris hadn't said a word since he awoke. He nodded *yes* or *no* and displayed no expressions other than a rare, faint smile. Phryné became exasperated. He didn't even display pain.

She told him that in the days ahead, she could not stay in the cellar for long periods – not only because she couldn't raise any suspicions from the locals, postman or milkman, but she had obligations with the cinema.

She locked the cottage door each time she went into the root cellar, just in case the Luftwaffe Captain stopped by out of schedule. Phryné believed that she would have enough time to scramble up the ladder, close the trap door and slide the rug back across the floor.

The Englishman's eyes grew to the size of hard-boiled eggs when she mentioned that Dieter Dientz visited about twice a month. When she saw his initial reaction, she thought it best not to mention any of the German's overnight stays.

In the days and nights that followed, she read to him from *The Great Gatsby* and bits and pieces of articles from old French magazines that she retrieved from the movie house. The printed material wasn't timely, so she heavily relied on imagination and improvisation to enhance her translation and the stories.

Because Morris managed to utter only a dozen or so sentences during his first days in the root cellar, Phryné believed that the trauma he suffered wasn't just physical. The second day was the only time that he seemed to indicate by nod and eye blinks that he wanted a morphine tablet.

When Phryné asked if he was comfortable and able to sleep well, his eyes and nod said "yes".

On Thursday, Morris swallowed his pride and permitted her to wash him. Heating the water and carrying it up and down the ladder was more laborious than she anticipated. His right ankle did look swollen but it wasn't the sack of potatoes that Renée had mentioned.

Words escaped his lips now and then, but they weren't anything like an encyclopedic dissertation. A statement of thirst was "water" and hungry was "food". "Thank you" was the equivalent of a full paragraph.

Phryné began to read his eyes, and believed that she could reach him in that way. Little inflections meant a lot; like the curl at the end of his mouth or the squint in the corner of an eye, the widening of a pupil or the strength of his stare. An occasional smile came across his usually stoic face and she answered with one of her own. She desperately wanted to reach Morris. She was hungry to know him.

When she read to him F. Scott Fitzgerald's words describing the character Daisy's feelings, and how she decided not to hide her love for Gatsby, he reached out his right hand and placed it on hers. Phryné was caught by surprise, stopped reading and remained motionless.

She dove into the Englishman's eyes and searched for his thoughts and only after a few seconds did she turn her hand to hold his. It was a fleeting moment of tenderness without a spoken word. He answered her with a soft caress along the length of her fingers and back of her hand. His eyes strained, and asked her for understanding. She replied in kind.

It was a magic moment for Phryné. She didn't realize that quiet could be so loud and clear. There was so much more to be said.

A week went by without a word from Renée. Dieter wasn't due to deliver any new film for at least another week, and Phryné didn't get any questions or unusually long stares when she picked up her ration of bread, two eggs, six potatoes and salt pork from the grocer. On a whim, she purchased a little pack of paper and a pencil for the flyer. She thought, *perhaps he can form his words on paper.*

Before she went to bed that night, she kept to routine, grabbed her torchlight and went down the beaten ladder to the root cellar to check on Morris. He had unscrewed the light bulb on his own and was sound asleep. He looked at ease and without worry. She watched him for a few minutes, longing to read his dreams.

Phryné went to bed contented. She felt happy in her skin.

We'll Meet Again
Sunday, July 25, 1943

He beamed when she gave him the writing materials, and revealed for the first time what his real smile looked like. For Phryné, it felt exceptionally good to feel good. His central method of communication went from squints, smiles and winks to the written word. Morris seemed at ease putting his thoughts down on paper. She didn't understand why, but for Morris the spoken word was easier formed with his fingers around a pencil.

Daily, he scribed little riddles and rhymes that went nowhere but gave elusive clues to his world. Phryné spent hours reading and trying to understand what each little line meant. It was tiring, exasperating and tedious. Most of all, it was mysterious. She saved every one of his little notes, and committed each line and every word to memory.

Above clouds of doubt
And below so deep
I beseech aloud
My treasures you keep

If only we could
Search o'er the world
Forever a day
Find a place to stay
Oh, if that we could
Forever a day
Forever we would
Have a place to stay

Please forgive
Once and forever
And did not ever
I dare not live

Words so simple
Yet hard to speak
Whose tongue is strong
Must remain in cheek
For only the mute
Dare taunt the meek
To allow one day
True hearts to speak

Phryné discovered that she could talk to Morris for hours. It was communication, not conversation. She would stop and ask if she was boring him, getting too personal or blindly rambling. He would smile and motion his hand for her to continue.

During his third week in the cellar, Phryné opened her heart and detailed bits of her life she thought she had forgotten or locked away. She believed that she had told all of her life secrets to Gael until she heard the words she spoke to Morris. Like an intimate chest of drawers, she exposed everything that her heart held close.

"My life in Hollywood was all wrong. I didn't know any real people. I lived among a small clique of movie moguls and picture people who I saw every day. Sure, they were talented and charming, but they sure weren't normal. People in Hollywood put false importance on every little relationship and all life's little indiscretions and insults. They go through life not knowing what's important.

"And here in France, before the war began, even after the Germans walked right through Poland and the Low Countries[**], people kept on living like nothing would ever change and everything would forever stay the same. Well it did and it won't. I lost what faith I had in humanity and I began to wonder if human nature is truly capable of compassion.

"All my adult life, every day, all the while I was searching for love, my heart was being teased and fooled into believing that parties, lust and sex could satisfy my hunger for lasting love and true romance. How wrong I was and how late I learned."

His eyes gave empathy that no words could ever relay.

She took his hands in hers and held them to her breast.

"Thank you for listening to me ramble, Morris. Thank you."

The wound on his arm was healing without any sign of infection and the piercing pain he suffered from the collar bone crack had subsided. The ankle had improved, but was still swollen. However, he did manage to hobble around the cellar and perform latrine functions with minimal assistance from Phryné. It seemed apparent that his days in the Boos

219

basement were numbered. All interested parties knew that the timing and transport out of France was the sticking point.

The fourth full week of Morris' basement holiday came and went without a visit from the German Dientz. No one knew for sure and there were no messages, but Phryné could only assume that he had more pressing matters on his agenda than canisters of old Nazi film. Every second or third night, flights of American B-17s traversed the skies over Boos on their way to Germany. There were whispers that the targets were in and around Hauptmann Dientz's hometown of Stuttgart.

Phryné sold two tickets for *Vienna 1910* on Friday and none for Saturday's showing. It came as no surprise that no one asked what would be playing next.

However, real-life drama did come to Phryné's little country cottage in Boos on Monday, July 26, 1943, at about two o'clock in the morning. Renée-Ffion Delacroix and knocked strong and sharp on the brightly painted blue entry door.

The moment Phryné slid the bolt and freed the lock, Renée pushed the door open, entered with her workhorse cohort Gitan Chegal and wasted no time or words, "It's time for Morris to leave. We need to move now."

Phryné turned without hesitation, took three steps across the floor, rapped on the trap door, opened it and announced, "It's me, Morris. It's time for you to go home. You've got to hurry, you know. Hurry." She stood at the entrance hole, holding an ages-old candlestick and providing flickering light along the rickety ladder and down into the dank cellar.

Phryné struggled to retain her composure. It wasn't easy. Her eyes moistened. She was about to lose her closest friend.

Thirty-five days after Gitan and Jules carried him into the root cellar, Morris was able to pull and hobble his way up the shaky homemade ladder and step out of his dirt dungeon and back into the world above. Renée and Gitan moved to him like flies to sugar.

The big Frenchman steadied the flyer with an arm under the Englishman's right armpit. Renée stood close behind and wasted no words, "We have an opportunity for your extraction back to England very early this morning from a hay field about three kilometers south of Rouen. A de Havilland Hornet[**] is in the air and on its way from Southampton. We have to hurry, Lieutenant Sutcliffe. We have only about an hour."

Morris blinked rapidly, chasing and clearing the fog of sleep. He had only seconds to gather his senses, react and respond. He answered Renée, "Yes, of course. I am ready."

He frantically searched the room with his gaze and found Phryné's eyes. His voice cracked, "We will meet again."

Those four words were the most he had strung together since he arrived.

Phryné could only manage four of her own, "Yes. Please stay safe."

She knew her words were sincere and wanted to believe that his were also, but acknowledged it was all pure poppycock. She had no idea where he called home or hung his hat.

Wondering and Waiting

The days and weeks that followed the Englishman's departure tested Phryné's emotional stability and physical stamina. Every minute not spent in restless sleep was nothing but torturous worry about Morris and Renée. The nights were alive with the unrelenting growl of American B-17's and exploding German flak.

Dientz arrived in back Boos nearly two weeks after Renée and Gitan had spirited Morris out of the root cellar. His mood

221

was depressed and weighed with the deaths of his parents during an American bombing raid in Karlsruhe, near Stuttgart, Germany. During an emotional farewell, he told Phryné that he and his 88 mm anti-aircraft unit were moving closer to the Rhine River to bolster defenses for The Fatherland. He vowed he would return to Boos after the war.

Exactly one week after Hauptmann Dientz left Boos for Germany, Renée-Ffion knocked once again on Phryné's front door. They had an emotional reunion that lasted halfway into the next morning and made a party of a jar of pickled beets, a loaf of stale sourdough and two bottles of German wine.

That night, Phryné got the bit of good news she awaited. The extraction of her British flyer in the early morning hours of July 27 went off without any snags. More importantly and true to his mysterious ways, Morris left Renée a cryptic note to pass on to his American nurse maid. It contained puzzling clues as to how she could find him in England after the war.

Dodging Bullets, Bombs and Bankers

For the first time in years, Phryné had a reason to hurry tomorrow and hold optimism for her future. She trusted that she held enough glue to put the pieces of her life back together. As frivolous and preposterous as building castles in the clouds and baking pies in the sky may be, the longing and promise that such dreams bring cannot be discounted. Even the most stubborn jackass can be led by a carrot dangled in front of its nose. Hope fuels a lot of traffic along life's road.

Eleven months after Morris climbed out of Phryné's root cellar, the Allies invaded Normandy on D-Day, June 6, 1944.

After another eleven months, on May 8, 1945, Germany signed the unconditional surrender that ended World War II.

In August, 1945, Phryné was once again able to access to her Swiss banking accounts and make travel plans.

9. MARGATE, KENT
(THE WAR HAS ENDED)
~ 1945 ~

Love Letters

6:30 PM, Friday, August 31:
Inn at The Flying Pig,
Corner of Market Street & Newby's Alley, Olde Towne

Desmond swallowed the last of his pint.

Phryné picked up her glass of sherry, swirled its contents and briefly studied the honey-colored liquid before relishing the last drops. With a nearly silent sigh of satisfaction, as if she had just completed an arduous task, she relaxed back into the tall-back wooden chair. She had finished her story.

A chance meeting inside a public house on a quaint back alley in an aging nineteenth century English seaside village offered Phryné Truffaut and Desmond Cuttleford an uncommon and precious opportunity: to become intimately familiar with a total stranger.

Over the three hours that the pair spent together, the customers inside The Flying Pig had watched Desmond and the lady traveler with strained curiosity as the unlikely pair privately conversed, smoked and nursed four rounds of drink. The crowd inside Olde Towne's most popular public house had grown steadily in size, as it usually did on Friday evenings. That evening, however, there was the added feature of the unexpected presence of an attractive female traveler who had been talking in low tones with one of the village's best known and respected seasoned citizens.

Although Phryné's words were fully heard by Desmond's ears alone, the whispered suppositions of the pub clientele became presumptions and were given credence regardless of fact or findings. Rumor and innuendo took wing like a flock of magpies inside the alehouse.

For whatever the reason, Roger, the innkeeper remained relatively mum about the woman's identity and purpose. Even when heartily egged on by loyal clientele, he managed to keep his lips tight. Perhaps he felt the mystery sold more frothy pints and spicy spirits. So far, The Pig's customers had only been able to glean two meager bits of information from the long-faced landlord: the newly arrived female guest was American citizen Phryné Truffaut who had been living in France for several years before the World War broke out. Those two simple facts were enough to feed the tapestry of conjectures, theories, and local legends that were being spun and woven within the walls and under the terra cotta roof of The Flying Pig.

Phryné felt relief. It felt good to tell her story. Once again, she had made her life an open book and her tale was repeated to a man she had just met. She had outlined her decisions and believed that her explanations had, at the least, made her choices clear to Desmond.

"That's it. That's my story, sir. That's my life wrapped up as an event-driven screenplay full of self-indulgence, bad decisions and twentieth-century pathos. It all boils down to a cheesy script for a tawdry, back-lot picture. A Hollywood B-Movie** starring a washed-up chorus girl.

"The whole story could be set in Paris, in a back-street cabaret or at the Moulin Rouge and maybe Edith Piaf** could play the lead and do the soundtrack.

"It would be perfect. Throughout my life, I have acted as a stand-in player for unscripted and uncredited roles; sometimes acting the self-righteous heroine, charitable humanitarian, rakish gold-digger or miscreant."

Desmond looked across the table and reached for her soul with his steely, blue-grey eyes. "Please, don't diminish your life, Phryné. I admire your bravery.

"What you have lived through, conquered and escaped is nothing to dinghy* away. From mobsters, heartbreak, and tragedy, to Hollywood, all across America, to New York City, to Paris, to London ... in these troubled, war-ravaged times of ours, you've traveled many miles on rough roads, rickety rails and indeed, across a stormy sea. Not many others can claim that and end up warming their toes and soul inside a fine public house in beautiful seaside Kent such as The Flying Pig!"

She allowed a brief, faint smile to cross her lips and raised her hand, signaling to Roger for yet another refill. "Fiddlesticks! My memories are not milestones. The miles I've traveled aren't a roadmap to be followed.

"When I left Paris for Boos, I vowed I wouldn't ever again allow a man to tempestuously steal away my heart. Then your English flyer fell into my life and scattered the dust every which way. All I have to show for my efforts are a few short, tattered, read and re-read love letters and silly poems written in what may as well be some kind of slipshod, unmetered, Shakespearian poetic code."

Desmond saw his chance to change the course and tone of the conversation. He pressed, "Well, you haven't yet detailed to me what the latest one says ... the one that inspired your journey here to Margate in the first place and brought you here inside this humble public house."

She nodded, brought out a small packet of folded letters and notes from her little black clutch. She untied the string around them, selected one off the top and placed it on the table.

225

Phryné watched as Desmond took possession of her personal correspondence and explained, "I received that note from Renée nearly three full weeks after my convalescing flyer had left for England ... about ten months before all Hell broke loose on D-day[**]. Those last days he spent in Boos fell through my fingers like the fine grains of white sand through an hour glass. I've felt cheated and tortured for more than two years and never found out if he made it safely back to England. He never shared any information with me about how I could get in touch with him. We were living a private fantasy in that root cellar in Boos and never gave tomorrow the time it deserves. And after the liberation last August ... almost exactly a year ago ... it took weeks for me to digest his last puzzling note and months to build up enough nerve to leave France and make the trip across the Channel and try to find him."

Phryné became silent.

Roger's backup barman appeared from nowhere and delivered their drinks. Desmond hurried his greeting to him, "Thank you for the refills, Jack, my man," and he temporarily claimed Phryné's private, tattered poem as his exclusive property. Slowly, methodically, Desmond began unfolding it, while keeping an eye on Jack, politely watching and waiting for him to turn and disappear back to the bar.

Secure and alone once again in the company of the enigmatic American beauty, Desmond's eyes raced across the worn, six-by-eight inch piece of paper.

For my shining star Phryne,

Please come and stay

The sky was dark as night the day
I fell broken into your world
Duty-bound I could not stay
A paradise reunion we did arow
Healed at last I must leave you now
Please come to me
Come near I beg
Come nearer please
Please come to stay
Passage for a pittance
From London a tuppence
To Dreamland on Victoria Station rail
Where all England comes to sail
Come to me I await
Come to me and Margate
At the pig that flies ask and see
Where the cottage lane may be
Please come and stay
Come live and love with me
at King's Mews number forty three.
So happy we shall be.

M.

227

Phryné spoke as Desmond finished reading, "It was easy enough to figure out about taking the train from London, once I found Victoria Station. The ticket agent explained that the Dreamland** funfair was here in Kent, but he couldn't help me with 'the pig that flies'. I had to wait until I got here in Margate for that."

Desmond formed a smile from ear to ear, and emphasized his excitement by wriggling the paper in his hand as he spoke, "I know that address. I believe I know the bloke who wrote this ... what's this fellow's name? Did you find him at King's Mews? Is this the flyer who you took under your wing beneath your country cottage in Boos?"

It was the most pressing string of questions that Desmond put to Phryné that afternoon or evening.

Although the slightest glimmer of hope appeared in her eyes, her reply was monotone and void of emotion, "The pilot's name was Morris. I knew him as Lieutenant Morris Sutcliffe, Royal Air Force. He flew Spitfire** escorts for American B-17 bombing missions."

Desmond perceived that her voice had signaled a blue, pensive melancholy. He hoped to encourage her, "That's his name! We all know him as *"Cliffy"* around here, but I'm guessing that you didn't talk to him or met him yet ... have you? You couldn't have. That's just daft*. He'll still be working at the ferry foundry until seven."

He checked his watch. "He works until seven. Just about now. And the pay envelopes are issued today, so any minute Cliffy will stop in for his pint before he turns to home for his evening tea and bickie*."

"Cliffy had some trouble when he came home from France, but you have a smashing reunion coming, Miss Phryné!"

She looked at Desmond with disbelief and said, "Oh sir, you must be mistaken. I learned my lesson in Paris years ago.

Men lie as a matter of convenience. Oh no, I don't think Morris is working. I saw him seated outside in a wheelchair in the front yard at 43 King's Mews. And I saw his wife and two small children, too."

Desmond leaned in toward her and quietly spoke, "Things are not always as they appear. You didn't see your Morris in his front garden. The man you saw in the wheelchair was Morris' older brother, David, with his wife Margaret and their children Dennis and Penelope. David was crippled by the Hun[*] at Dunkirk in the early days of the World War, during the Phony War[***]. They live on the ground floor of the cottage because of David's knackered back and legs. Cliffy lives in an upstairs flat that he sorted[*] for himself when he got back home.

"So, I believe you should keep one eye on the door. Like I said, you have a smashing reunion coming. Just like the one your Morris ... Cliffy ... promised in that letter I just read."

"La fin."

Phryné's story continues with:

Phryne Crossing

Also, you may enjoy:
Fables, Foibles & Follies

* THE WORDS *

(DE)	German
(EL)	Greek
(ES)	Spanish
(FR)	French
(IT)	Italian
(JI)	Yiddish (Jewish)
(UK)	United Kingdom (English)
aft	(nautical) at or toward the rear, or stern of a ship
à la votre	(FR) cheers, skål
aigu	(FR) accent mark { ´ }
allô	(FR) hello
aux femmes	(FR) women's
AWOL	(US slang) absent without leave
bandoneón	(ES) a concertina; type of accordion
bangers	(UK) sausages
Bastille Day	National Day in France, July 14th
beguine	music from island of French Martinique
bickie	(UK) biscuit, cookie
bijou	(FR) jewel, precious item
blitzkrieg	(DE) "lightning war"
blue-nosed	(US slang) snobbish
boche	(FR) German soldier (disparaging)
bollocks	(UK slang) nonsense, BS; literally = testicles
bonsoir	(FR) good evening
bourgeois	working-class
bowler	round, short-brimmed hat
brig	(nautical) ship's jail
C'est la fin des haricots	(FR) {literally} this is the end of the beans (this is the last straw)
cabeceó	(ES) invitation (nod)
calcified	arthritic; a condition of arthritis
can (in the)	(motion picture) (UK and US) finished
chèvre	(FR) a type of goat cheese
cinq-à-sept	(FR) liaison, affair (literally = 5-7 PM)
consist	the collection of rail cars in any train
cortina	(ES) a short song between tango dances

coup de gras	(FR) the last stroke, the deathblow
crème brûlée	(FR) baked cream desert with caramel crust
daft	(UK) foolish, absurd
dago	(disparaging) Italian or Spaniard
danseur	(FR) male ballet dancer
danseuse	(FR) female ballet dancer
Der Führer	(DE) the leader; ref: Adolf Hitler
digestif	(FR) alcoholic drink to aid digestion
dinghy	(UK) ignore, overlook
elevenses	(UK) midday snack or business lunch
entrée	(FR) main course of a meal
excusez moi	(FR) excuse me
faire la bise	(FR) [make the] kiss
faux pas	(FR) blunder, mistake
fleur-de-lis	(FR) floral heraldic symbol of France
fortnight	two weeks
French Huguenots	French reformed Protestants
fromage	(FR) cheese, usually soft
gams	(US slang) attractive legs, usually in stockings
gaucherie	(FR) insensitivity, crudeness
gumshoe	detective {after rubber-soled 'sneakers'}
Gypsy	nomadic people (can be taken as derogatory)
hawser	(nautical) heavy mooring rope
hallo	(FR) hello
hauptmann	(DE) captain
hoi polloi	(EL) the common people
hors d'oeuvre	(FR) appetizer
Hun	(UK) German, Germans (derogatory)
Il Duce	(IT) the leader
ingénue	(FR) an artless, innocent young woman
joie de vivre	(FR) joy of life
kilometer	1000 meters = .8 USA miles
le brunch	(FR) brunch (first use about 1915)
luftwaffe	(DE) airforce
(The) Maid of Orléans	Joan of Arc
magnifique	(FR) magnificent
maître d'hôtel	(FR) restaurant/hotel manager, head waiter
midship	(nautical) center of ship
mews	(UK) apartments built above stables or garages

mercurochrome	merbromin antiseptic
paper-mâché	a newspaper and flour paste used for crafting
paramour	lover
pasada	(ES) 'pass'; a tango move
pâté	(FR) paste, dough
pièce de résistance	(FR) outstanding item; showpiece
port(side)	(nautical) left side of ship, facing forward
postie	(UK) letter carrier
première classe	(FR) first class
profiterole	(FR) pastry similar to a creampuff
pub	(UK) bar, tavern (public house)
punter	(UK) guest, ordinary customer
Reichmark	German unit of currency; about 50¢ (1943)
relevé	(FR) ballet term, a turn on the ball of the foot
salida	(ES) walk, promenade (tango dance move)
scat	(US) improvised, sometimes nonsense, jazz lyrics {ex: skooby-di-do-wop-wop-di-do}
schmooze	(JI) idle conversation, chatter, gossip
Schwäbisch	German dialect used in and around Stuttgart
sherry	a Spanish wine fortified with brandy
shiksa	(JI) a non-Jewish woman (disparaging)
shilling	(UK) monetary= "old" shilling = 20 shillings per pound £ = 12 pence per shilling
solicitor	(UK) attorney
sorted	(UK) arranged, established
starboard	(nautical) right side of ship, facing forward
stern	(nautical) rear of ship
tanda	(ES) a group or set of tango songs
tea	(UK) hot beverage; also various meal-times
tête-à-tête	(FR) private, intimate conversation
toodles	(US slang) bye-bye
touché	(FR) acknowledging a telling remark (gotcha)
tripper, day tripper	(UK) tourist, vacationer
tuppence	(UK) two pence
unteroffizier	(DE) corporal
vis-à-vis [face-to-face] (sofa, love seat)	(FR) an *S* shape sofa so two people can face one another and carry on a conversation
(get) wiggle on	(US slang) hurry up

** THE END NOTES **

Phryné's namesake was that of a feisty Ancient Greek champion of women's rights born about 370 BC. She was a *hetaira:* an educated, beautiful and worldly courtesan. "Phryne" (Ancient Greek = Φρύνη = "toad") was the name commonly given to courtesans or prostitutes as a reference to their yellow complexion which was the result of olive oils used as body lotion. Today, the ancient muse would be considered a high-end escort or call girl.

In Classical Greece, Phryne was accused of blasphemy (punishable by death) and defended in court by Hyperides. Ancient accounts of the trial claim that after her legal counsel exposed Phryne's breasts in open court, the jury found it impossible to convict anyone with such beauty. She lived during the age of Alexander the Great and the wars between the city-states of Thespiae and Thebes. Because of her perfect form, Phryne was the model for several statues depicting love goddesses such as Philotes and Aphrodite.

Phryné Truffaut's middle name was Althea, also Greek, which means *one who heals.*

ONE ..... MARGATE, KENT

Zeppelins were lighter-than-air rigid airships named after Count Ferdinand von Zeppelin, a German, who developed the idea at the  beginning of the twentieth century and patented the design in 1895. During World War I, the German military used them for aerial surveillance on the battlefield and bombing raids over Britain. During the 1930s they were used for trans-Atlantic travel until the Hindenburg disaster on May 6, 1937 all but ended their use. Thirty-eight people died when the airship crashed and burned in New Jersey. Zeppelin LZ59 was over 700 feet in length, 80 feet wide and had a maximum speed of about 100 mph.

The Home Guard was a division of the English military from 1940 through 1945. It consisted of nearly two million volunteers who were either physically unable or too old to serve in the conscripted services. The original ranking system varied from that of the military, but in 1942 it came in line with that of the uniformed military.

Pint is the common volume of beer ordered and consumed in Great Britain's pubs. It needs to be noted that it's not the sixteen-ounce liquid measure used in the USA. The Brits use "Imperial" measure which is twenty ounces (four-ounces more!). Whose round is it?

Whist is a traditional English card game which is based on tricks and a trump suit. It was widely played from the eighteenth and early twentieth centuries, but like most parlor games has fallen by the wayside in modern life. The rules are simple, but experienced, devoted players develop complicated strategies and partnerships.

V-1 "Buzz-bomb" was the first guided missile, (actually a rocket-propelled flying bomb) and used by Nazi Germany from 1944-45. It had an explosive warhead of about 1800 pounds, a speed of 400 mph and a range of about 150 miles. The weapon was aimed at the target, launched and when it ran out of fuel, it would plummet to earth and explode. About 12,000 were launched: 9500 at south-eastern (Kent and Greater London) England and 2500 at Antwerp and other targets in Belgium.

Battle of Somme lasted from May 1 until November 18, 1916. Well over one million men were killed or wounded on the battlefields near the Upper Somme River in northern France.

Flu Pandemic of 1918 killed a quarter of a million people in Britain and fifty million worldwide. It was especially tragic for young teenage victims to the age of twenty-five, who could appear to be healthy in the morning and dead by nightfall.

Toad-in-the-hole, shepherds' pie, bangers and mash are traditional English suppers. They are: sausages baked into a biscuit batter, pot-pies of ground beef or lamb with a top layer of baked mash potatoes, or sausages and mashed potatoes served with mushy (mashed) peas.

The French Line (Compagnie Générale Transatlantique) was a French shipping company formed in 1855 by brothers Issac and Émile Péreire and commissioned by the French government to transport mail to the Americas. The company grew quickly and expanded into transatlantic passenger service. During the American years of Prohibition, the company catered to tourists seeking luxurious travel to and from Europe with entertainment, superb service, gourmet meals and the free flow of alcoholic beverages.

Pathé Frères Productions (Pathé Brothers) was founded in 1896 and remains in business today as Pathé.

In the early twentieth century, the company was a leading pioneer in the film, movie camera and phonograph industry with such innovations as hand-colored film, newsreels, and serial shorts. *The Perils of Pauline* created villains of pirates and Native Americans while stereotyping helpless young women as damsels in distress. The company opened its own movie theaters and by 1910 had a virtual monopoly throughout Europe.

In 1896, the Vitascope Theater, 305 Main Street, Buffalo, New York became the first to show Pathé films, and arguably became the first motion picture house in the United States.

Bromo Seltzer was first introduced about 1890. In its earliest form it was effervescent granules that dissolved in water. It contained bromide tranquilizers and the analgesic acetanilide, which is now considered dangerous. It was often used as a cure for hangovers and the company used poetic verse in its advertising such as: *With nerves unstrung and heads that ache, wise women Bromo Seltzer take.* The product was manufactured in downtown Baltimore, Maryland and sold in cobalt blue bottles. The Bromo-Seltzer tower with its iconic clock still stands at 21 South Eutaw Street, Baltimore.

The Hays Code was Hollywood's self-imposed censure guidelines from 1930 until 1954. The Hays Code was named after Presbyterian elder Will Hays, who helped develop the standards. After many the release of many risqué films, sensational scandals and the rape and murder trial of Roscoe 'Fatty' Arbuckle following the death of Hollywood sweetheart Virginia Rappe in 1921, the public demanded higher standards. Although it was not enforced until 1934, it remained the production guideline until the late 1950s. Due to the introduction of television, the code weakened and became ineffective. In 1968, it was replaced by the Motion Picture Association of America's movie and television rating system (G, PG, R, X).

 Clapper board (or slate board) is the little blackboard that the production crews snaps down at the beginning or ending of a scene or take. It is used to coordinate the editing of clips and the synchronization of sound to the film.

Café Trocadero opened in 1934 on Sunset Strip, in free- wheeling Hollywood, outside the city limits of Los Angeles. The club immediately became the place to be and be seen in Hollywood. Hollywood's A-list flocked to the night spot. Billy Wilkerson named his new club after the Trocadero Plaza at the Eiffel Tower in Paris, thus giving Sunset Strip an instant European flair. The restaurant and night club was advertised as 'the only high-class restaurant in Hollywood' and promoted dinners for one dollar at the height of the Depression.

The Garden of Alla was built in 1913 as the private residence of real estate mogul William H. Hay and was soon leased by silent screen star and Russian actress, Alla Nazimova. After her career began to slide, she built 25 rental units on the property. She sold it in 1928 and returned to the Broadway stage. The new owners added the "h" to Alla and the upscale hotel began to gain notoriety. A few of the famous residents of the units were F. Scott Fitzgerald, Greta Garbo, Errol Flynn, Artie Shaw, Benny Goodman, Marlene Dietrich, Groucho Marx, Lauren Bacall and Ronald Regan. It was demolished in 1959.

Phryné's September, 1935 divorce settlement of $2000 cash would be $36,000 in 2017 dollars. Her $20 monthly alimony equals $360, and the $50 stock debenture *was* worth $900 at the time of issue, but Paramount filed for bankruptcy later in 1935 and the debenture became worthless.

American Austin made small, two-seat, sporty automobiles under license from the Austin Motor Company of England from 1929 until 1934. Quick on the take-off and efficient with gasoline, the 747cc, 45cu, 40 hp, 4 cylinder, in-line engine hummed along at 50 mph and sold for $450 in 1934. The company went bankrupt in 1935 but later designed and built the first Jeep that proved so versatile for the US Military.

Hollywood Reporter is the oldest entertainment trade publication in the US. It was founded in 1930 by William (Billy) Wilkerson as a daily newspaper that was issued 6 days a week until 1940 when it reverted to Monday thru Friday. For more than fifty years its main officers were located on Sunset Boulevard in Hollywood. In its heyday, the Reporter sent reporters all over the world to cover film and its stars.

Technicolor was the most widely used process for color film from 1922 until 1952. The perfected process filmed on three separate strips of black-and-white film, each of them recording a different color of the spectrum. After Eastman Kodak and Agfa developed color film in the mid 1930s, the use of Technicolor film cameras rapidly faded. However, the process is still highly used in restoration and archival work.

***Triumph of the Will* (Triumph des Willens)** is a 1935 German propaganda film financed by the National Socialist Party (Nazi) and directed, produced, edited, and co-written by Leni (Helene) Riefenstahl. She alone edited 61 hours of footage down to 2 hours for the final film. *Triumph* and her 1938 film *Olympia* received worldwide acclaim and several awards in Germany, USA, Sweden, Austria, Italy and France. Both films are considered some of the best propaganda films ever made. Riefenstahl used many innovative techniques including boom cameras, sweeping, panoramic scenes of massive crowds and moving scenes from aircraft and locomotives. Her work was a favorite of Hitler and it was rumored that the two were romantically involved. Near the end of her life, she proclaimed that *"(meeting Hitler) was the biggest catastrophe of my life. Until the day I die people will keep saying, 'Leni is a Nazi'."*

Until her death in 2003, she denied any knowledge of Nazi atrocities. At age 60, she began a relationship with a cameraman 40 years her junior. They filmed and photographed native peoples in Africa, the 1972 and 1976 Olympic games, Mick and Bianca Jagger, and Siegfried and Roy among many others. They remained together until her death at age 101, in Pöcking, Germany.

The German Chamber of Film *(Reichsfilmkammer)* was the Nazi agency for regulation of the film industry. Adolf Hitler recognized the propaganda potential in film long before he came to power. In his book *Mein Kampf* (1925) he declared: "One must also remember that of itself the multitude is mentally inert ... (in a short) time, at one stroke I might say, people will understand a pictorial presentation of something which it would take them a long and laborious effort of reading to understand."

Place de la Révolution is a moat-encircled park on the eastern end of Champs-Elysées. At 20 acres, it is the largest public square in Paris, France. During the French Revolution of 1789, the new government erected a massive guillotine in the square. King Louis XVI, Queen Marie Antoinette, Princess Élisabeth, Charlotte Corday, Madame du Barry, Georges Danton, Camille Desmoulins, Antoine Lavoisier, and Maximilien Robespierre were among those executed there. The last *public* beheading by guillotine was held in 1939, but the last execution was performed on September 10, 1977 at a prison in Marseille, France. The guillotine blade alone weighed 40 kilograms (88 pounds).

Chateau Marmont is an upscale hotel-restaurant on the Sunset Strip in Hollywood. Built in 1929, it replicates a Gothic chateau on the Loire River in France, has nine Spanish-style cabins or cottages on the property, and has been home to many of Hollywood's elite. Not quite the same as the neighboring Garden of Allah, the property served mainly as a residence hotel. There is still an upscale restaurant at the hotel.

Jubilee is a musical comedy written by Moss Hart with words and music by Cole Porter. It opened on October 12, 1935 at the Imperial Theater. It was well received, critically acclaimed and the songs *Just One of Those Things* and *Begin the Beguine* became popular music hits. It has been taunted as one of the great theatrical events of the 1930s.

Gaulois Bleu (Gaul Blue) is a brand of French cigarette that was linked to patriotism during both World Wars. Advertising campaigns of the unfiltered cigarette featured images of soldiers fighting in the trenches or facing oncoming tanks. The brand was preferred by the French resistance fighters of World War II.

THREE ..... "LOS ANGELES LIMITED"

The Los Angeles Limited was a premier named train for the Union Pacific Railroad and became their flagship overland Pullman service starting in 1905. A typical steam consist was 10

Pullman sleepers, a dining car, baggage car and observation-lounge car. Steam power, until 1936 was usually a (**4-8-2**) (4 lead, 8 drivers, 2 rear wheels) coal-fired, Mountain locomotive. In 1936, Union Pacific modernized the fleet and put streamlined diesels into service with lightweight passenger cars, reducing the trip time to Chicago to 36 hours each way.

The Broadway Limited was an elite named train of the Pennsylvania Railroad from 1912 until 1995. For many years, it ran in direct competition with New York Central's *20th Century Limited.* In 1935, the travel time was eighteen hours over the rails from New York City to Chicago. The train's name had nothing to do with its destination, but rather the right-of-way to four sets of railroad

tracks (the *broad way*) that the Pennsylvania Railroad owned along much of the route. In 1905, the train recorded the amazing speed of 127 mph. For many years, the Broadway Limited used Pullman sleepers with no coach service. In its heyday, it was an integral part of coast-to-coast travel for Hollywood and its social trendsetters.

The Fates can refer to any group of three or more goddesses in various cultures of European paganism and polytheism (the worship of many gods or goddesses). They were often depicted weaving a tapestry that dictated the fortunes of men.

Checker manufactured taxicabs from 1917 until 1982 in Kalamazoo, Michigan. Sturdy and reliable, the units became best known for the checkerboard pattern along the sides. In the mid '30s, Checker Cab became the first company to hire African-Americans and pick them up as customers. The Checker and Yellow Cab Companies of New York City used Checker vehicles almost exclusively.

Pennsylvania Station was the historic hub of the Pennsylvania

Railroad and considered an architectural master-piece of the Beaus-Arts style. It was put into service in 1910 and demolished in 1963 to make room for Madison Square Garden. It covered two complete blocks between 7th and 8th Avenue and 31st to 33rd Streets, blanketing eight acres. Massive arched glass ceilings and two cavernous concourses made it one of New York City's landmarks for decades.

Ronson began as a metal-plating and art metal works firm in 1897. In the 1910's the company began to expand into the automobile industry and made hood ornaments for the top brands. In the 1920's the Aronson Company developed the Ronson De-light pocket lighter with the slogan *one click and it's lit; release and it's out"*. The company also marketed a cigarette case--lighter combination, with the lighter on top and

room for 10 cigarettes. In the 30's production expanded to *touch-tip* table lighters in a modern Art Deco style which became wildly popular.

Technicolor was the most widely used process for color film from 1922 until 1952. The perfected process filmed on three separate strips of black-and-white film, each of them recording a different color of the spectrum. After Eastman Kodak and Agfa developed color film in the mid 1930s, the use of Technicolor film cameras rapidly faded. However, the process is still frequently used in restoration and archival work.

Saks was incorporated in New York in 1902 and opened its Fifth Avenue location in 1924. The multi-billion dollar company now has retail outlets across the world from Bahrain to Mexico City.

Sardi's restaurant first opened in 1927 on West 44th Street, New York. It serves a continental menu and is renowned for the caricature portraits of show business, film and theatrical personalities that adorn its walls.

FOUR ..... "SS NORMANDIE"

SS Normandie *(The Ship of Light)* was an ocean liner laid down in 1931 for the French Line. Her maiden voyage was on May 29, 1935 from Le Havre, France to New York. She was rivaled by the British RMS Queen Mary, but held the speed record for transatlantic travel at 4 days, 3 hours and 14 minutes. Her top speed was about 32 knots (36 mph). The ship made 139 round trips from France to New York until the onset of World War II. In February 1942, while moored at Pier 88 in New York harbor, the Normandie was capsized and destroyed by fire. It was rumored that organized crime (Lucky Luciano) was to blame.

When the ship entered service in 1935, she was the largest (1029 ft long, 184 ft tall) and fastest passenger ship on the sea. The luxury liner immediately became the preferred transoceanic travel mode for the social, political and entertainment elite. Some of her famous passengers were: Ernest Hemmingway, Marlene Dietrich, Cary Grant, Gloria Vanderbilt, Walt Disney, Salvador Dali, Joseph P. and John F. Kennedy, Douglas Fairbanks, Jr.,

 James Stewart, Bing Crosby, the von Trapp Family Singers and of course, Phryné Truffaut. As of today, the ship remains the most powerful steam turbine, electric powered ship ever built. The French Line built the ship for exclusive first (848) and second class (670) passage, with only minimum third class (454) availability. The opulent décor was the modern glass, bronze

and stainless steel of the Art Deco era. The glass-walled and chandelier-filled dining room of the Normandie was the largest afloat and earned the liner the title *Ship of Light*. At over 300 feet long, 80 feet wide and 30 feet high, the First Class Dining Salon reflected more light and measured out larger than the Hall of Mirrors at King Louis' XIV Palace at Versailles. Dinner was served at 8 PM by a staff of over one hundred to all the First Class passengers at once, seated at one-hundred-fifty tables.

Considering 80+ years of inflation, Phryné's $335 one-way, 1935 transatlantic ticket would be equivalent to $6035 in 2017.

The Empire State Building became the world's tallest building at 1,250 feet (102 stories) when it was completed in April, 1931. In 1970, it was surpassed by the World Trade Center's *North Tower*. More than 5,000 men were employed for its construction.

Kepi hats (French = *képi*) are round, flat-top hats with a visor that are associated with French police, military and the French Foreign Legion. In the United States, both sides of the War Between the States used them as part of their uniform. They can be likened to a short, squatty version of the stove-pipe hat.

Paris-Soir was the most widely circulated paper in Europe prior to World War II. It was printed from 1923-1944. During the war, it was published under German control and was used to spread Nazi propaganda. When France was liberated in August, 1944, the entire editorial staff was arrested by the FFI, the Free French resistance forces.

Luminal was the brand name of a Phenobarbital marketed by Bayer in the early twentieth century. Early barbiturates such as *Veronal* and *Barbital* were first marketed for use as a sleeping aid, but by the mid-30s, the misuse of these new prescription drugs became widespread. Popularity and addiction created a greater demand that brought stronger, highly addictive Phenobarbitals such as **Secobarbital** (1934) to the market.

Je suis partout (I am everywhere) was a right-wing, nationalist newspaper in France from 1930 until 1944. It was sympathetic to German interests prior to World War II and became a propaganda tool for the Nazis during the War. It was disbanded when the Germans were pushed out of France in 1944.

Grauman's Chinese Theatre opened in Hollywood in May 1927 when it premiered Cecil B. DeMille's film *The King of Kings.* The theatre quickly became world famous for its star-studded, red-carpet premiers and presentations. Grauman's concrete sidewalks and entryways play home to the foot and hand prints of hundreds of stars.

Romani Gypsy Jazz (also Gypsy Swing, Jazz Manouche or Hot Club Jazz) emerged in 1930s Paris. It was stylized by guitarist Django Reinhardt and violinist Stephane Grappelli. Contrary to common belief, Romani gypsies did not originate from Romania. Recent scientific study has revealed that the Romani (Roma) gypsies are a clan of iterant people with DNA roots back to Northern India. Mass migrations from the Indian subcontinent occurred from 500 – 1000 AD. Over the centuries, large clans were formed and spread throughout the world. Nearly every nation on Earth is home to a large Gypsy population.

Gold Diggers of 1933 was a pre-code Hollywood musical presented by Warner Brothers. It was released in several edited versions to side-step censorship rules in the US and Europe. Musical production numbers included thinly veiled nudity termed "lewd and lyrical". One critic proclaimed that star Joan Blondell's performance was "cheap and vulgar".

Camay is a brand of soap first made and marketed by Proctor and Gamble in 1926. The company was established in 1837, in Cincinnati, Ohio by immigrant British candlemaker William Proctor and Irish soapmaker James Gamble and gradually became an international soap, food, pharmaceutical and manufacturing conglomerate. Camay was touted as *the soap for beautiful women, the white, pure soap for women; and the soap for a beautiful complexion at any age.* The brand has been sold to the Dutch firm, Unilever and is no longer produced or distributed in the US. The bar soap had a distinctive, soft, alluring scent that has driven its loyal American customers to purchase European-produced product from the internet.

Gillette safety razors and blades were developed by American inventor King Camp Gillette. In 331 BC it was a Greek (Alexander the Great) who ordered his legions to shave their beards and a mustached American (Gillette) who perfected the safety razor two thousand years later in 1901. Following World War I, American women began trimming body hair. Some have suggested that this uptick in feminine  personal grooming was due to returning American soldiers. French prostitutes were known to shave their legs and other intimate areas, prompting Gillette to develop the *Gillette Décolleté Milady* compact shaver for women. It was first marketed at the end of the Great War. Subtle magazine and newspaper advertising convinced American women that smooth legs were in fashion and shaving their armpits would help keep them dryer and odor-free.

Lalique glass was created by French *art nouveau* jeweler and sculptor René Lalique. The style was widely copied and became the standard for *art deco* glass during the first half of the twentieth century. It remains highly collectable.

Foie gras is an indulgent food product made from the liver of a duck or goose. The process became regulated in the later part of the twentieth century, and French law states that the bird may only be force-fed corn through a feeding tube. The process (*gavage)* fattens the liver up to ten times its normal size and has been the source of much debate between animal rights activists and food connoisseurs. Regardless, the entrée remains a popular delicacy in French cuisine. French law (the Rural Code) states "Foie gras belongs in the protected cultural and gastronomical heritage of France."

Evian mineral water has been bottled in France since 1908. It is sourced from the French Alps in Évian-les-Bains, on the south shore of Lake Geneva.

French West Africa was a union of eight French colonies. Upper Volta gained its independence from France in 1960 and was renamed Burkina Faso in 1984. The country is land-locked, has no access to the sea, and is primarily Muslim.

Nautical miles are used to measure distance in marine and aviation navigation. It is defined as one-sixtieth of one degree of latitude, or 1852 meters or 1.15 miles.

Fougère Royale (Royal Fern) is a woodsy fragrance for men created by Houbigant Parfum of France and widely marketed in Europe since 1900. Although it was available in the US, American men were reluctant to use colognes until the later half of the century.

Vine cuttings ensure consistency in the propagation of wine grapes. Vines are productive from 10 to 30 years, making the propagation of plants an essential part of the winery business. Varieties are often area and climate based, and therefore unique. Plants from seeds are not reliably worthy because of the inconsistency of pollination and the uncontrollability of genetic lineage.

Catgut string is preferred by many violinists because of the sound quality. Despite its name, it is not made from felines, but rather the intestines of cattle, mules, sheep or horses and usually wrapped in copper or silver wire for strength. Horse hair is used for the violin bows.

Rive Gauche (Left Bank) is the southern bank of the river Seine flowing through Paris. It was the epicenter of Europe's twentieth century counter-culture.

d'Artagnan is a romanticized, fictional swordsman created by French author Alexandre Dumas in his historical adventure novel "The Three Musketeers" (*Les Trois Mousquetaires*).

Johnny Weissmuller was a five-gold-medal Olympic athlete and film star. He is best remembered for his roles in the *Tarzan of the Jungle* movies. Many others have played the part, but Weissmuller is the best known. He made Hollywood studios millions for his twelve *Tarzan* and thirteen *Jungle Jim* films. His "Tarzan yell" is world famous. He was married to the "Mexican Spitfire", Lupe Vélez, from 1933 – 39.

Tango is a style of music and dance that originated about 1880 in Buenos Aires, Argentina and Montevideo, Uruguay. European, Caribbean and African cultures contributed to its evolution. The dance became popular in the early 1900's in Europe and the USA. Today there are several genres of tango, each with a specific and exacting set of rules.

Tanda is a set of three or four Argentine tango songs. It is customary to dance the entire tanda with one partner and is considered an insult otherwise. The tanda is usually ended with a short musical interlude of about sixty seconds or less of non-tango music called a cortina[*]. It is considered especially rude to dance during the cortina.

Carlos Gardel was an Argentine singer, composer and actor, and was one of the most influential figures in tango. He suffered an early death in June, 1935 in a plane crash.

Corte de pierna abierto (Open leg finish) is a dramatic last move in a tango. The following partner ends with open legs, oftentimes with one wrapped high around the lead dancer.

Two beds were standard in the First Class staterooms of the ocean liner Normandie. The larger would compare to a King and the smaller was a bit wider than a Twin.

Godthåb was founded in 1729. With a population of 18,000, it is the largest city as well as the capital of the Danish territory of Greenland. Translated into Danish, the name Godthåb means "good hope". About 80% of Greenland's total population of 58,000 are native Inuit.

Charlie Chan was created as a fictional detective in the 1925 crime novel, *The House without a Key* by Earl Biggers. Beginning in 1926, the brainy character became central in motion pictures and since then, nearly fifty have been produced around the world. The Chinese detective was also featured in several radio shows and comics. The lead role in the earliest popular Hollywood films was played by Swedish actor Warner Oland in yellow-face makeup for Fox film. Pathé was the first to produce a silent film in 1927 and was followed by a second silent release by Universal in 1928. Both silent films are considered lost. Fox Film, Monogram and 20th Century Fox released more that three dozen movies from 1935 until 1981.

Ball lightning is rare and unexplained, but proven as a dangerous, natural phenomenon that exhibits unpredictable form and behavior that can occur with or without an accompanying thunderstorm. Until the 1960's it was considered by most scientists to be unproven conjecture and a folk tale handed down by wild stories. Like other unexplained oddities, stories of the supernatural and spiritual abound. The first written account of ball lightning was recorded in England during a thunderstorm in 1638 and was followed by countless other documented sightings over the centuries. Because it has been successfully reproduced in laboratory conditions on more than one occasion, it is now considered very rare, but existing. Scientific data is scarce due to its sporadic occurrences. Although ball lightning has been produced in the laboratory, its properties have not been defined. The first photographic evidence of ball lightning was recorded by high-speed video in 2014. Modern natural sightings have been affirmed by police, fire departments, and airline pilots. Witnesses often report the odor of burning sulfur or strong agricultural fertilizer.

Le Havre Prison (La maison d'arrêt du Havre) was in use for one hundred and fifty years from 1860 until it was finally razed in 2010 for urban development. From 2009-2012, the French prison system underwent a cultural and institutional Renaissance and closed many suffering facilities that were built in the nineteenth century and still in use. Several cities were involved, including Le Havre, Toulouse, Lyon, Alençon and Rennes.

The prison in Le Havre underwent only minimal renovation or architectural changes until after World War II, when repairs were necessitated by damage suffered to several of the buildings from Allied bombs. For centuries, the French prison system suffered from unsanitary conditions that bred sickness and disease. There were no sanitary sewer or shower facilities available at Le Havre prison until after World War II. Earlier, bathing availability was limited to one tub per one hundred or oftentimes, more inmates. Although the prisoners were segregated by sex, hardened convicts and first-time offenders were housed together in the communal dormitories.

Renseignements Généraux (RG) was the intelligence gathering arm of the French National Police that was formed in 1907. In the 1930's it became active in the fight against the militant fascist groups that were forming across France, Spain and Italy that threatened national security. The division was dissolved when Germany invaded France in 1940. After World War II, it was reborn and took on the role it had in the 1930s; most notably that of fighting decolonization terrorist forces in Africa and Indo-China.

Popular Front of Catalonia was one of six revolutionary combatants that were part of the Republican Coalition during the Spanish Civil War of 1936-1939. Socialist, Communist, and anarchist groups formed a fragile alliance to fight against the Nationalists which consisted of monarchists, Roman Catholic Carlists and Spanish fascists. A simple characterization would explain the conflict as the clash of revolutionary forces of the far-left and far-right. With the support of Italy's Mussolini, Germany's Hitler and Portugal's Salazar, General Francisco Franco's fascist party was the victor.

Citroën Traction Avant was a luxury sedan manufactured by  French automobile company Citroën from 1934 to 1957. It earned automotive innovation awards for its front-wheel drive, welded unibody construction and four-wheel independent suspension. In France, the popular car was called "Queen of the Road".

SIX ..... BOULOGNE~BILLANCOURT, PARIS

Associated Actors and Artistes of America (4As) was founded in 1919 as one of the first trade unions to represent performing artists in the United States. In 2012, the 4As and the Screen Actors Guild merged with American Federation of Television and Radio Artists.

Pigalle is the high-stepping, dancing, can-can, night-club, theatre and red-light district of Paris, France, located within two miles of the Eiffel Tower and Arch of Triumph. It was named after sculptor Jean-Baptiste Pigalle, but gained the moniker of *'pig alley'* because of its adult-oriented night life. The world-renown cabaret Moulin Rouge is within the Pigalle district.

Fred Astaire was an American choreographer, dancer and actor. At age seven, he began dancing in vaudeville shows with his sister Adele, and broke onto Broadway at age eighteen. His first films were in 1933: *Dancing Lady* with Joan Crawford and *Flying down to Rio* with Ginger Rogers.

Celluloid was first created from cellulose fibers (found in trees and plants) as *Parkesine* (after its inventor Alexander Parkes) in 1856, and is considered to be the first thermoplastic. Its main use was in the manufacture of movie and camera film. Celluloid film was highly flammable and was replaced in the 1950s by acetate safety film. It is no longer widely used, but can be found today as table tennis (ping pong) balls.

Moulin Rouge is a cabaret in Paris that was first opened in 1889 and was the birthplace of the provocative can-can. The dance was created by the women who worked under its roof and grew to become the trade-mark of cabaret entertainment around the world. Today, the Moulin Rouge is located at 82 Boulevard de Clichy, and is one of the most popular tourist attractions in France.

Gitanes (Gypsy Woman) is an unfiltered French cigarette formulated with strong, 'brown', fire-dried tobacco with a heavy, distinctive odor. The packet features a tambourine-playing, dancing female. The brand was launched in 1910.

Franc (F) was the unit of currency used in France until 2002 when it was replaced by the Euro (€) of the European Union (EU). In 1936, Phryné's French franc was worth about four US cents (4¢).

Jean Sablon was a French singer and actor. He began his career as a cabaret singer in Paris at age 17. By the late 1930s, he had won numerous awards, had left the cabaret circuit of Paris and worked on Broadway with Cole Porter and George Gershwin. He remained in the US until the end of World War II.

Mistresses have been known across all civilizations and cultures since the written record began. *Kept women* have been a part of human society since the Creation. In the Book of Genesis, the word "womenservants" is used.

Through the ages, mistresses have had varying levels of social standing, but always rose above that of prostitutes. In some of the royal circles of Europe, they were held in high esteem and in fact, venerated and given positions of power. French royalty were by far the most prolific keepers of women. Charlemagne = 8, Louis XIV = 17, Louis XV = 16, Napoleon = 1, and the winner is: Henry IV = 32! The French royalty even had a title for the "official mistress": *maîtresse en titre.*

The best-known contemporary mistress may be the Duchess of Cornwall, Camilla Parker Bowles, now married to Prince Charles, heir apparent of the British throne, who asked, *"Do you seriously expect me to be the first Prince of Wales in history not to have a mistress?"*

The late Sir James Goldsmith Charles, once a member of the European Parliament, married his mistress, Lady Annabel Goldsmith, after the death of his second wife. He said to his peers, *"When you marry your mistress, you create a job vacancy".*

French author Alexandre Dumas (*The Count of Monte Cristo, The Three Musketeers*) claimed: *"The chains of marriage are so heavy that it takes two to bear them, sometimes three."*

Wordslinger Edward R. Hackemer expounded, *"Mistress Husbandry may have all the qualifications to be the quintessential oxymoron, but through the ages it has endured as a cultural anomaly."*

(Due to a lack of financial resources and to preserve domestic tranquility, this author has no further opinion on the topic.)

Maxim's de Paris was founded in 1893 as a bistro. The owners filled the place with beautiful women to attract customers. In 1913, French film maker Jean Cocteau wrote, "It was an accumulation of velvet, lace, ribbons, diamonds and what all else I couldn't describe. To undress one of these women is like an outing that calls for three weeks' advance notice, it's like moving house." Maxim's has grown in popularity and stature since. Today, it is not only one of the largest tourist attractions in Paris, the restaurant handles its own branded merchandise and has expanded over the globe with restaurants in seven other countries. The restaurant was a stepping stone for young chef Wolfgang Puck.

Tinker Bell is a fictional fairy created by J.M.Barrie in his 1904 play *Peter Pan.* Norwegian ice-skater Sonja Henie (Olympic gold medalist in 1928, 32 & 36) had a signature *'Tinker Bell tip-toe walk'*.

Radio Cité (Radio LL) was a pioneering radio station in Paris from March 1926 until 1935 when it became Radio Cité broadcasting at 1095 kHz. From 1920 until the television age of the 1950s, radio was akin to today's internet, and was the cutting edge of news and information for millions. All French radio was either private or public until June of 1940 when the German occupation began broadcast control. After World War II, all French radio became nationalized. It wasn't until 1981, under President François Mitterrand, that private enterprise could once again own some time on the air.

SEVEN ..... POISSY, ÎLE~DE~FRANCE

The French Government essentially split into two entities when the Germans invaded France in June of 1940. The official government moved to Vichy, in southern France and became a puppet regime of the Nazi Third Reich. Some military personnel and government officials fled to England, where they established a government in exile and commanded the Free French resistance movement under the direction of General Charles de Gaulle.

Reich Chamber of Film (Reichsfilmkammer) was controlled by the German Reich and prohibited Jews and undesirable foreigners to be part of the German film industry or cinema distribution. It was answerable to Joseph Goebbels and the Propaganda Ministry.

Waffen SS was the armed military division of the SS (Schutzstaffel). It was formed in 1925 and was commanded by Heinrich Himmler from 1929 until the defeat and collapse of the Nazi Third Reich in April of 1945. During World War II, the SS conducted brutal security and surveillance enforcement and spread terror throughout Germany and German occupied Europe. Thousands of prominent leadership and rank-and-file members of the SS were tried and convicted of war crimes at the Nuremberg Tribunals in late 1945, and were sentenced to death or life imprisonment.

251

Ufa is the German film production company formed in 1917 as *Universum-Film Aktiengesellschaft (Ufa)*. During World War II, Ufa was the largest producer and distributor of propaganda films in the *Reichsfilmkammer* (German Film Institute). Today it is known as Ufa, or Universum Film AG.

Junkers JU-87 (Stuka) was a gull-winged, dive-bomber aircraft used by the German Luftwaffe from 1936 until the end of World War II in 1945. The Stuka made its combat debut in 1937 during the Spanish Civil War. The aircraft was instrumental in the destruction of Guernica in northern Spain. About 6500 units were manufactured through 1944.

Looney Tunes was founded in 1933 as an animated film production company to directly compete with Walt Disney. Over the decades, it gained popularity with its main characters Porky Pig, Daffy Duck, Bugs Bunny and Elmer Fudd.

Bombing of Paris on March 3, 1942 was conducted by the British Royal Air Force. 223 aircraft bombed targets in and around Boulogne-Billancourt and Poissy on a night raid that lasted nearly two hours. About 450 tons of bombs were dropped. A *Renault* factory was the target, but over 600 civilians lost their lives. One British aircraft did not return to base: a Wellington long-range bomber with a crew of six.

Horch was an automobile manufacturing company founded in 1910 by August Horch of Cologne, Germany. From its humble beginnings, *Horch Motorwagenwerke* grew into the *Audi* brand we know today.

EIGHT ..... BOOS, ROUEN, NORMANDY

Bright Eyes is a 1934 Fox Film starring Shirley Temple. The film was released on December 28, 1934 and featured the song *On the Good Ship Lollipop*. Shirley was under contract to Fox Film for $1000 a week, and her mother for $250. Both were fabulously high sums in 1934. In February 1935, Shirley Temple was awarded the first ever "Juvenile Oscar" for her performance.

Boeing B-17 Flying Fortress was a four engine heavy bomber developed for the United States Army Air Corps. About thirteen thousand units were produced from 1936 until 1945. The plane performed extensive duty in the European theatre of World War II  and was the work horse of the US Army Air Corps. Most missions were flown from airfields in England with fighter escorts provided either by the British Royal Air Force or American fighter aircraft.

Rouen is a city in Normandy, France with a rich history dating back to the Middle Ages. The city is a historical treasure with a cathedral that is as magnificent as Paris' Notre Dame. Inside the Rouen Cathedral is a tomb that holds the heart of King Richard the Lionhearted (1157-1199), King of England and Duke of Normandy. Also within the city is *Place du Vieux Marché,* where Joan of Arc was burned at the stake on May 30, 1432. There is a small, modern Catholic church at the site. During World War II, about 45% of the city was laid waste.

Low Countries is a term referring to the Benelux countries of Belgium, The Netherlands and Luxembourg.

De Havilland Hornet Moth was a single-engine  biplane used by the RAF during World War II as a trainer and utility, multi-purposed transport. About thirty are still flying today.

Lucky Strike was founded as a brand of chewing tobacco in 1871. By 1905 it evolved into cigarettes. The brand was the largest selling cigarette ('Luckies') in the US during the 1930s. Packaging was originally green, with a red circle and the name in black. In 1942, the company changed the pack to white with a red circle and the brand name in black. An advertising campaign *Lucky Strike has gone to war* claimed that the company made the change to save copper (in green ink) for the war effort.

NINE ..... MARGATE, KENT

B-Movie is a low-budget film originally produced during the Golden Age of Hollywood to fill the lower half of a double-feature for theaters.

Edith Piaf was a French singer, cabaret act and film actress who became one of France's most widely known and admired talents. Her music oftentimes reflected her own personal struggles with lost love and sorrow.

D-day was the culmination of *Operation Neptune,* the invasion of Normandy, France by the Allied forces of WWII on June 6, 1944. It was the largest seaborne attack ever on land forces and led to the liberation of France, Europe and the defeat of the Nazi Third Reich of Adolf Hitler.

Spitfire was a single-engine fighter plane manufactured in Great 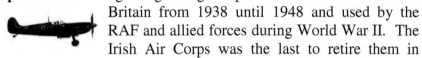 Britain from 1938 until 1948 and used by the RAF and allied forces during World War II. The Irish Air Corps was the last to retire them in 1961. The versatile fighter had the highest production of any British aircraft. Of more than 20,000 units built in Birmingham, West Midlands, England, about 50 are still flying.

Dreamland is a seaside funfair and tourist destination that opened in 1880 in Margate, Kent and is still popular today, despite several receiverships, transfers of title and hard economic times. It was home to the Scenic Railway rollercoaster and many "sea-land" amusement rides.

*** THE ODD STUFF ***

The White Cliffs of Dover are imposing cliffs of chalk on the southeastern coast of Kent, facing the English Channel. Written by Walter Kent and Nat Burton, the song was released by British songstress Vera Lynn in 1942. Although the lyrics taunt "there'll be Blue Birds over the White Cliffs of Dover", there are no "blue birds" native to Great Britain. It is supposed that the "birds" to which the song refers are the blue uniforms of British RAF flyers.

Flying Pig (sometimes used as *when pigs fly*) is a hyperbole taken to extreme lengths as to indicate the impossible. The saying transcends time and cultures over the world. British author Lewis Carroll (*Alice in Wonderland* and *Through the Looking-Glass*) used the phrase in 1865 and 1872. American novelist John Steinbeck (*The Grapes of Wrath* and *Cannery Row*) was once criticized and told he would never be a successful writer. After that jibe, he opened his books with *"Ad astra per alas porci"* (Latin for: to the stars on the wings of a pig).

The winged porcine pictured in the back of the book was hand-carved from American basswood by Cecelia Hackemer in 2001. *"Porkette"* measures about nine inches long tongue-to-tail and four inches high. Fly to the stars, Miss Porkette!

Fishnet weave stockings were first introduced in the US from France in 1908. Performing dancers wore them primarily for cooling ventilation while still presenting the semblance of hosiery. They are often associated with the high-stepping cancan dance of the early and mid-nineteenth century, but no verification is available.

Harlem stride piano is a rhythmic style of playing in which the left hand is free to improvise. Unlike ragtime, jazz stride players often moved their left hand further across the keyboard and played a wide range of tempos that encouraged creativity and individual riffs. James P. Johnson, Luckey Roberts, Willie Smith and Thomas (Fats) Waller pioneered the style which oftentimes included added lyrics and ad-libs.

Champagne cocktail is a sweet, classic drink concocted from whatever tickles the taste buds. Ingredients can be added or subtracted to personalize, but a classic stand-by is made from 8 ounces of champagne, 1 ounce of brandy, one or two sugar cubes, a dash of bitters and a maraschino cherry.

Peter Ibbetson was released by Paramount Pictures on October 31, 1935. At sixteen minutes, twenty-five seconds (16:25) into the film there is a curious on-screen reference that immersed author Edward Hackemer into a bizarre déjà-vu experience. When young Peter Ibbetson is hired to work at an architectural firm in London, England, the camera focuses on a brass plaque on the building that reads: "Throckmorton and Slade, Architects." The full given name of architect *Throckmorton* is not revealed in the film and remains an enigmatic, cinematic quirk.

The role (Mary, Duchess of Towers) that Guilermo's acquaintance, Nancy Kenyon, auditioned for was eventually awarded to actress Ann Harding. However, Nancy did secure a non-speaking role in the film as a housekeeping maid with the Forsythe Estate.

Gimlet is a simple, basic cocktail. *Tanqueray* is a leading brand of British gin and *Rose's* is the brand of lime juice likely used in the first gimlets. During the Roaring Twenties, the drink was described as "equal parts of Tanqueray and Rose's" until Prohibition when it was nicknamed "gin and sin". A modern variant is the Vodka Gimlet. Additional ingredients such as syrups or mint can be added.

Bilge and wastewater were simply emptied into the open ocean once a ship was 3 miles or more out to sea. It wasn't until the late twentieth century that sewage and grey water was either treated or filtered aboard ship or transferred to sewage plants at ports of call.

Cointreau is a brand of triple-sec, orange liquor made in Saint-Barthélemy-d'Anjou, France. *Red Stockings* is a popular cocktail consisting of 1½ ounces Cointreau, 1 ounce cranberry juice and a ½ ounce lemon juice.

Mary Pickford was a popular 1930s cocktail named after the famed Hollywood actress who was one of the first stars secured under contract by Famous Players Paramount Studios. At the peak of her career, she was known as *America's Sweetheart, the girl with the curls* and the *Queen of the movies.* The drink recipe contains 1½ ounces white rum, 1 ounce pineapple juice, ¼ ounce grenadine and ¼ ounce maraschino liqueur. It is usually prepared shaken with crushed ice and served with a maraschino cherry on top. The last ingredient can be replaced with additional grenadine.

The Quintette du Hot Club de France is likely the most significant jazz group founded in France. It was formed in 1934 by the legendary band leader and violinist Stéphane Grappelli and guitarist Django Reinhardt. Django was born in 1910 of Romani (Gypsy) lineage in Belgium, and eventually became the most influential jazz musician to come from Europe. In 1928 he nearly lost his life in a caravan fire that left him severely burned and permanently disfigured. He was partially paralyzed but was able to walk again a year later. However, the third and fourth fingers of his left hand remained deformed, paralyzed and curled into the palm. He taught himself to manage the strings and neck of his guitar with only a thumb to two fingers.

Pousse-café [poos-ka-**fey**] (*French*: literally "coffee pusher") is an elaborate cocktail formally served at the end of the evening or after the "Coffee Course" (last course) of a seven-course meal. The classic recipe consists of equal amounts of these six liqueurs: grenadine, maraschino liqueur, crème de menthe, crème de violette, yellow chartreuse, and brandy; each added separately. The drink is occasionally used to test a bartender's knowledge, pouring skills and steady hand. The ingredients are carefully added into a special pousse-café (or a tall, thin, champagne) glass in the order listed. When presented, the drink has a colorful, multi-colored "rainbow" layered effect.

Bénédictine and Brandy (A "B&B") is a cocktail that originated about 1930 in New York City and became instantly popular despite prohibition in the United States. It is made with equal amounts of DOM Bénédictine liquor and a brandy of the connoisseur's choice. It may be served with ice, neat or warmed. Traditionally, it is savored rather that gulped.

Phony War *(British spelling: Phoney – American: Phony)* was the term used by journalists for the early days of World War II (1939-1940). It began by the declaration of war against Germany by France and England on September 3, 1939 after Hitler's invasion of Poland. The Allies launched no land or air offenses other than an invasion of the Saar region of Germany by French troops. The offensive fizzled out and the French withdrew. The embarrassing British withdrawal from Dunkirk, France marked the end of the Phony War after the German *Blitzkrieg* stormed through the Netherlands, Belgium and Luxembourg.

Music To Consider

~~ All Music is Contemporary to Story ~~	
The White Cliffs of Dover	Vera Lynn
I'm Forever Blowing Bubbles	Ella Logan
Let's Misbehave	Irving Aaronson & Commanders
Crazy 'Bout My Baby	Fats Waller & His Rhythm
You Oughta Be in Pictures	Chick Bullock
Masculine Women, Feminine Men	The Savoy Havana Band
Let's Do It	Billy Holiday, Eddie Haywood
A String of Pearls	Benny Goodman & Orchestra
Dream a Little Dream of Me	Teddy Raph & Orchestra
Pennsylvania 6-5000	The Andrews Sisters
Puttin' on the Ritz	Fred Astaire
Lovely to Look At	Eddy Duchin & Orchestra
Oh! Look at Me Now	Helen Forrest, Benny Goodman
Begin the Beguine	Artie Shaw & Orchestra
Let's Sail to Dreamland	Dick Roberson & Orchestra
Anything Goes	Bing Crosby
Si j'aime Suzy (If I like Suzy)	Stephane Grappelli, Django Reinhardt & the Paris Hot Club Quintet
Fidgety Feet	Bob Crosby and his Bob Cats
I've Got My Fingers Crossed	Thomas (Fats) Waller
Le mer (The Sea)	Stephane Grappelli, Django Reinhardt & The Paris Hot Club Quintet
Tango Negro (Black Tango)	Libertad Lamarque, Rodolfo Biagi Orchestra
La valse de l'amour (Waltz of Love)	Édith Piaf
Head over Heels in Love	Edythe Wright, Tommy Dorsey
J'ai deux amours (My two loves)	Joséphine Baker
How Deep Is the Ocean	Peggy Lee, Benny Goodman Orch

Was That the Human Thing to Do	Boswell Sisters
Accentuate the Positive	Irene Daye, Charlie Spivack Orch.
But It Didn't Mean a Thing	June Christy, Glenn Miller Orch
J'suis Mordue (I'm hooked)	Édith Piaf
Le jour où je te vis (The Day I Saw You)	Jean Sablon
Don't Do Something to Someone	Kay Starr
Boum! (Boom)	Charles Trenet
My Last Affair	Billy Holiday
Ich Nenne alle Frauen Baby (I Call all Women Baby)	Horst Winter
As Long as You Live (You'll Be Dead if You Die)	Edythe Wright, Tommy Dorsey Orchestra
We Three (My Echo, My Shadow and Me)	Kay Starr
American Patrol	Glenn Miller Orchestra
Tears in my Heart	Edythe Wright, Tommy Dorsey Orchestra
We'll Meet Again	Peggy Lee, Benny Goodman Orchestra
Love Letters	Vera Lynn

"The end of Time"

Venez dans mes bras
(Closer to me, dear)
Donnez-vous à moi (Set aside all fear)
Restons enlacés, pour l'éternité
(Yes, you shall be mine, 'til the end of time)

Lyrics: "The End of Time" by Charlotte Gainsbourg - 2012
Music: "A Maiden's Prayer" by Tekla Bądarzewska-Baranowska - 1856

CINEMATIC SUGGESTIONS

Paris in Spring (1935)	(starring) Tullio Carminati & Ida Lupino (director) Lewis Milestone
Morocco (1930)	(s) Marlene Dietrich & Gary Cooper (d) Josef von Sternberg
The Devil Is a Woman (1935)	(s) Marlene Dietrich & Lionel Atwill (d) Josef von Sternberg
Becky Sharp (1935)	(s) Miriam Hopkins & Frances Dee. (d) Rouben Mamoulian
The Gay Bride (1934)	(s) Carole Lombard & Chester Morris (d) Jack Conway
Triumph of the Will (1935) (Triumph des Willens)	(s) Adolf Hitler & Heinrich Himmler (d) Leni Riefenstahl
Peter Ibbetson (1935)	(s) Gary Cooper & Ann Harding (d) Henry Hathaway & Ray Lissner
Anything Goes (1935)	(s) Bing Crosby, Ethyl Merman (d) Lewis Milestone
Gold Diggers of 1933 (1933)	(s) Joan Blondell, Ruby Keeler, Dick Powell, Ginger Rogers (d) Busby Berkeley
The Gilded Lily (1935)	(s) Claudette Colbert, Fred MacMurray (d)Wesley Ruggles
Tango Bar (1934)	(s) Carlos Gardel, Rosita Moreno (d) John Reinhardt
Girls Dormitory (1936)	(s)Simone Simon, Herbert Marshall, Janet Gaynor (d) Irving Cummings
Murder at the Vanities (1934)	(s) Jack Oakie, Kitty Carlisle, Victor McLaglen (d) Mitchel Liesen
Bright Eyes (1934)	(s) Shirley Temple, James Dunn (d) David Butler

Post Script

The Title Spring:

"Phryné isn't French. The name is Greek. She is an American."
~ Hugo-Henri Grétillat, June 1940, Poissy, Île-de-France ~

This novel was created with 100% recycled thought.
Some of it was green ... some of it wasn't.
>>All thoughts are Earth-friendly, processed unicorn flatulence.<<

Thank you!

"Elvis has left the building."

Charter member of the Flying Porcine Air Defense League.

Filename:	PhrynéIsn'tFrench2-12-20.doc
Directory:	F:
Template:	
	C:\Users\Administrator.DESKTO
P-	
3HJP19I\AppData\Roaming\Microsoft\Templates\	
Normal.dot	
Title:	Phryné Isn't French
Subject:	
Author:	Edward R Hackemer
Keywords:	
Comments:	Copyright 2018 Edward R
Hackemer	
Creation Date:	2/12/2020 9:00:00 PM
Change Number:	2
Last Saved On:	2/12/2020 9:00:00 PM
Last Saved By:	Edward R Hackemer
Total Editing Time:	1 Minute
Last Printed On:	2/12/2020 9:01:00 PM

As of Last Complete Printing

Number of Pages: 278

Number of Words: 70,477 (approx.)

Number of Characters: 401,725 (approx.)

Made in the USA
Columbia, SC
27 August 2020